D.S. JOYCE

Out of Shot

A CLAIRE ARMSTRONG MYSTERY

D.S. Joyce

For Mum

Out of Shot

PROLOGUE

MONDAY 1ST MAY

The kayakers don't realise what they've found, at first.

The sea throws up all sorts of debris along Scotland's fractured coastline, barely noticed most of the time. If it hadn't been such a pristine beach, the holidaymakers might never have gone to investigate the tangle of red and black cloth.

But, humped between the flat calm turquoise sea and the smooth white sand, these rags strike a discordant note, a reminder of the grubbier world they thought they'd left behind.

Having already eaten their sandwiches they decide to collect the rubbish, stow it in the hold of the kayak, and dispose of it when they get back to the village.

The girl is ahead, and her scream seems too big for her fragile body, escaping to possess the wider world around it, bouncing off the rocks and grass towards the sky. Her partner, rushing to join her, is already reaching for the phone, cocooned in its waterproof cover, on a lanyard around his neck.

Damn. No signal.

"Go and sit by the kayak. I'll head uphill until I can get a signal and call the police."

She nods, stumbling back across the beach, her footprints swallowed noiselessly by the dampness. As she spews up her

1

breakfast and lunch sandwiches all over the perfect, pale sand, she can hear him shouting instructions, forcefully, into the air above.

She prays that help will come quickly; and without her having to re-assemble her trembling limbs into the plastic prison of his two-man kayak.

Overhead, the gulls continue their languidly swooping ballet, in the vast blue dome of the blameless summer sky, sly eyes on the treasure down below.

CHAPTER ONE

7 MONTHS EARLIER

'd been there for less than three months, but I was already regretting my decision to move to the middle of nowhere. And things were about to get worse.

"I hear there's snow on the way tonight."

These words were not addressed to me. I'd popped into the village shop after walking along the beach – the quickest way to get there, from my rented cottage - and was standing at the counter, twitching impatiently as my hair dripped onto the beige lino. The two women in front of me showed no sign of moving any time soon.

"Aye – so they say. It's early this year mind."

"We're in for a long one alright."

I shifted my weight from one foot to the other, shivering at the thought of snow. Although at least it would make a change from lowering skies and drizzle. Might even make the place look better – cover up some of those grey pebbledash buildings.

Finally Mairi, the shop's owner, turned her attention to me.

"Still wet out there, is it?"

I nodded, wiping raindrops from the end of my nose to press the point home, and draw attention to the packet of chocolate biscuits I was clutching in my hand. The other women hadn't bothered turning round to see who'd spoken – my accent was about as obvious as a drum-kit in a string quartet.

"Is that all you're wanting?" Mairi inclined her head towards the biscuits.

"Yes." I wanted to say aye, like a local, but didn't dare try it out.

"That'll be a pound."

I handed over my coin, irritated by the blatant rip-off – the packet stated clearly 79p – but loathe to prolong the transaction.

"Enjoy your biscuits now won't you," Mairi said, putting my hard-earned cash into her till. "And I don't know if you've heard but......"

"There's snow on the way. Yes, thank you. I heard."

I attempted a smile, but it fell from my face before I'd even finished composing it, as Mairi switched her attention back to her other customers.

As I opened the door to leave, I heard her say

"I see he's arrived then......"

I was already halfway out, so I couldn't stop to find out who had arrived, or why. I pulled up my hood against the wind and the rain, leaning on the exterior stone wall at the corner of the shop to get my balance; and then jumping away, as a lump of pebbledash fell with a dull splash into a puddle.

Stuffing my biscuits into the deep pockets of my waterproof coat, I strode towards the beach, trying to ignore the wind that slapped my cheeks. It had an icy edge that hadn't been there a few moments earlier, and I was anxious to get home. As I walked, I mulled over my latest impetuous move. The one which had brought me here.

*

Rash decisions – something I'm prone to, according to those who know me best. This one was made during an idyllic holiday week – I'd come to Kylecraig with my brother and his kids for a break at Easter. The sun shone every day, the sea sparkled, the islands called to mind Greece, rather than Scotland. I felt like I'd discovered paradise, and when I heard that the village school was threatened with closure, I had an idea.

Back in Manchester, I'd asked my boss to allow me to make a fly on the wall documentary. The department had some surplus cash, for once, and he'd said yes almost immediately. I'd been thrilled, initially, but then frightened by the amount of responsibility I'd taken on. By which time it was too late to change my mind – the programme was commissioned, and the next year of my life was to be lived in the extreme north-west of the British mainland.

*

I glanced at my watch, as I paced beside the water's edge. 3pm on a Saturday afternoon, and already it was starting to get dark. What would I be doing, if I was back in Manchester? Shopping? Cinema? A nice meal out, with friends?

Tears bubbled up in my eyes, and my nose dribbled onto the saturated sand.

"Pack it in, Claire," I admonished myself. "It's not forever."

At least I could rub my eyes with impunity. I'd given up wearing mascara a few weeks earlier, unable to find one that was genuinely waterproof when faced with the bitter wind whipping in off the Minch.

Carrying on, my foot stubbed against something lumpy, half-buried in the sand. Looking down, I saw the tiny, inert body of a puffin. The first one I'd ever seen, and it was a corpse.

I crouched down and examined the bird closely. There was no blood, and nothing seemed broken, but there was no more life in those eyes than in the stuffed toy I'd owned as a child.

I was startled by a voice from just a few feet away.

"Too far from home."

Jumping to my feet, I saw a man watching me.

"Me?"

He laughed.

"The bird. Off track. Should have left months ago."

"Oh. I know the feeling." I wiped a hand across my face, smearing salt and snot into the sleeve of my jacket.

The man took a step forward, and held out his hand.

"Surely not, you've only just got here."

I shook his hand, but I was puzzled. I was sure we'd never met.

"I'm Jackson. The new teacher. And judging by your accent, you must be Claire."

Of course. This was who the women in the shop had been talking about.

"I heard there was another infiltrator in the midst," he carried on, smiling. Sure enough, his voice sounded as un-local as mine. "You've been here since the school term started, is that right?"

"Yes. I'm here for the year."

"Excellent. It's really good to meet you."

"You too," I said, automatically, trying out another smile.

He had a wild look about him, with his curly hair on the wrong side of long, and his beard unkempt rather than trimmed. He didn't look much like a teacher. Not like any of the ones I'd had, at any rate. More like an explorer, a mountaineer, a bit of a hippy.

There was silence, apart from the waves and the pattering of rain on my hood. Un-nerved by Jackson's level gaze, I looked back down at the broken puffin, and kicked sand over its battered face.

"Giving the little fella a proper burial?"

"Something like that" I muttered. "Poor thing. Anyway, I should probably head on home. There's bad weather on the way."

He gave a funny little smile, and a wave.

"Apparently so. Stay indoors, would be my advice. But I'll see you on Monday morning."

"Oh you will. There's no avoiding me, or my camera."

His expression darkened as I said this, so I turned quickly and continued on my way. When I looked back a moment later, he'd vanished from sight, as though he'd never even been there.

CHAPTER TWO

I t snowed all day on Sunday, and it was still snowing on Monday morning, when I next saw Jackson. I was at the back of the classroom adjusting the settings on my camera and didn't notice him come in. It was the quietness of the children that alerted me to the new presence in the room.

Having spent almost every day of the past three months in the tiny West Coast school, I was familiar with the noisy morning routine. The children were used to me too and had stopped greeting me every time they saw me, finally heeding my requests to "...just pretend I'm not here."

Now there was a new reason for them to nudge one another. Jackson was sitting at the teacher's desk, moulding a piece of clay, seemingly engrossed. He paid no heed to any of us, and I was able to study him, this time noticing the silver amongst the head of curls and beard. He was older than I'd thought.

Some of the children looked at me as if for clarification, but I just shrugged back at them. My job was to observe and record, not to interfere.

It fell to the bravest – and cheekiest - boy in the class to ask the question. Standing up, Murdo Mackay strode to the front of the room and stood beside the desk.

"Are you the new teacher?"

There was no sign that he'd even heard, at first. He just carried on moulding the clay, didn't look up.

Murdo coughed, showily. "I said….."

He got no further.

"I heard what you said. But it's more about what you didn't say."

A look of confusion came over Murdo's face.

"So," Jackson continued, patiently. "What did you not say?"

The boy hesitated. "Please?"

Jackson looked up now, blue eyes sparkling, and cracked a smile.

"There you go – not hard is it? A little bit of politeness goes a long way. I hope you'll remember that."

"I will, sir" promised Murdo. I doubted that very much.

"Shall we try again?"

"Please, sir. Are you the new teacher?"

"Yes, I'm Jackson," he said. "Not Mr Jackson; just Jackson. Now sit down, please."

The other children clearly had no idea what to make of this encounter. Too baffled even to whisper now, they were pulling exaggerated faces at one another instead, shrugging their shoulders and raising their palms to the ceiling.

The new teacher seemed unfazed by the strangely quiet classroom. He carried on shaping his clay for a few moments, and then set it down on a corner of the desk. It looked like nothing, just a lump, and I wondered whether he'd been using it as some kind of stress relief.

"Right." He scanned the classroom, ran a hand through his hair, smiled. "Let's begin today's lesson. It seems like it's finally stopped snowing out there now."

I glanced towards the window and saw that he was right. The storm clouds had cleared and the snow had settled. It was shaping up to be a beautiful day.

"So, who wants to go outside and make a snowman?"

There was a flurry of gasping and then a host of hands shot into the air.

"Come on then – I'm guessing you all have coats and boots."

The children, who'd only just rid themselves of these garments, couldn't wait to get back into them. The decibel level rose back to a more normal level as they stampeded out of the classroom.

I picked up my camera and followed them into the snow.

*

When school finished at 3.30pm, it was already dark, and shaping up to be one of those crisp, cold evenings which seem to freeze the breath from your body before it even hits the air. I scraped ice from my car windscreen for the second time that day, and sat in the driver's seat waiting for a clear enough view to head out onto the single-track road.

As I sat rubbing my hands together, I saw Jackson. He was bundled into a brown tweed overcoat, hands thrust into pockets, beard hidden beneath a thick woollen scarf, and he seemed to be heading somewhere on foot. I wound down my window.

"Jackson," I called. "Can I give you a lift somewhere?"

Without breaking stride, he shouted back to me.

"Thank you, I appreciate the offer. I like to walk though. I find it clears the brain."

Reaching the school gate, he turned not left, towards the road, but right, in the direction of the beach. There were no street lights on the road, but the beach seemed even darker, somehow, and he was soon out of sight. I tried to think where he might be heading but couldn't think of any buildings along that way. Maybe he was planning to take a short cut across the dunes – but in the dark?

I drove off slowly, full of curiosity.

*

"Ceol na Mara" was the single-storey cottage I'd rented for a stupidly low price, unseen, from a post on the internet. At least the price had seemed stupidly low – it fell within my limited allowance anyway. But it was really me who'd been stupid, failing to realise that what made for an idyllic summer holiday home would be either ridiculously cold or ruinously expensive to heat through a Highland winter.

No wonder the owner had nearly bitten my hand off when I asked for a long-term rental, seduced by the translation from the Gaelic – "Music of the Sea." To add insult to injury, I'd be evicted at the end of March, just as the place started to get bearable again. According to the landlord, I might be able to hire a static caravan from March until the end of the school year. I could hardly wait.

I let myself in, and, still wearing my coat, went through the nightly ritual of clearing out last night's fire and then piling up paper, sticks and coal to make a fresh one. Every day I vowed to do it before leaving for school – and every day my bed proved just too tempting.

The lounge, once the fire was going, was pretty cosy. The tiny galley kitchen could be warmed up easily enough as well, by lighting the oven. In the main bedroom, I'd resorted to a portable oil radiator which I left on overnight, trying not to think about the bills I'd have to face in the spring.

As for the second bedroom, which I had originally intended to use as my editing suite and office, I'd quickly realised that it was a cold, damp and gloomy space that was never going to function as a working environment. Instead, I had set up my computer on the dining table in the lounge.

Having got the fire going, I fetched my camera from the boot of the car and plugged it into my computer to ingest the footage. I hunched over my laptop, working my way steadily down a bottle of red wine as I looked through the pictures. The shots were mainly of grinning ruddy-faced children building snow-people (they were very right-on, these kids.) I could see that they were cute pictures but I had no real interest in them. Had it been a film about a zoo then I'd have viewed the animals with the same kind of detachment.

Watching my material, I was struck by just how cleverly Jackson had evaded me. He'd expressed some reluctance to appear in front of my camera, and for a tall man, he had an amazing knack of disappearing, even amongst children in a schoolyard. There were just a handful of glimpses of him – it seemed that each time I'd adjusted my focus, he'd sensed it, and had moved or turned away from me.

After a while, my head began to ache as the middle of the screen began to fizz and jump around. I rubbed at my eyes, willing them to work properly, but jagged lines were now radiating across my vision, until I could no longer see clearly. Groping in my bag, I found my tablets, and washed a couple down with the rest of the wine.

I held the edge of the table to steady myself as I stood, and snapped the lid of my laptop closed. Experience told me that there was no point in trying to work through a migraine – the only way to shake it off was to go to bed.

Besides, there was only so much you could learn about a man from studying a still-frame of his back.

CHAPTER THREE

Leaving the cottage in the murky half-light of the following morning, I found that my car had all but disappeared under a fresh fall of snow. It would be quicker to don my wellies and walk than to try and dig it out.

Head-torch on and camera in its backpack I set off. It was tough work trudging along the lane, especially feeling as nauseous as I did, and I was relieved when I heard the sound of an engine.

An ancient khaki Land Rover came ploughing through the snow, overtook me, braked, skidded a bit, and came to a halt further up the road, the windows so fogged with steam that I couldn't even tell who was driving it. As I reached it, the driver's door opened and I saw that it was Mairi Morrison, from the shop. She was carrying four or possibly five children in the back and a couple more on the passenger seat.

"I think we can squeeze one more in," she said. "You two hop in the back now, and let Miss have the front seat."

There was much hilarity as Calum and Rory, the two boys who'd been in the front, joined the gaggle of girls in the back, and I clambered gratefully, if somewhat inelegantly, aboard, thanking Mairi as I did so.

"I was worried I'd be late. Where I grew up they'd have cancelled school on a day like this."

"Aye, well, that I can believe."

Mairi was obviously not a woman who was going to let a bit of snow – or the lack of a clear windscreen – stop her from going about her daily business.

"Heater's knackered," she explained, using the sleeve of her jacket to wipe a clear square on the windscreen.

We reached the school gates a few minutes later to find the car-park empty.

"Well," said Mairi. "I suppose I'm the only one brave enough to hit the road today. The others will be waiting for the plough coming through."

We were all piling out of the Land Rover by now and Marnie, one of the two female teachers, was teetering across the snowy playground to greet us.

"Morning Mairi, morning Claire. Come on kids, go inside and get warmed up."

To us, she added;

"Jackson was already here when I got in twenty minutes ago. He's dug that path to the door, gritted it, and got the whole place warmed through – I was worried we were all going to be sitting in our coats until the boiler fired up."

I took the opportunity to quiz Marnie.

"What do you know about him, the new teacher?"

"He's not from round here, that's for sure. But then they'd advertised that job all over the place, they were getting desperate. He's living in a camper."

"A camper?"

"Aye, campervan you might call it, where you're from. We get lots of folks taking advantage of the wild camping laws see; anyone can camp anywhere they choose. You get used to weirdos pitching up here."

"I'm not sure we want a weirdro teaching our children" said Mairi Morrison. "Where's he parked this van of his?"

"Billy Mackenzie's land, next to the dunes. Billy offered to rent him that cottage of his but he didn't want it. Said he loves the simple life in his van."

The older woman frowned and looked at her watch.

"I'll be needing to get back and open up; I'll have a queue forming at the door."

With that, she was back into the Land Rover and reversing wildly onto the road, still unable to see but clearly desperate to impart the latest gossip to her customers.

"Good job there's not much traffic," I said.

"They probably all stay off the roads when the snow comes. Not for fear of the snow but for fear of Mairi Morrison in that death-trap. I can't believe you took a lift from her."

Watching the crazed zig-zag path of the Land Rover weaving back down the lane neither could I.

*

The morning assembly was underway as I sneaked into the hall, and there was a buzz around the room that bordered on hysteria. All eighteen pupils were gathered around the piano, stamping their feet and belting out the Proclaimers' "500 Miles." Over the top of the upright, I caught a glimpse of Jackson's wild hair.

"What do you make of our new teacher then, Claire?"

Janey Macleod the head teacher had walked into the hall and now stood beside me.

"Doesn't really matter what I think does it? The kids love him already."

15

I turned to look at her as I said this, expecting a smile, but her face was impassive beneath the heavy make-up she always wore.

I set up my camera as quickly and discreetly as I could, but as I hit the record button, Jackson brought the tune to an abrupt halt.

"Okay kids – that's enough. Let's get you off to class, now that I've warmed you up."

He jumped up from the piano and swept out of the room, leaving the doors swinging behind him.

The kids groaned and so did I.

"Wily bugger," I thought. "I wonder what he's hiding."

And I remembered what my friend Leonie had said when she'd first heard of my plan to leave Manchester for the Highlands of Scotland.

*

The conversation had taken place in the beer garden of our favourite canal-side pub.

"You're running away, Claire. And hats off to you, you've chosen the right place. The Highlands is full of people who've run away."

"What do you base that theory on?"

"Plenty. Plenty of holidays anyway. All those idyllic little West Coast communities, they've all got their share of incomers. English folk who go up there to start new lives as potters, painters, writers, whatever. And all of them are running away from broken relationships, the tedium of suburbia, the nine to five….."

"Who'd blame them?" I'd interrupted. "That makes perfect sense to me."

"It might do in the summer. Just wait till the winter when you're lonely as hell, freezing cold and bored out of your skull. You'll be over-eating comfort food and hitting the bottle."

"No, I'll be working. I'm going up there to make my film, you know that."

Leonie had fixed me with her favourite look. Her "yeah, right" look.

"And the reason you're going to make this film in a far-flung corner of Scotland? It's got nothing to do with Tom?"

"Why would it have? He's not going to care, is he?"

"No, Claire, he's not. That's kind of my point. Because I'm your best mate, and I care. In fact I'm really worried about you."

I'd been touched by this, but had carried on with my own argument.

"I'm only going for a year, and I'll be busy busy busy. Anyway, you can come and visit."

"Of course. And I know we can chat on the phone. But I just want you to remember one thing. Wherever you go, you take yourself with you."

"That's fine. I'll be perfectly happy with my own company."

"So you're not running away?"

"No. Absolutely, categorically, NOT running away."

The waiter had arrived at this point to see if we were ready to order and, by the time he'd gone, I'd been able to change the subject.

Just days later I'd loaded up my car and headed to Scotland to start my new life, determined to prove that I'd be happy on my own. I hadn't told Leonie that she'd hit the nail on the head; because at that point I'd genuinely believed that she was wrong.

*

Packing away my camera and collapsing the tripod took only a couple of minutes but when it was done I was already alone. Leaving my kit in the hall I took a wander around the classrooms, to see what was going on.

The local council had opted for practicality over aesthetics when renovating Kylecraig School, replacing a charming but dilapidated pre-war building with an ugly grey pebbledash one. Three classrooms opened off the central hall, and triple-glazed windows did their best to deal with everything the Atlantic threw at them.

I peered through the internal windows into each classroom in turn. In the first, a music lesson was taking place, with Annie instructing the youngest four children in the recorder. Even to my inexpert eye Annie looked almost ready to give birth, judging by the strain of her belly against her brightly knitted jumper. Mind you, I couldn't blame the baby for staying inside with that racket going on.

In the second room some kind of geography lesson seemed to be taking place. The whiteboard held a picture of a World Map, and the oldest children – those who would be off to the High School next year – were pointing at places with a laser pen. Marnie, over-seeing them, kept glancing at her phone.

It was the third classroom which interested me, since Jackson was there. He was in the centre of the room, perched on a tiny desk with half a dozen children on chairs in a semi-circle around him.

Frustratingly, I couldn't hear what they were talking about, and was about to head off when I was spotted. To my consternation, Jackson slid off the desk, came striding over to the door and opened it.

"Claire. How can I help you?"

"Oh, I was just taking a look around, you know, to see what's going on."

"No camera?"

"No. I thought I'd look first, see if there's anything worth filming."

"Well you're very welcome to come in and join us, as long as you DON'T bring the camera in. We're writing Haikus and I've a feeling it might stifle creativity…"

Never mind stifling creativity, I had to stifle a laugh.

"Much as I'd love to come in and write poems, I've got a job to do. And I need to keep some distance between myself and the kids – I can't be joining in one minute and then expect them to pretend I'm not here the next."

Jackson nodded.

"If only more of us had enjoyed ourselves at school the world might just be a better place. Did that ever occur to you Claire? "

"But I'm not at school, am I? I'm at work, just like you are."

He looked at me for a moment then turned, abruptly, to walk back over to the children.

"Come on you lot. Who's going to read me their Haiku first?"

Clearly our conversation was over.

*

I'd been shocked when I arrived by the lack of a staff-room in the school, but the teachers seemed quite happy to take their breaks and lunches with the children. Some of the local mothers took it in turns to come in and cook, and I was glad to find Eilidh Ross in the kitchen. In the short time I'd known her she'd proved adept at sharing local gossip and giggles in roughly equal measure. Unlike most of the others.

"Morning Claire, how are you?"

"Good thanks Eilidh, yourself?"

"Aye, can't complain. Glad it's Friday though. Alasdair will be home tonight, that'll give me a wee bitty break for a few days."

Like many of the local men, her husband worked offshore, spending two weeks on an oil rig in the North Sea and two weeks back in the village. They owned a croft with sheep and cows – hard work at any time of year but particularly gruelling through the winter. Eilidh worked harder than anyone I'd ever met. Not only did it fall to her to look after the croft whilst Alasdair was away, she was also mum to three children under ten and worked as a driver on the local mini-bus one day a week as well as cooking at the school. Just thinking about it made me want to hibernate.

"That's good. Will you get a lie-in tomorrow then?"

She laughed.

"No chance, but I might get a cup of tea in bed. Talking of tea, I'm guessing that's why you're here?"

"Please."

Handing me a mug of tea, Eilidh appraised me.

"What do you make of the new teacher then?"

"Difficult to know what to make of him; nobody seems to know much about him. I hear he's living in a campervan."

Clearly this wasn't news to Eilidh.

"Aye. Strange, eh?" She looked around, as though expecting spies, and lowered her voice until I could barely hear her. "I hear he's come up from London".

"So why has he come here?

"Who knows? Maybe something happened to blot his copybook, eh?"

"They'd hardly just let him into a classroom if that was the case. Any new teacher has to go through some pretty rigorous background checks."

Eilidh looked disappointed at this inconvenient barrier to her conspiracy theory.

"I guess he must have passed the DBS stuff, right enough. Anyway, they've been trying to get someone to stand in for Annie for months, so it's just as well he's here."

I was eager to move Eilidh onto further revelations, but she knew as little as I did.

"He might be a bit of a weirdo" she said, "but I think it'll do this place the world of good having a man about. Far too many women here already - teachers, head, you, us lot. The lads need someone to have a kick-about with."

I nodded, but I already had my doubts about the new teacher as a typical male role model.

*

It was too pure a day to be cooped up indoors and Jackson and the other teachers were by now outside, doing a spot of beach-combing with the children. He was at the centre, and, as I looked over, the two young women seemed to be laughing at something he'd just said, whilst the kids ran amok all around them.

I deliberately walked away from them at a fast pace, enjoying the sharp sting of salt-chill air on my face and the constant nagging of the surf in my ears. Up above, a skein of geese noisily made their way eastwards, in a ragged "V" against the pale sky. I kept in a straight line along the edge of the water, sending oystercatchers skittering upwards, to re-group behind my back once I'd passed.

I'd have missed the van completely, were it not for the fact that the low winter sun was causing light to bounce and glitter off the windscreen, which caught on the very corner of my vision. At first, I thought my migraine had come back, but, shielding my eyes, I could just make out a beige vehicle, almost completely camouflaged by the dunes over to my left.

One quick glance along the beach showed me that everybody else was engrossed in scouring the shoreline. The children were offering their finds over to Jackson and he had his hands full, so I seized my opportunity, heading quickly in the direction of the van.

When I got closer, I wondered how Jackson could bear to be cooped up in something so tiny. I'd pictured a large, American-style camper-van, but this was far more old-fashioned – it looked like the kind of thing my gran might have dreamed of back in the 1970s, with bug eyes for headlamps and bright orange curtains pulled fast across the windows.

I couldn't imagine spending a night in it, let alone a full Scottish winter.

CHAPTER FOUR

S aturday was another ice-cold day, which could have kept me in my bed longer than planned. But I could only put off the inevitable for so long - a trip to the supermarket had become a necessity. I didn't want to drive home in the dark and the fifty-mile journey to Ullapool would take almost two hours on winding single-track roads.

I defrosted the car, shovelled away the snow that had built up around it, and inched cautiously along the pitted icy street towards the school, hoping that the snow-plough had made it as far as the main road.

Luckily it had; and pulling out of the junction, I could almost feel my tyres sighing with relief as they relaxed onto the heavily gritted tarmac. I accelerated up through the gears, until I reached the dizzy heights of 40 miles per hour.

That was when I saw him.

Jackson was walking along the verge a couple of hundred yards ahead, one thumb stuck out into the road.

I pulled up alongside and wound down the window.

"Can I take you somewhere, Jackson?"

"I don't suppose you're heading for Ullapool are you?"

"I am."

"The planets are in my favour." He folded himself with some difficulty into the passenger seat. "Although a more benevolent alignment might have granted me the comfort of a larger vehicle."

"And a less benevolent one would have seen you in there," I responded, as Mairi Morrison pulled past us in her Land Rover, swerving gently onto the snowy verge opposite before correcting the vehicle and continuing on her way.

"Ah yes. More space; but also far more need to fear for one's life. On balance, I'd rather take my chances with you."

I asked him why he wasn't driving to Ullapool.

"Have you seen my van?"

I nodded, not trusting myself to lie.

"Well, that should answer your question. The speed she goes at, there just aren't enough hours in the day. Besides, I'd have to tidy all my stuff away."

I was about to ask him why he chose to live in a van, but he got in ahead of me.

"How are you finding life in Kylecraig? A bit too quiet?"

"It's fine," I said, firmly. "It's all about the film; and I want it to make the case for keeping the school open. That's why they agreed to let me in. It'll make a lovely programme. You can't really go wrong with scenery like this."

I waved my arm expansively at the general beauty ahead of us – the long narrow line of tarmac glinting dark against the brilliant white of the snow, the strange domes of hills rising straight up out of the moor like abandoned space-ships, the gleaming strip of sea shining bright on the horizon.

I was so busy waving my arms and marvelling at the glory of it all that I failed to spot the stag which had wandered, majestically, into our path.

Luckily Jackson had spotted it, and he grabbed the steering wheel, turning it violently to the left, just in time to avoid a collision. The car skidded around the animal and into a convenient Passing Place, whereupon I instinctively slammed on the brakes. Luckily the gritted road held firm beneath us.

"Never slam on the brakes," Jackson shouted. "Not in these conditions. You need to steer, not brake."

"I know." I yelled back. I did know, I'd just forgotten and panicked.

I glanced into the rear-view mirror, where I could see the stag calmly completing his crossing of the road, followed by two does. For some reason I had a flashback to Jackson on the beach, with the two female teachers beside him.

"Maybe I'd have been better off with Mairi Morrison after all."

His tone was lighter now but it was as though he was trying too hard to make a joke; and it was that shout that resonated in my head long after we were moving again.

*

By the time we reached Ullapool, it was almost midday. We'd caught up with the snow-plough a few miles out of town and I'd elected to follow it rather than take my chances on an un-salted road.

I parked up and we agreed to meet in an hour. Jackson levered himself awkwardly out of the passenger seat, straightened his coat, and strode off. I watched until he was out of sight, wondering how I'd failed to prise any information out of him about his personal life. Some journalist! Two hours in the car - and still I knew nothing more about him.

In the drinks section of the supermarket, I tried to calculate how much wine I would get through before my next visit, and came up with an alarmingly high figure. I took about half the amount I wanted, which still looked like quite a lot, then put in a couple of bottles of single malt whisky, figuring I would drink that more slowly. Filling boxes at the checkout, I reflected that there was an awful lot of bottle-clinking going on.

"I'd never have had you down for a secret drinker Claire."

Jackson's voice came from just a few feet away, but when I looked up and saw him at the next checkout I barely recognised him.

"Wow – you look….different."

Jackson had clearly paid a visit to the barber. The beard was now trimmed close and his curls had been cropped away from his face.

I began cramming bottles hurriedly away.

"Yes, it's been a while since the barber had the pleasure of my company. You've taken a long time over your shopping."

"I like to make sure I'm getting the best deals on everything" I said.

"Especially the wine, it would appear."

The woman on the checkout laughed out loud at this, as I fumbled in my bag for my purse, trying to hide my embarrassment.

*

Steering the car up the steep hill above Ullapool harbour a short time later, I was finally able to ask one of the questions that had been forming in my mind.

"I've been wondering - why did you arrive midway through a school term?"

"Circumstances beyond my control."

I persevered.

"I was just wondering what the delay was? I know they've been looking since the summer."

"I'm sure they were trying to find somebody local."

"That doesn't matter to the kids. They've accepted you far more quickly than they did me."

"Ah well – I'm not hiding behind a lens, am I?"

"You're a really good teacher." I persisted. "Your last school must have been sorry to lose you. Was that the delay?"

From the passenger seat, Jackson snorted. Looking at the road, I couldn't tell whether he was amused or angry.

"Let go of it, Claire. I'm not in an interview now – you're not at work and neither am I."

I could feel myself flushing, but I tried to keep my voice steady.

"I'm not interviewing you, Jackson. I'm just curious. Human beings talk to one another, share life experiences. That's how we get to know one another."

Now there was definitely annoyance creeping into his voice as he replied.

"I've nothing to tell you. Isn't it enough that, for whatever reasons, we're both here?"

"Not really, no."

"Why not? Why isn't that enough? We're winding our way north through some of the most beautiful scenery on the planet as the sun sinks into the sea beside us. There are deer grazing at the side of the road….." (I took an anxious glance but he was right, they were just grazing) "…and before long the stars will come out and we'll actually be able to see them. What more could anyone need?"

It was probably the longest speech I'd heard him utter, but I stuck to my subject.

"Conversation. That's what I need."

27

"I'm happy to talk Claire, more than happy. I just don't want to talk about myself."

I was genuinely puzzled. I struggled to think of anyone I'd ever met before who didn't want to talk about themselves.

"Oh, come on. You rock up here out of nowhere, you don't live in a house, it's like you've created this great mystery…."

Jackson interrupted me.

"I think you're the one who's creating a mystery. And I'd have thought that in your line of work you'd have come across far more interesting people than me."

"Hardly. I worked in local news before I came up here, and it was all run of the mill stuff. Lots of court cases, rows about traffic, rows about planning applications. You name it, people row about it. That's partly why I came up here, I was just so bored."

"Well, now that you're here, don't you think it's time you opened your eyes to everything that's around you? I'm not telling you to stop asking questions, just to ask more interesting ones."

I concentrated on watching the sky turning pink, as the sun splashed the last of its weary efforts across the very tips of the hills. Then it vanished and, almost immediately, it was night.

*

The rest of the journey passed in a silence which felt awkward rather than companionable until we approached Kylecraig, its scattering of crofts and bungalows glimmering in the moonlight like cubes from an up-turned sugar bowl.

"Where should I drop you?" I asked. I'd no idea how to reach the place beside the dunes where the campervan was parked.

"It's quickest for me to cut along the beach, so just here is fine. I might borrow one of those."

Jackson pointed towards the side of the road. I pulled over and peered through the gloom towards a couple of sledges stowed at someone's back-door.

"Don't worry, I'll bring it back. Handy for lugging the shopping though."

"You're very resourceful."

"I have to be. And so are you, Claire, although you might not think it yet. I'm sorry if you think I've been hard on you but please, don't be hard on yourself."

All I could think was that we had barely spoken for the past hour, with all the promise of the day seeming to have evaporated along with that rose-pink sunset. Jackson was already prising himself out of the car.

Thinking about another long, lonely night in my cottage, I found the courage to speak.

"How about a drink?"

His face appeared back at the open passenger door.

"Great. I'll be with you in an hour or so."

"It's Ceol na Mara – the second to last house at the end of the road."

"I know."

His face vanished again, and the door was slammed shut.

Back at the cottage, I went through the usual rigmarole of lighting the fire before lugging my bags into the kitchen.

I made myself a cup of tea, sat in the chair by the fire to drink it, and promptly fell asleep.

CHAPTER FIVE

W hen a loud hammering noise woke me, I jumped and looked at my watch – it was after six o' clock, which meant that I'd slept for an hour. My pathetic fire was almost out and there was no time even to look in a mirror, as another thump threatened to bring the door down and possibly the house with it. Leaping up, I went to the kitchen and opened the door to find Jackson standing there, his face barely visible beneath a red knitted scarf and hat.

"Don't leave a poor old man freezing on the doorstep," he said. I was about to say something about this particular poor old man choosing to sleep in a van, but I suspected that he was teasing me.

He held out a 4-pack of beer, as though making a peace offering.

"Thanks. Although I must admit, I'm not really a beer drinker."

"I know. I saw you stocking up, remember? But I am. And just for you…" reaching now inside his coat, "I brought this along as well."

He handed me a bottle of wine. Red, Argentinian, Malbec. Ticked all of the boxes.

"Then I can impede your progress no longer. Welcome to my humble abode."

He stepped inside, seeming to fill my tiny kitchen. Without waiting to be asked, he stripped off his scarf, hat and coat, ran his fingers through his hair and winced.

"I quite liked it long. You see, I'm not so unusual. I still have some vanity about me, not to mention immense pride in having reached this grand old age with a full head of hair. It seems a shame to have been shorn of so much of it."

"I agree. I don't mean about the age, whatever that might be" I added, hastily. "And no, I'm not digging, but the hair suited you long and wild."

"Not according to our lovely headmistress. It was her who told me to get it cut."

He was already striding through to the living room.

"What's going on with this fire? Good grief woman. That wouldn't warm a guinea pig."

I watched as he knelt down and started blowing on the embers, then added sticks and coal. Within a minute or two he'd achieved a blaze the likes of which I could only have dreamed of.

"Thanks, Jackson." I handed him a bottle of beer.

He took the drink and we settled into the chairs on either side of the fireplace.

It occurred to me that Jackson was my first visitor. The locals, unsure of quite how to regard me, or just too busy living their lives, left me to my own devices.

"So," he said suddenly. "What do you want to know?"

He wasn't looking at me but was gazing instead into the flames.

"To know? About what?"

Because he was still gazing down I couldn't see the expression on his face.

"About me."

"Oh nothing." I could feel the heat spreading across my face. "Really, forget it. I shouldn't go poking my nose in other people's business."

He looked up at me, and his face was kind.

"Come on - it's your job. And you're not the only one with questions Claire; although you are the only one bold enough to ask me to my face rather than talking about me behind my back."

I thought back to my chat with Eilidh.

"Well – you can't expect to rock up in a place like this and not arouse curiosity. And I'm so boring they were desperate for some new material."

He smiled and shook his head. "Stop fishing for compliments. Go on, fire away. Ask me a question. This could be your only opportunity. Seriously, you want to seize it with both hands."

Of course my mind went blank.

"Um.....okay - where are you from?"

"Ah, the classic opener. Quite unlikely to tell you anything important about anybody."

He looked so smug, suddenly, that I snapped at him.

"Oh, stop being so bloody awkward. Just answer the sodding question, will you?"

"But it's such a hard question to answer. Take where we are now, for example. Most of the people up here come from here and have stayed here. And even if they leave, they will still say that they are FROM here, that this and nowhere else is home. I envy that, because it gives them a simple answer - and I don't have one."

I could see his knuckles straining white against the brown of the bottle in his hands, although his beer remained untouched.

"Can we just say that for the time being, this seems like as good a place as any to call home?"

He sat back in his chair and took a long swig of beer.

I was about to ask him about the rumour that he'd come from London, when the phone began to ring. I ignored it, until Jackson said

"Hadn't you better answer that?"

"Oh, it'll be Mum. I'll call her back."

"You should always answer the phone to your Mother." He sounded almost angry.

"If I do, she'll be on the phone for an hour. Honestly, it'll be fine, I'll call her back."

The phone carried on its plaintive call for a while longer, then stopped. I breathed a sigh of relief.

"Would you like some supper?" I suddenly wanted to keep Jackson in the house for as long as possible, but he'd already drained his beer and was now standing up.

"It's a tempting offer. But I don't want to get too cosy by this fire. I might fall asleep and start snoring, and then what will you think of me?"

Without waiting for a reply, he carried on. "Thanks for your hospitality and for the lift earlier. And I'm sorry if you think I'm winding you up, it's just that I value my privacy."

By now, he had retrieved his coat and scarf and was preparing to leave.

"What about the rest of your beer?" I indicated the three bottles still on the table.

"Oh, save those for next time. I know they're safe here, since you don't like beer. I must go and do some lesson plans for Monday morning. But do pop in to say hello tomorrow, if you're passing."

He headed to the door, and before I'd even registered it opening and closing, he was gone.

I stood still in the middle of the kitchen, looking at the emptiness of the space where he'd been just a moment ago and trying to shake some sense back into myself.

"Impossible man," I said, aloud. "Belligerent, awkward smart-arse." And sparkly-eyed and mysterious, I added silently. Dangerous.

I took a long, slow sip of wine, and pinched myself, hard, on the thin skin on the inside of my wrist.

Then, interrupting the silence, there was a loud thump at the window, which made me grab the top of the table. A lump of wet snow was sliding down the outside of the glass.

Must have fallen off the roof, I thought, knowing even as I did so that it was way too cold for the snow to melt. Curious to see if this was some kind of test that Jackson was setting me, I opened the door, half-expecting to see him standing there, laughing at me. But the street was deserted. It had started snowing again, heavily.

I was about to go back in when I glimpsed a dark shape below the window, where the pile of snow had settled. It was hard to make out, but it looked like some kind of creature. Perhaps a bird had flown into my window?

I ran back into the kitchen and fetched my torch, stepping back out towards the thing as carefully as though it were about to jump up and bite me, although the fresh snow had already almost covered the body. I scraped some away, then recoiled at the feeling of cold damp fur and something sticky under my fingernails.

A rat.

There was no residual warmth in the body, so it must have been dead for some time before it hit my window.

I flashed the torch around me, but all that was picked out by the beam was swirling snow, falling hard and fast. There was no sign of movement, and there was just one set of footprints leading to and from the cottage – Jackson's. There were none leading round to the back of the house, where the kitchen window was, so someone clearly had a good aim on them. Someone who'd found a reason to come out in this blizzard, conceal a dead rat in a snowball and hurl it at my kitchen window.

Holding the torch up to the glass, I saw that the streaks of snow were stained with blood the colour of cherries. When I shone the torch back out at the street, it was still deserted, and the new snow had already blurred the edges of Jackson's footsteps.

CHAPTER SIX

The following morning, I stepped from the cottage into a glowering, grey-skied world. The wind was whipping sand from the shoreline across the road, and the old snow that had been roughly cleared to the sides had hardened into treacherous lumps of gritty grey ice. Pulling up the hood of my warmest down jacket and digging my hands into my pockets, I told myself that this was just the thing for a hangover, as the gusting bursts of wind pushed me towards the beach.

After being blasted by sand for ten minutes, I was on the verge of going home. On a good day, the beaches around Kylecraig looked like the Caribbean - only this was like being there in hurricane season. I couldn't tell whether the pounding in my ears was coming from the waves, the wind, or the over-zealous workings of my body, processing yesterday's red wine. I'd hit the bottle with a vengeance after receiving that unexpected present against my window. It had worked too – three glasses in, I'd convinced myself that it was just a daft wind-up by one of the local kids.

As I thought about turning around and going home, I caught sight of Jackson, in the distance. Unlike me – stooping, hunching, and hating the weather – he was embracing it. He stood alone in the middle of the beach, halfway between the dunes and the sea, facing out towards the mountainous island of Greagha. He wore no hat and his head was raised to the sky.

As I watched, the clouds split for a moment and a burst of sunlight tumbled like an avalanche towards the sea, sending shivers of sparkling light across the waves.

I thought I heard laughter, but it could have been the wind.

Then the clouds closed over once again and the light vanished, like God turning off a light switch.

Jackson lowered his head and turned to face me, and I walked as though hypnotised towards him.

*

As he boiled water on a camping stove for coffee, I perched on one of the foam covered benches and studied the belongings which filled the inside of his campervan. Books were piled up on every surface, including both driver and passenger seats. I could see why he wouldn't have been able to drive to Ullapool very easily.

There was a rudimentary clothing rail in one corner, holding an assortment of jumpers, shirts and neatly-pressed trousers.

Placing two mugs of coffee onto the pull-down table, Jackson apologised for the lack of fresh milk.

"I take mine black. So I just keep powdered milk for visitors."

"And do you have many of those?"

He said something, but his words were lost in the latest violent blast of wind attacking the sides of the van.

"Thank God I love books," he shouted. "They're not just the carriers of civilisation; they're the only things keeping this tin can from tipping over. Anyway" he sat down opposite me, "tell me – did you call your Mother back?"

"What? I – no I didn't. I forgot. That is to say, I got distracted."

I explained as best I could, over the howls of wind, which rattled every nut and bolt on the van, what had happened after he'd left me the night before,

"I wondered if maybe you'd done it, as some kind of joke."

The look on his face told me that whoever had chucked that gory present at my window, it definitely wasn't Jackson.

"What on earth would I do something like that for? It'll be schoolkids, playing a good old-fashioned prank. That's what happens with vivid imaginations running wild and not enough to do. The creature was dead already, you say? They probably just found it, and they thought it would be a bit of a laugh. You've not taken it personally, I hope?"

I paused for just a beat, and then shook my head. "No, of course not."

*

We listened to Desert Island Discs and then a play on Radio 4, all the time watching the angry waves through the snow spatters on the windows, and we shared a very good chicken curry, which Jackson heated up on the little camping stove. He showed no sign of minding my company, but I couldn't work out if I was getting in the way of his routine or slotting nicely into it. So, as the skies started to glower with the first real hint of night, I stood up to leave.

"I'd better get home while I can still find my way there."

He looked up from the book he'd immersed himself in, and seemed surprised, for a moment, to find me still there.

"Oh, yes. Good idea."

He remained where he was, only getting up to help me when I struggled to push the door open against the force of the wind. I half fell out of the van onto the beach, a vicious sting of salt and hail bringing tears to my eyes as I staggered back towards my cottage.

*

A long telephone conversation with a good friend was called for - I needed to re-connect with the 21st century again, to remind myself that there was a world outside Kylecraig, and people in that world who cared about me.

"Claire!" Leonie sounded gratifyingly pleased to hear from me. "How ARE you? I thought you'd fallen off the face of the planet. You haven't been on Facebook in days!"

"I know. It's weird up here, it gets dark so early and the weather's pretty wild. It seems to take all my energy just to get out of bed and struggle through the day.

"November's always a crappy month. It's not that great here, to be honest. So, when are you coming home? We need a night out on the town!"

She pointed out that, with Christmas less than a month away, there were plans to be made. And so we chatted and plotted and gossiped about all the people we'd see, the people we definitely did NOT want to see (Tom) and so on. That is to say, Leonie chatted and plotted and I listened and agreed. It was impossible to get a word in edgeways, but there was something reassuring in that. After Jackson's comments, I'd started to wonder whether it was me, not him, who had a problem. An hour flew by, and then Leonie apologised and said she had to go.

"I'm meeting Jill and the others for Book Group - except we're going to the cinema to see *Anna Karenina* – you know how we've always talked about reading it? Now we've all realised we're never going to get round to it, and there's a special screening on as part of some classic films season, so this seems like the perfect compromise. But I wish you were coming, Claire."

"Me too."

I thought, longingly, of a night in our local independent cinema. There would be glasses of wine and gourmet burgers in the trendy café to start the night, and then the great joy of watching a film from a comfortable reclining seat with another glass of wine close at hand.

I wished Leonie a good night out, then cut her off, wishing I was having one myself. It occurred to me that of all the Book Group members, I was the only one who did have sufficient time at my disposal to tackle not only *Anna Karenina* but *War and Peace* as well. Perhaps Jackson would lend me some of his great works of literature?

In the meantime, I called Mum, just to alleviate any lingering feelings of guilt, only to discover that she was out. Everybody, it seemed, was having a better Sunday night than I was, and so I left a message, cracked open a bottle of wine and whiled away yet another evening watching nonsense on my laptop.

I had turned off the downstairs lights and was about to lock the front door when I became aware of an orange glow outside, visible through the glass pane in the top of the door. This was odd – Kylecraig had no street lighting. Instinctively, I shrunk back against the wall, listening. There was a slight scuffling noise on the other side of the door, and the light bobbed around for a moment or two, then faded.

I stood there for a few moments longer, trying to steady the thumping in my rib-cage, then slowly opened the door. Nothing but silence and darkness.

I was about to close it again, when I noticed an acrid smell drifting up towards me from the ground. Turning on the outside light, I saw a cigarette butt, stubbed out in the pile of snow I'd shovelled away that morning from my front step.

*

I tried not to over-think the mystery of the late-night cigarette-smoker – probably nothing more than a drunken neighbour returning home I told myself, firmly. Maybe the same one who'd hurled a dead rat at my window. But it was hard to raise my spirits, and the weather didn't help my black mood. Stormy winds had chased away the last of the sunshine, blue skies and snow had given way to wet and squally days and the gloomy grey sky seemed to squash the village like a too-low roof. Daylight was a brief interlude of slightly paler grey. It was no longer nail-bitingly cold, but it was dreadful light to film in.

Inside the classrooms, the lessons which I'd found such fun to film back in August now just made me yawn. There was no conflict, no jeopardy – no reason why anybody should care about what happened to the children of Kylecraig, or their school. As the calendar flipped over from November into December, there were several days when I thought about calling my boss to cancel the whole project. Only the knowledge that he'd committed a large chunk of his budget kept me from pulling the plug.

My tea-breaks and lunch-breaks got longer and longer, and I was grateful that nobody was supervising me. I took care to always have pen and paper to hand.

"Scripting," I would explain, airily, if anyone threw me a curious look. The truth was, my project was at risk of grinding to an ignominious halt if I couldn't find some inspiration from somewhere.

CHAPTER SEVEN

The sun chose a Saturday morning to return. I was so pleased to see it that I went out straight after breakfast, strapping my camera and tripod onto my back and heading for the hill-path behind the cottage. This had become one of my default walks since I moved here, and for a small hill, the view from the top was spectacular. On a clear day like today, it stretched for miles.

To the west, just a mile or so off the coast, was Greagha, with its rugged interior and tiny jewel-like coves. I hadn't been there but was looking forward to visiting in the spring. Looking south towards Ullapool I could just make out the strip of tarmac road wending its way between peat hags and tiny lochans, some of them no bigger than ponds. A brief glint of silver indicated the progress of a car heading along the road.

To the north and east, an imposing range of domed mountains prevented long vistas, but they were enough of a sight in themselves, especially with the brightness of their highest snow-topped peaks making a stark contrast with the gloomy corries on their rugged flanks.

I wrestled with the stiff, cold metal clips of my tripod, wincing as I pinched the skin between my fingers on one of them. Even with fingerless gloves on, this was always the most fiddly, least fun part of my job, and I cursed under my breath as I tried to stabilise the tripod on the snow-crusted, tussocky ground. But once the camera was set up, and the view framed to my satisfaction, I could relax and enjoy myself.

I was so engrossed in my work, that I didn't hear anybody approaching, so when a female voice greeted me I jumped, bashing my eye-socket against the viewfinder in the process.

"Sorry. Thought you'd seen me coming."

Rubbing my eye, I shook my head, trying desperately to place the woman standing in front of me.

"Catriona Mackay. Murdo's mam."

She didn't extend a hand, but stood with them both in her pockets, surveying the view as though she was looking at it for the first time.

"Of yes, of course. Sorry – I know who all the kids are, but I haven't got the parents sussed yet."

"Nae bother. What is it you're doing up here then?"

"GVs," I replied, without thinking. "Sorry – it means General Views. It's just some pictures of the scenery, to illustrate my film."

"Oh, aye. And how's it all going, the film?" She pronounced it "fillum."

"It's going really well," I lied. "The school is a great subject; it's such a contrast to where I come from. I think lots of people will be amazed that this kind of place still exists."

"Is that right?"

She turned to face me now, and there was no getting away from the hostility in her eyes.

"And what's in it for us, like? Those that live here, I mean?"

"Well…." I thought rapidly, aware that I'd have to choose my words carefully. "I'm sure you're aware that funding is always an issue, for schools like this, in the more remote areas of the highlands. And budgets are really stretched at the moment. The film is not exactly going to be a PR exercise, but my hope is that it will show what a valuable asset it is. I think it would be very hard for the council to close Kylecraig School, if my film hits the right note."

The school had held meetings with the parents before I arrived, so I was only repeating information that would have already been imparted. I'd got quite used to explaining myself when I'd first arrived, but thought that by now everybody had accepted me, or at least knew why I was there. Obviously not.

"Aye, well. Just make sure you don't go sticking that camera in any places where they're not wanted."

There was a wild look about her now, her red hair blowing messily around her face, her cheeks flushed by the cold.

"Of course, that goes without saying". I tried to smile, to catch her eye, but she was looking away from me now. I could see slivers of silver light dancing in the centre of my vision, and cursed inwardly; I had no pills with me to ward off the migraine that I knew was coming.

"Jimmy MacIver's parents had the right idea, keeping their lad out of it. Wish I'd done the same an' all, but I guess it's too late now."

"Yes it is," I said, firmly. Not being able to film Jimmy made my work harder than it needed to be, but I was duty bound to respect his parents' instructions. "Murdo's one of the most engaging of the boys on camera," I continued, trying to win her over.

"He's a wee divil is what he is. What do you know about the new teacher? He's one of you, isn't he?"

The abrupt change of topic took me unawares.

"One of us?"

"Aye. English. Murdo minds him just fine, but I'm still not sure myself. How can you have a teacher living in a van on the beach like that? It's no kind of example to set the kiddies."

"I don't know much about his background, but he's a great teacher. All the kids love him."

"Aye, well, we'll see. Just you remember what I've said now."

By now, the slivers had turned to daggers, slicing my vision into a kaleidoscope, so that I could do little more than nod. It seemed Catriona had said what she'd wanted to anyway, since she was already walking away.

I sunk down into the heather and put the palms of my hands over my eyes, waiting for the worst of my migraine to pass, oblivious to the fact that behind me, my camera was still rolling, recording her unsteady progress back down the hill towards the village.

*

The migraine was a bad one. I'd waited for almost an hour on the hillside for the aura to subside, and then I'd stumbled home, taken my pills and headed straight to my bed, sleeping until early evening.

As a result, I was all over the place on Sunday morning. Tentatively opening first one eye, and then the other, I was surprised to find that it was still dark outside, until a glance at my watch showed that it was only just after 8am.

Waiting for the kettle to boil, I peered out into the gloom, trying to look for clues as to what the day had in store. I was obsessed with checking the weather every five minutes in Kylecraig, whereas back at home in Manchester it had hardly even registered. But all that I could see was my ridiculously tousled head looking mournfully back at me from the ice-crusted window. After several cups of tea, it was hearing the music for Desert Island Discs that finally spurred me into action.

I bundled myself into my down jacket, hat and scarf and headed off, determinedly, along the beach towards Jackson's van.

But as I got nearby, I could hear voices, snatches of laughter, carried towards me in fragmented bursts.

I slowed right down. The icy wind was making my eyes water, but I could still make out the figures outside Jackson's van. Four of them – Murdo, Calum, Jimmy and Rory, standing on tiptoes, faces pressed against the windows, daring each other to knock. They paid no attention to me as I walked behind the campervan, intent as they were on finding out what was inside it. The orange curtains were tightly drawn, and I wondered if Jackson was even there. Certainly the boys seemed to think so, since one of them was calling his name.

I passed on by, then headed for the dunes, and crouched down, waiting to see what would happen next. After a short time, the door opened, and Jackson appeared. I expected him to shout at the boys, tell them to go away and stop disturbing him, but instead, he came outside, and stood, hands in pockets, chatting, whilst they took it in turns to try and nip behind him, to see inside his van. Ineffectively, as it turned out, since his imposing figure was too much of a barrier.

After a short while, Jackson disappeared back inside, shutting the door firmly behind him. The boys stayed where they were and a few moments later he re-appeared, a bundle of red fabric in one hand. This, he flung up into the air, where it revealed itself to be a kite. The boys, their attention diverted, tried to grab hold of this instead, but Jackson just laughed and ran with it. Further and further away from me he ran, the four boys laughing and following, until they were just distant dots of colour – five on the beach and one, the bright red diamond of the kite, twisting and slicing through the air.

When they rounded the corner and disappeared from view, I heaved myself up from my crouching position and headed for the van. It was un-locked, so I let myself in, figuring that I'd just sit there and wait for Jackson to come back.

Radio 4 was burbling away in the background, and there was a tantalising smell of freshly ground coffee in the air. A hardback book was placed, facedown, on the table. I lifted it carefully, and checked the cover. "The Silver Darlings" by Neil M Gunn. I'd never heard of it. Jackson was clearly enjoying it – there was a marker towards the end of the book. I opened it, carefully, and saw that it was a train ticket. My heart beat a little faster, as I took in the information printed on it – Newcastle to Inverness. Dated November 1st.

I did some clumsy calculations in my head and worked out that it was five days later that I'd first encountered Jackson on the beach. Either the gossips were wrong about him coming from London, or he'd had some other reason to travel from Newcastle.

Placing the book back just as I'd found it, I peered through the closed curtains, but there was no sign of the kite flyers returning. I scanned the inside of the van, hungry now for clues, but seeing nothing else that would help me. A pile of local OS maps, some teaching plans, some photographs of the local area. A box of 20 Christmas cards, as yet un-written. At least this was a clue, of sorts – he must know people to send them to. But there was no address book, smartphone, or laptop that I could see. Nothing that would tell me anything more about the new teacher or what had brought him to Kylecraig.

Looking out of the window again, I saw a bright dot of red appear in the sky above the curve of the dunes, and five figures coming around the corner down below. Seeing Jackson's imposing figure approaching, I got cold feet about my plan to surprise him. Leaving the van un-locked was hardly the same as issuing an invitation, after all, and I'd barely seen him recently. So I let myself out, wincing as the door banged behind me. Luckily the sound of the wind and the waves was powerful enough to mask any noise that I might make.

It was only when I got back to the cottage and kicked off my boots, scattering clumps of damp sand all over the rug in the hall, that I realised how stupidly I'd incriminated myself.

*

But when I saw Jackson at the school on Monday morning, he didn't mention any incursion into his personal space. Maybe he assumed that one of the children had been the sandy-footed culprit.

Instead, he asked me about my plans for the Christmas holiday.

"You'll be heading off I take it?"

"Yes – I'm planning to pack up on Thursday and drive down early on Friday morning."

"And that would be to where?"

"I'll be staying with mum for a few days, after I've seen friends in Manchester."

"That'll be a shock to the system, after four months in Kylecraig."

"It will. But I'm looking forward to catching up with people. How about you Jackson, what are your festive plans?"

"None to speak of. Other than the ceilidh of course, at Hogmanay."

I'd seen posters mentioning this event at the village hall, but I'd barely paid them any attention, figuring I'd still be down south. Jackson carried on speaking.

"I daresay you've already made your plans. But if you are coming back up here, maybe we could go to the ceilidh. What do you think?

This invitation was so unexpected that I was shocked into silence, until Jackson repeated himself.

"I'll think about it." I said. I wasn't going to give him any more than that.

*

When I got back to the cottage that night, there was a note taped to my door. I opened it at the same time as I was fiddling with my door-key, and so it took a while for the words to assemble themselves into a meaningful sentence.

"We don't need any more RATS in this village. Time to get OUT. "

The writing was clumsy, rounded, child-like, the capital letters scored over with biro several times, almost breaking through the paper.

I crumpled up the note, and threw it into the bin. Then I took it out again, smoothed it down, and tucked it inside my rucksack.

I was desperate for a glass of wine. But I made sure to lock the door, and to pull all the blinds and curtains tightly closed before I poured myself one.

CHAPTER EIGHT

The last day of term came and went. I filmed the carol concert, hoping that there would be thirty seconds in there which didn't make people's ears bleed. Still, I guessed that viewers would think the kids looked sweet dressed up as elves and reindeer. I'd brought in a bottle of sherry and a box of mince pies to share with Janey, Marnie and Jackson, but although the mince pies all went, I was the only one drinking the sherry. I took the rest of the bottle home with me and finished it whilst watching a DVD of "The Holiday" and wishing I was Kate Winslet.

As a result of the excessive sherry intake, Thursday was rather more chaotic than I'd hoped it would be. I didn't surface until noon, which gave me precious little time to wrap the presents I'd ordered online, write my cards, and pack.

By late afternoon, the zig-zag aura of another migraine was blotting my vision, so I nursed it with pills and peppermint tea; but at 7pm I gave into it, and went to bed. I'd done all that I could do in any case. I set my alarm for 6am and went to sleep.

*

Sometime during the night, I woke, in a panic. I was sweating, but when I threw off the duvet the room was like an ice-box, so I pulled it back around me. My stomach hurt and there were waves of nausea sweeping through my head. When I tried to get up, the room swam around me, so I collapsed back into my bed. Strange noises filled my head – voices, and laughter, and then a vehicle's engine starting up.

51

"Shut up and go to bed, losers" I muttered. My head was burning up, and I longed for something cool and soothing to wipe over my face. Images of Mum and Leonie swam around inside my skull. "Just sleep, Claire, you're over-excited, that's all". Who was this now? Oh, I knew her. It was me. What a sensible woman, I thought.

I fell asleep.

*

There was no escaping my alarm. I'd set it to its loudest, most strident, setting, knowing how much I hated getting up in the dark.

Throwing myself out of bed before I could change my mind, I sleep-walked through to the kitchen, put on the kettle, went into the lounge and opened the curtains.

It took me a while to register what was outside.

Which was, nothing.

That is to say, where I had parked my car last night – where I always parked my car, right outside my front door - there was just an empty space.

"That can't be right," I thought. "Come on Claire think. You must have left it somewhere else." But I never did; and I knew, even in my fuzzy-minded state, that I'd loaded it yesterday afternoon, putting bags of Christmas presents and a suitcase in the boot and throwing extra coats and boots onto the back seat, with a sleeping bag, just in case.

The noises I'd heard in the night came back to me then. In my delirium, I'd thought myself in Manchester, where cars were always starting up and where people shouting in the street faded into the general ambience. But I wasn't in Manchester, I was in Kylecraig.

And my car, it seemed, wasn't.

I rushed back through to the kitchen looking for my handbag, with my car-keys in it.

Gone.

I raced to the back door, tried the handle. It opened.

In my haste to get to bed, it seemed that, for the first time since arriving in Kylecraig, I'd forgotten to lock up. Someone had walked in, seen my bag on the table, found my car keys and taken the car. They must have thought it was their lucky night.

I picked up the phone and, with a shaking hand, dialled 999.

*

Ten minutes later, whilst I was sitting waiting for the police, my phone rang.

"Hello?"

"Hello – is that Miss Armstrong?" A woman's voice, soft and soothing, perfect for breaking bad news. "It's the police here. I'm sorry to have to pass this onto you, but we've just had a report from the Fire service. They've an engine out on the scene of a vehicle fire in the woods near the bridge, about a mile out of the village. I'm awful sorry to say this Miss, but it sounds like it's your car."

"What?"

Very patiently, the woman repeated what she'd just told me. She was just finishing when there was a knock at the door.

"I'd better go, I think the police are here. The other police. Thank you."

I replaced the receiver, and went to the door.

Outside, was a man with a kind looking face, the only sort of face you'd want to have standing on your doorstep at 6.30am in the morning after something bad has happened.

"Claire? I'm Iain Cameron, local police officer. There's a colleague coming up from Lochinver, a female, if you'd prefer to wait?"

But I'd already opened the door wider. I didn't want to be on my own in that house for one second longer.

*

By seven o' clock, there were three of us sitting around my kitchen table, Iain having been joined by Kirsty from Lochinver. We were onto our second cup of tea. Their verdict was that my car had been stolen for fun, driven at speed up and down the main road a few times, and then dumped in woodland and ignited. Carefully chosen Christmas presents for my friends, my nieces and my Mum had all gone up in flames. Along with most of my clothes, my only pair of smart boots, and a very good down sleeping bag.

"But why?" I asked, for the tenth or possibly twentieth time.

Iain and Kirsty exchanged a look.

"Hard to say for certain, but probably high on drugs, booze, or both. Tried a few doors, found yours open. You were just unlucky."

"But this is the Highlands, not inner-city Manchester." I still couldn't believe what had happened. I'd lived for thirty five years in a city, and never been burgled, and I told them as much.

"It's not a common occurrence Miss, rest assured" said Iain. "But there are always a few bad examples in every community, and the last Friday before Christmas……"

He tailed off, leaving Kirsty to finish his sentence.

"People get a wee bit – over-excited. It doesn't necessarily lead to criminal activity mind – just a few sore heads the next day. As Iain's said, you've been unlucky."

"You're sure I haven't been targeted?"

They looked at each other again, as if deciding who should answer that question. Once again, it fell to Iain to do so.

"Do you know of anybody with a grudge against you?"

Only the whole village, I thought, remembering some of the suspicious looks I'd had over the past few weeks and months. Then I saw, on Iain's face, a look of such concern that I felt ashamed.

"No, I don't think so."

Five minutes ago, I'd been planning to tell both of them about the dead rat, the mysterious cigarette smoker, the note on my kitchen door. Now, I decided, I would keep silent, fearing that I'd just sound like a spoilt outsider who couldn't cope with life in a rural community.

Whoever took my car could have hurt me, if they'd wanted to. They'd been in my house, after all, and there were drawers full of kitchen knives, if they'd felt inclined to use them. So either the police were right, and this was just a case of bad luck, or they were wrong; in which case, I would need to find out who was trying to frighten me away.

And to make sure that they didn't succeed.

CHAPTER NINE

The news about my car was all round the village in no time, and I spent the rest of the morning answering the door to villagers. Some seemed genuinely concerned for my safety; others seemed to be more worried that their own cars and homes might be at risk. All professed to be horrified that this had happened in Kylecraig.

"That kind of thing just never happens here," was a phrase I heard more than once.

"Well – it's happened to me," became my stock response.

People brought me home baking, and freshly laid eggs from their hens. I was even invited to a "Drinks and Nibbles" event on Christmas Eve. After a few hours of this, I just wanted to be left alone, so that I could make some phone calls to try and get my life sorted out.

First of all, I tried to find a way of getting to Manchester, but this seemed to be impossible. Apparently, there were train strikes scheduled for the next few days. As a result of this, all of the flights out of Inverness were fully booked. As for hiring a car, since I no longer had a credit card, that was a non-starter.

It looked as though I would have to resign myself to spending Christmas in Kylecraig.

I'd just managed to get through to my insurance company when there was more hammering at the door. I ignored it, and continued my phone call. It took about twenty minutes to go through all the details of what had happened, and what would happen next. By the time I came off the phone, I realised that I was hungry, so I walked through to the kitchen where the home baking had been piling up, and jumped about a foot in the air when I saw a familiar figure sitting at my table.

"Jackson – what the hell do you think you're doing?"

"Well….the door was open. Round here, that seems to be an invitation to step inside."

Maybe he did suspect that I'd been in his van the other day after all.

"Haven't you heard what happened to me this morning?"

"Of course I have. That's why I'm here. And I did knock."

I recalled the hammering I'd heard at the door.

"Well, I didn't answer. In my book, that means please leave me alone. I don't need any more visitors or any more cake. In fact, please take some away, I can't eat it all."

"Relax, I'll clear off if you don't want me here. I just wanted to check that you're alright."

"I'm fine," I snapped. "I've just lost my car, my driving licence which was in my bag, along with my purse, bank cards, and all the Christmas presents that I'd bought for my family. How could you possibly think that I wouldn't be alright?"

Jackson stood up.

"Okay. I'm going to go now, since I can see that there are things you need to get on with. But I know you will have cleared your food stores out, so if you want to come over to the van for dinner, please do. There will be wine."

I hesitated, and then nodded, slowly.

"Thank you. That would be really – helpful."

"Oh, and I brought you this," he passed me a bottle of milk. "It's from Billy Mackenzie – he thought you might not have any left."

I took the milk without a word, and watched as Jackson picked up a Tupperware box full of chocolate brownies.

"Are you sure you don't want these?"

"Take them," I said. I'll see you later.

When he'd left, I locked the door behind him and sat down at the table, as the shakiness I'd been feeling all morning evaporated into tears. I allowed myself five minutes of this indulgence, and then I slapped myself, hard, on the side of my head, to remind myself that I was on my own here – so I'd just have to toughen up and get on with it.

*

Once the initial shock of realising how much I'd lost had worn off, I found myself being thankful for what hadn't been taken. My camera and tripod were locked securely away in an upstairs cupboard, along with the laptop and all of the material I'd shot, which was backed up onto an additional hard drive. Everything else was replaceable. And although she was shocked to hear what had happened, Leonie was quick to reassure me, when I called her.

"It's just stuff," she said. "They didn't hurt you, that's the main thing. I know it must be a horrible feeling, but don't let it get to you. That kind of thing could happen anywhere."

"I know. It's just such awful timing, when I was looking forward to coming home."

"Think yourself lucky" she said, trying to lighten my mood. "I wish I had an excuse to opt out of Christmas. We're going to my sister's – which'll mean three nights sleeping on an air-bed under the desk in her study, in a house full of toddlers and flatulent Jack Russells. In fact, can I come up to Kylecraig and keep you company instead?"

"Please do," I laughed, knowing that it was all a bluff, since she loved seeing her nephews and nieces – if not the dogs – over Christmas.

After that, I had to make the call I'd been dreading – to Mum. Not wanting her to worry, I played down the whole incident, telling her only the minimum – that my car had been stolen, it was written off; there was no way for me to get home. I even lied about the loss of the presents, telling her that I'd been hopelessly disorganised and asking if she could please get gifts sorted out for my brother and my two nieces.

"It's not like you to be so last-minute dear," she said.

"There aren't any shops here" I bluffed, although I'd ordered everything online weeks earlier. "I was planning to stop on the way down and do it. I'm sorry you won't have a present but we can have a delayed celebration when you come up to visit me."

"Let's do that" she said. "It'll be fun. But Christmas Day won't be the same without you."

*

I was acutely aware of my emotions over the next few days and I kept myself busy. Luckily, there was plenty to get on with. Paranoid about losing my precious footage, I made duplicate hard copies of everything I'd already shot, and posted them to Mum, enclosing a very glittery Christmas card (the only type available in the village Post Office) and a note explaining that the rushes of my film were not being sent in lieu of a present.

I had to cancel and replace bank and credit cards, store cards, my driving licence, my work ID card, my NUJ card. At some stage, I would have to arrange to buy another car, but I couldn't, until I received the insurance money. It turned out that my policy didn't provide me with a courtesy car and so I was, effectively, stuck.

Swallowing my pride, I took Eilidh up on her offer to borrow some money, and travelled on the weekly community mini-bus into Ullapool. Whilst everybody else went for a boozy lunch, I did the most frugal shop I could; although half of the loan went on a 3 litre wine box. Food seemed less important at the moment – wine was the only thing that would get me to sleep, and that was what I craved more than anything.

Apart from that one dinner, on the night my car was stolen, I stayed away from Jackson. He'd been so kind that night that I'd felt myself come dangerously close to tears. I was terrified of going back to Ceol na Mara after we'd eaten, but I did my best to convince him that I wasn't concerned.

"It was my own fault," I said. "I always check that I've locked the back door before I go to bed, and it was only because I was ill that I didn't. There's nothing like being punished for a one-off event eh? At least it means I won't forget in the future. Besides, there's nothing left to steal."

I'd smiled until my jaw ached, told him stories about my previous job in Manchester, and drunk two large glasses of red wine very, very slowly. I'd refused to let him walk me home, though I suspect he'd followed me anyway, and I'd turned down his offer to cook for me until I was able to get to the shops.

"I've plenty of stuff in the freezer," I'd lied. I was damned if I wanted to beholden to him, or to anybody else.

*

On Christmas Eve, just as the Festival of Nine Lessons and Carols started on Radio 4, there was a polite knock on the door.

I hid the wine box and half-empty glass under the table and turned down the radio.

"Who is it?" I called. I'd stopped un-locking the door, wary of more gifts of cake, or splattered rats.

"It's Jackson. And I'm not going away until you open the door. I'll sit here all night if I have to."

I sighed, and opened up.

"Well?"

"How are you planning to spend Christmas Day?"

"I'm staying here. Junior Choice on the Radio, turkey-based microwave meal, I might even wrap a bit of tinsel around a slice of Mairi Morrison's fruit cake. Why?"

"I'm planning a good long hike. Wondered if you might care to join me. Thought it might do us both good to get a bit of fresh air, away from here. What do you think?"

"Okay." I said it before I'd had a chance to think about it.

Jackson looked surprised.

"Great. Well then, that's settled. I'll come for you at 10, Billy Mackenzie's given me the loan of his pick-up for the day. He said he'll be too pickled to drive it anyway, once he's done his early morning check on the sheep. I've never seen him touch a drop of drink, and I told him so. Apparently this is the one day of the year he does, so we may as well take advantage of his lack of sobriety. I'll see you in the morning."

Before I could speak he was up, and out of the door, but he rapped on it again after he'd closed it.

"Lock this door" he shouted. "Now."

I did as I was told, and listened to his footsteps receding along the path.

Turning up the radio, the clean, pure music of the King's College choir singing to a packed congregation filled the void of my remote Highland cottage. An image flashed into my head of me and Mum, making sausage rolls and mince pies with my nieces. That's what they would be doing – what I should be doing - right now.

I lifted the cloth, and crawled under the kitchen table. It was surprisingly cosy in there, the red of the cotton material lending a warm glow to the space. I remembered being a kid, playing at houses, in the days when my brother and I would happily spend hours in such a place. Thirty years on, at least there was wine on tap.

"What's good enough for Billy Mackenzie, is surely good enough for me," I thought, depressing the plastic nozzle until my glass was full again, and closing my eyes as the opening line of "In the Bleak Midwinter" drifted into the air.

CHAPTER TEN

"How would you normally spend Christmas Day?" asked Jackson.

We were bashing upwards through heather, apparently heading for Loch Dubh – the Black Loch. I'd been assured that it was prettier than it sounded.

"Binge-eating chocolate in suburbia. Since dad died, my brother and I have made a point of being with Mum. This is the first one I've missed. Alex and his wife split up last year, but he's got the kids for Christmas Day and I guess they won't be there next year. That'll be weird. I wish I could have got there."

"Sometimes it does us good to break a routine," said Jackson.

"What do you normally do at Christmas?"

"I don't treat it any differently from any other day. This time last year I was somewhere else. This time next year, who knows?" He looked down at his map, and raised a hand, pointing towards the horizon. "We need to bear right here."

*

He'd put on such a turn of speed that by the time I caught up with him he was leaning against a trig point, surveying the view.

"Better than the view from suburbia, I think you'll find" he said, as I panted over the lip of the hill.

Joining him at the cairn, I saw right away what he meant. Floating out to the west, the hills of Greagha seemed flattened and lowly, the whole island diminished by our lofty viewpoint. Beyond that, the sea stretched away into a void – next stop,

America. In every other direction were hump-backed hills and hillocks, bumps and tussocks, lochans and puddles. But something wasn't right.

"Where's the Loch? Isn't this the Loch Dubh path?"

"Well spotted. You might wish to consult your map."

I pulled the pink-covered OS map from the pocket of my rucksack and studied it.

"So, we're here?" I pointed to a trig point which was marked at a height of 674 metres.

Jackson nodded.

"Sgurr Creagan" I read. "No idea how to say that properly. So that means Loch Dubh – which I do know how to say, it's pronounced Doo….."

"Well – close enough."

I ignored him.

"Loch Dubh is about another two miles in the same direction."

"Correct. But as you can see from the contour lines we've already done all the climbing. The next bit is relatively flat. Come on."

I was still struggling to put my map away and my rucksack back on as he strode off.

The Black Loch lived up to its name when we reached it. Thanks to its situation, cradled amongst the peat hags, it glowered darkly even on a day as sunny as this one. There was a battered old fishing boat tied with bailer twine at one end, although how it had got up here was anybody's guess. A few yellowy looking reeds protruded from the water, but other than that, this was an unadorned, un-touristy, basic Scottish loch.

"Good place for Christmas lunch?" asked Jackson. "Breaking with tradition, we have cheese and Marmite sandwiches."

"Simple things," I smiled. "You don't have to spend much money to be happy."

"I actually paid quite a premium for the Marmite. It was the last jar on Mairi Morrison's shelf and I swear to god she put the price up when she saw me."

"That doesn't surprise me. Still, the sunshine and the views are free."

But before long we were feeling the cold, and re-traced our steps hurriedly across the hill. By the time we got back to the summit cairn, the skies had darkened dramatically over Greagha and we could see a squall coming in.

"It's going to be a race to get down before that weather," said Jackson.

He wasn't wrong. We were still about half an hour from our starting point when the first spots of rain dappled my coat, and by the time we'd reached the lay-by where he'd parked the truck we were soaked through.

"We need a decent dram and a log fire," said Jackson. "I know just the place."

We got into the car and headed north up the single-track road until we hit the coast again. We'd been driving for around twenty minutes when, rounding a sharp bend in the road, I caught sight of a tiny white building, huddled into a gap in the sea-cliffs.

"Wow. What is this place?"

I pulled the car into the one space in front of it.

"This is the Craggan".

"It doesn't look very open. Maybe they close on Christmas Day."

"Oh, it'll be open alright."

There was no pub sign, just a narrow black door, but sure enough this was unlocked, and we stepped from the road into a tiny space, no bigger than the kitchen in my cottage. The unmistakable sweet and sour smell of a peat fire grazed my grateful nostrils and I headed towards it like a moth towards a light bulb.

The room was empty, but Jackson seemed to know exactly where to go, heading for a serving hatch in the wall, where he picked up a huge old-fashioned hand bell. As the sonorous tones of the bell rang out, the floorboards creaked above my head, and before too long, a whiskery face with beady eyes appeared at the hatch.

"Two drams please," Jackson said.

"Any preference?"

"Anything from Islay," he told the old lady.

We heard her shuffle away, and a few minutes later she re-appeared with two glasses and two bottles of different Islay malts, which she plonked on the bar.

"Leave them back here when you've finished, save me coming round the outside."

Jackson brought the bottles and glasses over to where I was sitting, steaming, in front of the fire, staring at the sloping walls, which seemed to be carved from the rock.

"I've never seen anything like this pub," I said. "It's like a film set."

"Yes, well, I doubt it'll be here for much longer."

"Oh?"

"Well, you saw the old lady. Can't be a day shy of ninety, what do you think?"

Right on cue, there was renewed creaking of floorboards, causing us both to look up at the ceiling, which seemed in danger of crumbling on our heads. After a while, the noise stopped, and the only sound was the hiss of the fire.

"This place is spooky," I said.

"Cosy, I'd call it."

Jackson poured a couple of small drams, and we chinked glasses, but he seemed on edge, glancing up at the ceiling, and round to the hatch. I sipped my whisky slowly, and felt it warming me from the inside out.

"Do you think we could do this again?" I asked him.

"What?" He snapped round, stared at me.

"What we've done today. A walk, a drink. Conversation optional."

"I'm not sure it's a good idea. You know what people are like for gossip."

"Seriously, are we going to spend the next six or seven months avoiding each other?"

Up until then he'd been twitchy, his eyes roaming all over the tiny room, but now, he focused on me properly.

"We'll see. We've got the ceilidh at Hogmanay. I've too much to do to between now and then."

He was running a hand through his curls, which had gone wild and wiry in the rain.

I bit my lip. There was no point in pushing him. Besides, I had plenty to do as well.

CHAPTER ELEVEN

One week later, at exactly 6pm, Jackson knocked at my kitchen door. When I opened it, he took a step back and gave a mock bow.

"Goodness. The belle of the ball."

My hard work had apparently paid off. Solvent once again, since my new bank card had finally arrived, I'd cadged a lift into Ullapool with Eilidh Ross and visited a hairdresser for the first time in six months. She'd applied a new colour which emphasised the natural, coppery tones of my hair. She'd also cut it to a more flattering length, with layers that framed my face, and recommended a new grey eyeshadow to emphasise the green in my eyes.

Amazing to think that I'd often spent in excess of a hundred quid on a city salon hairdo, and the same on designer make-up – here I was after handing over £40 to a local stylist, who used her front room as her salon, and an extra fiver for the Avon catalogue eye make-up, and I looked better than I had in years. I'd concealed the shadows under my eyes, hidden some worrying thin red veins on my cheeks with blusher, and even painted my nails. I was grateful that I could still fit into my most flattering emerald green body-con dress – a frugal Christmas had some advantages.

As soon as we walked into the village hall, I wished I'd brought my camera. The place was a riot of colour and noise, and most of the parents and children were there.

I added some bags of crisps to the trestle tables at the back of the hall, embarrassed by the laziness of my offering against the vast plates of home-made pies, sandwiches and cakes. Jackson had gone off in search of drinks and returned carrying a bottle of red wine and two tumblers.

"Not the most elegant, but it's all that was left," he said, glugging wine into the glasses.

"I didn't know you were a wine drinker."

"I have many hidden vices," he replied. "This is just the one I can go public with."

We were soon surrounded. Mairi Morrison from the Post Office, Eilidh Ross, and a few other women had made a beeline for our table in the corner of the room. After expressing their shock at my car misfortune, and assuring me all over again that things like that never happened here, it was Jackson they wanted to talk to, and he received them with charming smiles, like the benign ruler of a small kingdom. Finally, Eilidh noticed that I was there as well.

"How are you doing, Claire?"

"Oh, I'm fine. Looking forward to my first ceilidh."

"Really?" She looked surprised. "I guess we grow up with them here, so it's funny to think of some folk never having been to one. All part of the learning curve for you."

"Yes, I'm learning a lot up here. To think I wasted all those years going to pubs and clubs when I could have been doing this."

Seeing a suspicious look flash across her face, I hurried to reassure her.

"I mean it. This is so much – nicer. Everybody here together, all ages from babies to grandparents, and everybody pitching in.

It makes me wonder why I've spent so much of my life in cities."

"Well, if you'd grown up here you'd be desperate for the city. We face it all the time with the youngsters. They can't wait to be off when they get to eighteen – Edinburgh, Aberdeen, Glasgow, even London – anywhere but Kylecraig."

"Yes, but some of them come back," I pointed out. "Look at Janey Macleod."

We both glanced across the room to where the Head was standing, slightly apart from the crowd. As we looked, her glance snapped to our table, although she couldn't possibly have heard her name over the noise in the hall. She seemed to hesitate for a moment, and then began to stride towards us.

"Well yes, she came back." Eilidh's tone had lost some of its warmth, I noticed. "But most of them stay away until they've families of their own."

Janey had now reached the table. Glancing around, and seeing that Jackson was still held firmly in the grip of local gossip, she lowered her voice.

"Claire – a word, please."

"Of course – why don't you join us?"

But she shook her head, beckoning me to follow her as she headed back across the room towards the main door. Reluctantly, I got up and followed her out to the lobby. There was nobody else out here when I reached her, but she still spoke quietly.

"I noticed that you and Jackson came together."

"Yes."

"You've become good friends then?"

"I wouldn't say that, exactly. But I guess we're both in the same boat." I tried not to sound too defensive. "We're both English, we're not from round here, so I think it makes sense that we're sticking together."

"You need to be careful."

I regarded her stern face, trying to work her out.

"What do you mean?"

She was about to reply, but at that moment, the doors swung open and a cluster of women burst through, giggling and gossiping. Janey switched on her widest smile to greet them, and I was left standing alone as they headed outside together.

*

Later, tired of not being able to get anywhere near Jackson on the dance-floor, I headed for the Ladies. I was about to go in, when I heard his name being mentioned by someone on the other side of the door.

"That Jackson's fair lit up the place tonight. "

"Aye. He's a good-looking fella all right. Mind, I'm still not sure myself. How can you have a teacher living like that? It's no kind of example to set the children."

"Janey Macleod seems not to mind any of that."

"Aye well....she'll have her reasons, won't she? After all....handsome man....ticking clock..."

Here, the voices lowered, and I could no longer hear what was being said. And the next thing I knew, two more women were jostling me. One of them was Catriona Mackay, flushed in the face and laughing manically. She was holding onto the tattooed arm of a pale, skinny woman. It took me a moment to place her, then I got it. It was Kelly MacIver, mother of Jimmy, the only pupil not allowed to be in my film.

71

"Come on you, whatever your name is, get in with you, I'm bursting for a pee."

She and Catriona pushed rudely past me, flinging open the door. The other two women who'd been gossiping inside made a great show of applying their lipstick in the mirror before heading back into the hall.

When I got in there myself I spotted Jackson, still dancing, leading the charge in the Dashing White Sergeant. I was glad to sit that one out – my feet, now used to wellies and walking boots, were protesting at being forced back into my glittery dancing shoes. They looked lovely but wearing them was torture.

Past caring by now, I took them off, and put my bare feet up on a chair but as I did so the music finished, and people started to pour off the dance-floor. It seemed the evening had come to an end.

Red-faced and grinning widely, Jackson appeared in front of me.

"Lightweight."

I took the insult on the chin.

"Absolutely. Us city girls aren't used to this hectic pace of life."

"I can see that. I take it you'll be ready to head home then?"

He didn't wait for an answer but disappeared, coming back a few minutes later with our coats. I tried to force my feet back into their shoes, but my toes had swollen into fat little sausages.

"Allow me."

Before I realised what was happening, Jackson was kneeling in front of me, one hand casually stroking the top of my foot as he tried to force my shoe back on. A shiver rippled right through me, in spite of the heat in the room.

"Cinderella, you shall go to the ball" he murmured on succeeding with the first one. "Although you might want to go to the shoe-shop and buy a bigger pair of shoes first."

He moved onto my other foot and somehow got the second shoe on as well. Standing up he towered over me, and there seemed suddenly to be something dangerous about him. Whether it was the look on his face or just a feeling I had after my earlier conversation with Janey I couldn't tell, but I got hurriedly to my feet, wincing at the pain in my toes.

"Steady on," he said. "Looks like I might have to carry you home at this rate."

"I'm fine," I snapped, hobbling towards the door.

"Claire wait – your coat."

I stopped, still facing away from him, but felt him come up behind me and wrap my coat around my shoulders. As he did so I caught sight of Janey Macleod. She was standing nearby, slightly apart from a group of school mums, and looking directly at me. I smiled and waved to show that all was well. But instead of returning my smile she frowned and turned away.

Shrugging Jackson off, and pushing my arms into my coat sleeves, I approached her as quickly as my crippled feet would allow.

"Janey." I tapped her on the shoulder and she swivelled round to face me.

"Are you heading home? Thanks so much for coming. I hope you've enjoyed your first ceilidh?"

"Yes, it's been great. But I really think I need to talk to you."

"I don't think so." Her expression, serene and polite, gave nothing away. "Goodnight Claire." She nodded in the direction of Jackson, who was waiting by the door. "Looks like your escort is ready to leave – you'd better hurry."

Chance would be a fine thing I thought, but I took the hint and headed for the exit. We walked out into a crisp cold night and started along the road to the cottage.

"What is her problem," I grumbled. "She seems to forget that I am NOT one of her pupils."

"Just ignore her."

I stole a glance sideways, but Jackson was looking up, rather than at me.

"Stop," he said a moment later. I kept walking, or rather hobbling. "Claire, stop. Look up, look at the stars."

"Oh right, the stars. And the sodding mountains and the stupid waves and the whole bloody sodding universe. Never mind what's right under your sodding bloody nose."

"Are you annoyed with me? Because I didn't dance with you, is that it?"

I did stop now, and tried to look at Jackson, but it was hard to make out much in the darkness.

"Why the sudden rage and anger?" He sounded perplexed. "Are you drunk?"

"Of course. It's the only way to cope with living in this this stupid sodding place where everybody knows everybody and nobody has any secrets except you, of course, and you have so many secrets and I don't know what they are but clearly they're only secrets from me and they must be pretty significant because everyone seems to give you just what you want and tiptoe round you. And then just when I think we have some kind of ….friendship…and just when I think I might have met someone here who I can actually talk to……"

Here I tailed off, realising that I was about to tell him that Janey Macleod had warned me to be careful. I didn't want him to know about that conversation.

"But we are friends, Claire. At least, I hope we are."

Without any warning, I burst into tears. I stood there, weeping, in the middle of that dead-end road on the outer edges of the Scottish Highlands, with the stars of the universe spread above me like a ballroom canopy and the sound of the waves washing into my brain.

Once I'd started weeping I found that I couldn't stop. I allowed Jackson to scoop me up into his arms and carry me along the road. And I breathed in the smell of the wool of his jacket, and felt the beat of his heart through the fabric, and the motion of his body as he strode along the road beneath that vast sky with me in his arms. Gradually my tears began to slide more slowly down my face, and my breathing slowed down.

And then there was just the sky and the stars and the sea and Jackson and all of it was spinning away from me.

CHAPTER TWELVE

For once, I was grateful for Jackson's reticence. We never spoke again about my tears at Hogmanay, or about the fact that he'd had to put me to bed (fully clothed) and sit with me through the night to make sure that I didn't choke on my own vomit. When I'd woken up the next morning, he'd quietly told me all of this before leaving me to stew in my embarrassment.

Humiliation aside, I'm not sure how I made it through January.

I became obsessed by the weather, and the sunrise and sunset times. Never before had I paid so much attention to the sky. It stayed stubbornly dark until 9 in the morning, returning to darkness by around 3pm. Sometimes the sky seemed barely to lighten at all, and I learned the true meaning of that most powerful and onomatopoeic of Scottish words, as "dreich" became my bête noire.

*

At least my life was slowly getting back on track. The insurance money for my car came through in mid-January, and I was able to replace it with a similar one that Eilidh's husband Alasdair was selling, although I refused to let him knock £500 off the value. I didn't want anybody taking pity on me.

My film was coming along again, too, and I scrutinised Jackson through my eye-piece even more closely than before. He definitely had a way about him, which meant that even the most restless child paid attention. Even the usually monosyllabic and sullen Jimmy MacIver contributed to Jackson's lessons (annoyingly, since I was not allowed to film him) and the normally hyper-active Murdo Mackay sat silent and rapt.

Not that it ever stopped him from wheeling out of the classroom at the sound of the bell, sometimes so fast that he almost dismantled my tripod in his desperation to be out of there.

That boy," Jackson said to me one afternoon, as Murdo made his hurried exit out of the classroom whilst the other children were still packing books into their bags. "If only he could learn to be still."

"He's a lot better than he used to be," I told him. "At least he listens during the lessons now. He never did that before you arrived, just sat there twitching and throwing bits of paper at the girls."

Meanwhile, Janey Macleod and I continued to skirt around each other – I used the camouflage of my camera to study her behaviour around Jackson, certain that there was some kind of tension between the two of them and curious to know the reason why. But whatever it was eluded me, since they always managed to be civil to one another; at least when my camera was anywhere near them.

*

When Jackson abruptly cancelled one of our weekend walks in early February, saying that he had to go to Inverness instead, I offered to take him in my new car. He refused me, politely but firmly.

"Why are you going there?" I persisted, long after I should have taken the hint and kept quiet.

He rounded on me, grabbing me by the wrist.

"For crying out loud Claire – I managed to live my life perfectly well before you came along. You never know when to stop, do you?"

Hours later, there were still red marks around my wrist. Sitting at my kitchen table, I rubbed them, thoughtfully, brooding on the fact that his mood swings had become more frequent, and more dramatic, over the past few weeks.

Finally, I realised that if I didn't get outside and grab some fresh air, it would be dark, and I'd have wasted the whole day sulking.

When I reached the beach, I was still burning with indignation, but even that wasn't enough to keep me warm. Although I'd dressed in a padded down jacket, gloves, hat and scarf, it was bitterly cold. Gradually, as my black mood evaporated, I became aware that the light was wonderful, a dusky orange sun filtering soft darts of brightness between scattered grey clouds and onto the water. Although the last few days had been almost apocalyptically wet there had been very little wind, so the water was flat calm.

Inspired, I ran back to the house to fetch my camera.

As I filmed along the shoreline, a few curious seals popped their heads out of the water, and a flock of oystercatchers bobbled about at the edge of the waves, gifting me some entertaining shots. In spite of the cold, I realised I was enjoying myself – it had been a while since I'd used my camera creatively.

Eager to make the most of the unusually kind circumstances, I headed round to Kylecraig's small harbour, which huddled at the foot of a rocky outcrop to the north of the school.

A fierce storm in the 1980s had demolished much of the structure and this, coupled with a collapse in the fishing industry meant that it was no longer in use commercially. But it was strangely picturesque in its own bruised and battered way. A few locals still used what remained of the walls to tie up small boats and dinghies, which added a welcome splash of colour.

I set up my camera on a low tripod to frame this pleasing scene, and had just hit the "Record" button when something moved at the periphery of my vision.

Looking up, I saw that in the furthest corner of the harbour, one of the boats was rocking steadily. Given that there was no wind, and no movement anywhere else, I wondered what had caused this. Could it be someone working on the boat? But then the dinghy next door began to move as well.

Curious, I bent my head to the eye-piece of my camera. The light was fading quickly by now, but I could just make out the small figure of a boy in a striped jumper, jumping from boat to boat. I zoomed in as far as I could, figuring it must be one of the kids from school – Calum, Jimmy or Murdo, to judge by the size and nimbleness – but I was too far away to tell for sure.

"Damn."

The motion was stirring up the surface of the water – I'd started off filming a perfect reflection, like a mirror, but now just had a shot of broken slabs of colour ripping across the startled sea. I hit the record button again, to stop filming.

The striped jumper had reached the end of the line of boats now, but rather than leaving, the boy turned around and began heading back the way he'd just come, jumping adeptly from deck to deck. Clearly this was going to come down to who got bored first – me or him - and having already lost the best of the afternoon light, I decided to call it a night.

As I packed away my gear, the game was still in progress. I tried to put away my annoyance - it was good to see children playing outdoors rather than staring at a computer screen after all – but I was frustrated that the actions of one small boy had ruined such a perfect shot.

My wrist was still sore, and worse of all, my vision was beginning to fracture and tear, meaning that a full-blown migraine was only minutes away.

About to head for home, rucksack on my back, I turned to take one final look at the harbour in the last shreds of daylight. The splintered slats of light in my eyes didn't present a clear image, although I could tell that the boats had stopped rocking, and I thought I could hear a snatch of shouted conversation.

I strained to hear properly and after a moment it came again, a gruff shout, followed by what sounded like a slightly strangled cry.

But I could see nobody else around; and the screeching of gulls had fooled me like that before.

CHAPTER THIRTEEN

Finally, inevitably, February sloped moodily away to be replaced by a benign, birdsong-strewn March. Temperatures didn't exactly soar but not long after the half-term holiday came the morning when I stepped out of my house and realised that I could dispense with my gloves and hat.

But then came the day that I had been dreading.

It was a Sunday afternoon. I was eating a very late lunch and flicking through a month-old copy of *Hello!* (sent by Leonie in an attempt to lower me down to her level) when there was a loud, impatient rapping at the door.

Opening it, I came face to face with a bald, red-faced man in a too-tight sweater. It was Mr Frazer, the landlord, who I'd met only once before, when I'd collected the door keys from him at his vast, modern home a few miles outside Inverness. He was peering around me, rather than at me, as if to see what I'd done to his house.

"Hi, Mr Frazer. What's this about?" As if I didn't already know.

"I'll be needing the cottage back. I've bookings for April and May, as you know."

Given that the cottage hadn't been exactly a home from home, I was surprised at how upset I felt at having to move out.

"I might have an idea for you though. If you don't fancy the static caravan, I hear Billy Mackenzie might be willing to rent his place to you for the next few months."

Billy Mackenzie? Something clanged in my brain, and then I realised why. It was on his land at the back of the beach that Jackson parked his van, and the cottage was on the same plot.

"I'll take you to the caravan now if you like, and then round to Billy's. Help you make your mind up."

The static caravan was every bit as dreary as I'd imagined it would be. It was beige and brown on the outside and even beiger on the inside. It was situated in one corner of a thistly field on the outside of the village, and it reeked of damp.

"Nobody's been in here since the summer," explained Mr Frazer. "Needs an airing."

"Needs blowing up," I muttered under my breath, adding "let's go and see Billy's place" in a louder voice.

We clambered back into Mr Frazer's shiny new BMW and drove even further out of the village. But I didn't mind the extra distance, knowing that this was the only house close to Jackson's van, and the perfect place from which to keep an eye on him.

Billy Mackenzie was waiting for us outside the cottage. I'd come across him a couple of times, including on the night of the ceilidh, but we'd never had a proper conversation. However, I'd heard enough from Jackson to know that he was a decent man. We shook hands, and he showed me round, without saying a word.

The cottage was similar to Ceol Na Mara, but nicer. Tall sand-dunes over the road meant that the sea was only visible from the upstairs rooms - but on the plus side, the garden would be sheltered from the worst of the westerly winds.

Inside, the layout was almost identical with the main door opening directly onto the kitchen. There was a lounge with a wood-burner and upstairs, two bedrooms. The bathroom was at the back of the house, downstairs.

"I'd love to move in, as soon as possible please," I told Billy Mackenzie.

By now, it was almost 5.30pm. Mr Frazer offered to drive me back to Ceol Na Mara, but I turned him down - the slippery leather seats and cloying scent of Vanilla Air Freshener over-laying stale cigarette smoke had made me feel sick. Billy and I watched him screech away as though he couldn't wait to be gone, and then we chatted for a while longer, agreeing on the rent and a moving in date. I could hardly contain my excitement as we shook hands on the deal.

I headed past the dunes onto the scrub land at the back of the beach, hoping to share my good news with Jackson. A charred pile of wood outside the van was still warm, but there were no other signs of activity, and the door was padlocked, so I carried on along the beach towards the village. By the time I reached the far end of the bay, most of the light had already drained from the sky.

He'd almost walked past me before I caught sight of him – he was walking at speed in the opposite direction a few feet away, his hands stuffed into the pockets of the usual overcoat, his face, unusually for him, jutting down towards the sand. I called his name and when he failed to respond, I ran after him.

"Jackson!"

I tapped him on the back and he spun round, clearly caught by surprise, his fists balled up as though he was ready for a fight.

When I saw his face, it was my turn to be startled. Even in the dim light, I could see that his eyes were bloodshot, the skin around them red and sore, as though he'd been rubbing at it repeatedly. There was tension in the angle of his jaw, and he quickly turned his face back towards the ground when he saw me staring.

"Claire - what are you doing out here?"

"I've been looking at Billy Mackenzie's house – he's looking for somebody to rent it and I'm looking for somewhere to live, so it's perfect. Anyway, where have you been? Out for a walk? Have you been far?"

Jackson remained silent, staring down at where his right foot was tracing an abstract pattern in the sand.

"Are you alright?"

"Fine. But it's getting dark, and there's a storm coming. You should get back home."

"Jackson….." my voice trailed off into the gloom.

"What, Claire? What is it? Do you want me to tell you where I've been, who I've been talking to, what I've been doing? What are you, my keeper?"

"I….Jackson….no, I….."

"Because trust me, that is not going to happen. Not now, not ever."

I could barely see his face by now, but I could hear choked-up emotion in his voice, though whether through fear, anger or grief I couldn't say. I tried to stay calm.

"Jackson of course not, you know I wouldn't want you to tell me anything if you don't want to. It's just that – well, I'm your friend, and I care about you."

"Well – that's your problem."

He turned away from me and carried on up the beach, his stomping feet stirring up whirlwinds of sand.

"Jackson – wait….."

I called after him, started to run, and then stopped as he shouted back at me.

"Go away, Claire. For God's sake, just leave me alone."

As his words reached me, darkness folded in and took him from my sight. With the wind already strengthening, and neither torch nor moonlight to guide me, I struggled to make my way home.

CHAPTER FOURTEEN

The storm kept me awake until the early hours of Monday morning. At least that's what I told myself. In reality, I was going over and over the encounter with Jackson, and the rattling window panes and lashing rain just provided an appropriate backdrop to my thoughts.

But the following day, it was as though nothing had happened. The squall had blown away, and Jackson waved at me when I tiptoed into his classroom with my camera.

"Come in, come in, you're just in time," he called, as half a dozen children turned to see who'd arrived. Most of them lost interest as soon as they saw it was me.

"We're just about to go and do some nature study on the beach. Care to join us?"

I tried to emulate his cheery tone.

"That sounds good. I'll fetch my coat and see you out there."

I decided to leave the tripod behind and just shoot hand-held, since my main motivation for going out there was to keep an eye on Jackson. Heading out of the main door, I bumped into Marnie, who had another half-dozen children in tow.

"Bloody Jackson," she said, under her breath. "As soon as my lot saw him taking his class out onto the beach there was anarchy in the classroom – or at least there would have been, if I hadn't agreed that they could come out too."

He certainly knew how to entertain the children, picking up huge fronds of seaweed and draping it in his hair to look like a monster dragged from the depths of the ocean. He ran after them trailing the slimy green and brown algae, and they screamed and ran away from him. "Nature study" was an interesting way to describe it.

Without the tripod it was tricky keeping my camera steady as I filmed, and with an eye to the viewfinder it was a few moments before I realised that Jackson had stopped messing around and was looking anxiously in the direction of the school.

I turned, with my camera still running, to see Janey Macleod and another woman who was carrying a toddler, half-walking, half-running towards us. When they got a bit closer, Janey called out;

"Murdo? Murdo Mackay?"

"Not here, Miss," shouted back a couple of the children.

"Jackson, is that true?" Her voice was sharp and anxious now.

He looked at her, and the woman beside her, who I now recognised as Murdo's mother, Catriona. Her face was puffy and wet with tears.

"Well – yes, it is. That is to say, I haven't seen him this morning. But he's often late, you know, because of the croft…."

His voice trailed off.

This was true – Murdo was late as often as he was punctual, but there was usually a good reason for it. Whether it was a sick cow or a ewe in labour in the small hours of the morning, ten-year-old Murdo was always on hand to help out in emergencies - even if it meant him snoozing his way through lessons the next day.

"He was meant to be at a sleepover last night," sobbed Catriona. "That's what he told me, yesterday afternoon. "I'm staying over at Jimmy's tonight, ma", that's what he said, "and I'll be straight to school in the morning". So when I found his gym kit in the hall just now I thought I'd best bring it in for him, seeing as he'd forgotten it."

Everybody turned and look at Jimmy, who seemed more confused than frightened, in spite of Catriona's obvious distress.

"I don't know nothing about it Mrs MacKay. He never came over last night."

I realised that I'd automatically trained the camera on him as he spoke, and quickly panned away from him, before Janey noticed. But she was otherwise engaged.

"We know that Jimmy, thank you, we've just rung your mother," said Janey Macleod, rather brusquely. "The question is, where is Murdo? And why on earth did nobody think to tell me that he was absent from school this morning?"

As her words sunk in, we all automatically looked to Jackson, as the only man, to take control. He seemed to shrink visibly under the pressure of our collective gaze, before rising up to meet the challenge.

"Like I said – he's often late, so I didn't think to question it. And he won't have gone far," he said finally, assertively. "He's probably just having an adventure. Boys will be boys, after all. I doubt he'd have stayed out long in that weather, so he's probably spent the night in a barn or something. He'll come home when he's hungry, like a cat. But we'll have found him long before that happens."

"We need to call the police."

This was Janey Macleod, who seemed flustered and out of her depth.

Jackson was quick to reply this time.

"They'll not thank us for wasting their time. We should just split into groups and look in the obvious places. Where does he like to hang around, Catriona?"

"I...oh I don't know. I've called his name all over the croft and there's no sign of him."

The little girl in her arms was being gripped so tightly that she started to wail.

"Can someone take her?"

Jackson looked over to where Marnie was standing.

"You could have the little one, couldn't you? And take the smallest children as well, back to the school. The rest of us will split into groups and look for Murdo."

Marnie stepped forward.

"Yes, I'll take Katie, she knows me a bit. Don't you, Katie?"

She plucked the screaming toddler from her mother's arms.

"Come on B1 – let's go back to the school and see if we can find some milk and cookies, shall we?"

The youngest children seemed to think that the appeal of cookies made up for missing out on the beachcombing, and eagerly followed Marnie.

Jackson now turned his attention to the rest of us, starting with me. I'd kept my camera running throughout the last few minutes, but now he glared at me.

"Could you turn that off and help, do you think?"

Cut by the tone of his voice, I obeyed without questioning. I suspected that even if I hadn't, Janey Macleod might have wrestled the camera from my grasp, since she was giving me daggers as well.

"Right."

Jackson looked around.

"There are four adults here and…" he did a quick head count, "eight children. So if we grown-ups each take two of the children and investigate an area that will give us maximum coverage. You'll see Catriona, we'll find him in no time."

Janey put her arm around the other woman's shoulder.

"So you just need to tell us where you think we should start looking."

Catriona was still sobbing but we all stayed quiet until she pulled herself together enough to speak.

"I don't know. What do you think? Maybe I should take Jimmy and Rory. I daresay you two know his hiding places better than I do."

The two boys looked nervously at one another.

Suddenly I remembered the incident that had interrupted my filming a few weeks earlier.

"Does he like to go down to the harbour?"

Catriona looked at me sharply.

"Why do you ask?"

I told her what I'd seen.

"The light was quite dim. I couldn't see who it was, but it was definitely a young lad. He was wearing a striped jumper….."

Jackson interrupted me.

"Murdo has one of those; I've seen him wearing it. We should go to the harbour and check straight away."

He turned to Jimmy and Rory.

"You two come with me and Mrs Mackay. Calum, Davy – you boys too. We need to see if he's hiding on one of the boats. The sooner we find Murdo, the sooner we can all carry on with our day. The rest of you - search the village, the school grounds, and the beach. Meet back at the school in one hour. I'm pretty sure we'll find him within the next ten minutes."

*

But we didn't.

Together with my two helpers, Kayleigh and Angela, I walked along the beach away from the school and village, calling Murdo's name. We found footprints in the sand, a few battered old lobster pots and even the remains of a wooden packaging crate with "Made in China" stamped proudly on the side.

But no ten-year-old boy, nor any sign of one.

After almost an hour of searching, we began to trudge back towards the school. The two girls who'd been helping me had started off being excited and full of wise-cracks about Murdo and what a devil he was. Now, they were quiet and tearful.

"Well done, girls," I told them, smiling, trying not to convey my own fears. "Don't worry now. He's probably decided it was too nice a day to bother with school and hitched a lift on a passing tractor or something. That's boys for you!"

There was quite a crowd at the front of the school when we reached it. News of Murdo's disappearance had clearly spread, and all those who were around had dropped whatever they were doing to join in the search. This included the policeman Iain Cameron, who I'd last seen when my car was stolen, talking earnestly to Murdo's mother. I eavesdropped on their conversation.

"This isn't totally out of character is it, Catriona? I know he's a headstrong lad. And chances are he's too frightened to come back now knowing he's caused so much fuss. I bet he's watching us from some clever hiding place right now."

"He's always causing me bother, you know that as well as anyone Iain," she said. "I just want to know where he is."

"Of course you do," said Iain Cameron. "Listen, I still think that we'll find him very soon, but I'm going to radio for some help from Ullapool. If we can get a couple of dogs up here, they'll soon track him down, and then we can all get on with our day."

As he reached for his radio, I caught sight of Jackson with Murdo's two friends, Jimmy and Rory. He was chattering away to them, but behind the steady façade I thought I could see something approaching panic.

"Nothing from the harbour," he announced to the assembled group, although he was looking at me.

"We checked all of the boats after what you told us, just to make sure Murdo hadn't hidden himself away on one."

He lowered his voice to a whisper, directed this time at me.

"What's he doing here?"

"Iain? I think he just saw Catriona and the others looking for Murdo, so he offered to help. Now he's calling for reinforcements."

"I'll go and have a chat with him," said Jackson, and then more loudly;

"Can you keep an eye on these two for me please? We don't want any more boys going missing."

He winked at Jimmy and Rory, but I once again glimpsed fear in his eyes, before he turned away to approach the policeman with an outstretched hand.

"Could we go inside and get a drink please, Miss?" asked Rory, and I was forced to tear myself away from watching the meeting between Jackson and Iain.

"Of course we can. Come on."

I smiled briskly and led the way, trying not to mind about being called "Miss", which always made me feel ridiculously old.

Eilidh was on duty in the kitchen, dispensing milk for the children, tea and coffee for the grown-ups, and homemade tablet and flapjacks for everybody.

"Where do you think Murdo's got to?" I asked her.

She looked at me shrewdly.

"I've no idea. If I thought I knew that, I'd have told somebody already."

I felt my face flush.

"Of course, I'm sorry. I didn't think."

"It's okay. No offence but you wouldn't really understand, not being a mother yourself. I don't think any of us will relax until Murdo's found."

"No, I can see that. I'm sure he'll turn up."

My words tailed off lamely.

"Well, let's hope so."

As we'd been talking, a queue had formed behind me, so I thanked her again and moved aside. I looked around the hall at the children, who were sitting in groups and chatting, under the watchful eye of Marnie (still holding Murdo's sister) and Mairi Morrison. Most of the other adults, those who weren't waiting for drinks, seemed to have gone back outside.

So began a wrestle with my conscience. Would it be wrong to take my camera out and begin filming?

I knew what the parents and teachers would think. On the other hand, I was here to record what happened at the school and, even more than Jackson's arrival, this was a dramatic event.

In an ideal world I'd have found Janey Macleod, explained my dilemma, and waited for a sympathetic and understanding response. Clearly that wasn't going to happen, so I made the decision to fetch my camera and take a few, discreet shots. This was the side of journalism that I'd always hated – hence my decision to turn my back on the door-stepping, inquisitive nature of investigative news, and move into features.

The irony of the situation did not escape me.

I decided not to hide the fact that I was filming, figuring that it would only leave me more open to criticism if I tried to disguise what I was doing. Of course, within a minute of setting up my camera on a tripod at the back of the hall, Marnie had made her way over to my side.

"What are you doing?" she hissed in my ear. "These children are upset. You can't seriously be filming them?"

Looking around the room, I saw little evidence to back up her statement. Most of the children were chatting away quite happily, enjoying the novelty of milk and snacks in the middle of the morning.

"I'm doing my job," I told her, firmly, "just like you. You're doing yours but I've been neglecting mine for the last few hours, because I wanted to help."

When Marnie continued to stand at my side, hands on hips, I lost my temper.

"Please, Marnie; credit me with a bit of intelligence. I'm not going to be intrusive or insensitive, but I do need to record what's going on."

"Fine. But I'm going to go and let the head know."

"I'm sure she'll understand," I snapped.

Waiting until she'd left the hall, I quickly filmed a selection of shots. Then I took the camera off the tripod and carried both outside, before Marnie had a chance to return with Janey Macleod.

The scene in front of the school was one of quiet unrest. Catriona was being comforted by one of the other mothers, with everybody else giving her a wide berth, as though they were scared of saying the wrong thing. But then what would be the right thing to say, in a situation like this?

Iain Cameron was talking on his radio. Beyond the perimeter fence, a group of villagers were walking in a line up the road, clearly looking for any clues as to Murdo's whereabouts.

I filmed just enough pictures to tell the story without wanting to push my luck too much, and then returned indoors and packed away my camera. I looked around for Jackson; but he was nowhere to be seen.

CHAPTER FIFTEEN

B y lunchtime, and with still no sign of Murdo, numbers in the village had swelled.

Two more police officers had arrived, along with a sniffer dog, and had been taken to see Murdo's bedroom, accompanied by Catriona and Iain Cameron. Jackson had re-appeared, and when I'd asked him, quite casually, where he'd been for the past couple of hours, he'd snapped at me.

"I've been looking for Murdo, Claire, what have you been doing?"

Stung, I'd sloped away, without trying to justify myself or to question him further.

By three o' clock, the end of the normal school day, it was clear that the police were now taking Murdo's disappearance very seriously indeed. They'd had the sniffer dog running all over the croft, the harbour, the beach and the main lane through the village, but no trace had been found. A loudhailer was procured from somewhere, and the chief police officer from Ullapool used it to gather everybody together at the front of the school.

"I just want to update you all on the situation," he said, when everybody was gathered around him.

"We still have no reason to believe that there is anything sinister or suspicious about Murdo's continued absence. However, the fact remains that nobody has seen the boy since yesterday afternoon, when he told his mother that he was going to a sleepover. As yet, we have no clues as to his whereabouts.

It is possible that he could have run away – and in the hours that he was presumed to be at his friend's house, he could have travelled quite a distance. Especially if he hitched a lift…"

Here, he was interrupted by an angry voice from within the crowd of villagers.

"Who'd give a lift to a ten-year-old boy? Nobody round here, that's for sure."

The officer put up a hand to silence the angry muttering of the crowd.

"Please. We are not discounting any of the options. Quite a few folk around here leave their vehicles unlocked so it's not impossible to imagine that Murdo could have climbed inside one – stowed away, if you like – and ended up a long way from home. I am just trying to keep an open mind, whilst in no way under-estimating the seriousness with which we are treating this ….event."

There were a few more grumbles from the crowd, but nobody shouted out, and after waiting for a moment or two, the police chief continued.

"Murdo's mother is at home now, with a trained female police counsellor. We have advised her that the best thing she can do is to stay there and await further news. In the meantime, I have requested further assistance from Inverness, in the form of experienced police officers. We are also in the process of organising a social media campaign, using a photograph of Murdo, to circulate his details as widely as possible as quickly as possible. Now I'm afraid that this will have the effect of drawing this event to the attention of the media and so I have to warn you that it is likely that journalists and photographers will arrive in Kylecraig within the next few hours……"

As he carried on talking, I felt movement in the crowd behind me, and then the faintest of touches in the small of my back. Glancing over my shoulder, I saw that Jackson was standing behind me. I was shocked by his appearance. His face seemed grey and sagging, his eyes devoid of the light that normally danced there whether in anger or humour.

"Are you okay?" I mouthed.

He shook his head.

As he turned to walk away again, I hissed at him.

"Jackson. Can we go somewhere and talk?"

He ignored me and carried on walking, but turning to me just before he was swallowed up by the crowd, he mouthed something.

I think it was "later" but I couldn't have said for sure.

*

The rest of the afternoon passed in a surreal blur of arrivals and departures. The little village took on the air of a war zone, with residents and police officers on one side pitched again journalists, television crews and rubber-neckers on the other. Yes there really were people, it seemed, who came just to look at the "media circus" as the tabloid newspapers like to call this kind of thing.

I moved around in a daze, bringing my camera out for about ten minutes each hour to try and capture some of the madness.

I'd had the briefest of conversations with Janey Macleod, who'd told me to, "...do whatever you want Claire, but don't get in the way."

I found myself uncomfortably straddling my two worlds, past and present. I was careful to keep away from the news camera crews, and to keep my camera out of sight when they were shooting. I watched from the side-lines, like most of the villagers, with a kind of disgusted fascination as satellite trucks filled the road outside the school, draping cables over people's garden walls and shining high-powered lights onto carefully groomed presenters as the natural daylight faded.

Mairi Morrison arrived back at the school at around 6pm and, with the help of her husband, set up an impromptu soup kitchen.

"We do what we can," she told anyone who cared to listen, stirring vats of chicken broth. "In a place like this, everybody pulls together."

"Aye. But some of us do it more publicly than others," said a voice in my ear.

I turned, surprised, to see Eilidh Ross.

"Sorry about earlier – I was out of order," she said.

An awful lot of people seemed to be apologising to me today.

"Don't be daft. There's no rule-book for dealing with something like this, everybody's just doing it in their own way."

"Aye – I make a brew and bake flapjacks and Mairi brings in the soup. Seems there's nothing can't be solved with food, eh?"

"Whisky might be more useful," grumbled Donald Morrison. "I told Mairi to bring some down, but she's got it in her head that people want soup. What can you do?"

He shook his head, sadly, and wandered off.

Eilidh and I looked at each other and then burst out laughing. It felt good to lighten the mood, even for a moment.

"Take care, eh? I'm off home to get the wee 'uns sorted."

To my surprise, Eilidh leaned forward and hugged me, then left in a hurry as though embarrassed by this show of emotion. I held onto the moment fondly for a while, and then got back to work, filming Mairi Morrison doling out soup to volunteers who'd arrived to join in the search for the missing boy, before guiltily taking some for myself.

*

Shortly after 10pm, Iain Cameron re-appeared at the school and told those of us who were still there to go home.

"Please go and rest," he said, clearly weary himself.

"You've all done everything you can. The best thing you can do for Murdo now is to go home, get a decent night's sleep, and be back here at first light in the morning. We'll resume extensive searches then, although we are continuing to comb the area with lights and dogs overnight. If he hasn't turned up by the morning, we'll be conducting one to one interviews tomorrow, to try and gather as much information as we can. Thank you all for your help."

It was only as I left the school, ducking past the glaring white lights of the television crews, that I realised how utterly exhausted I was. Not only had the surreal events of the day taken their toll but far more worryingly, my mind kept flashing back to my encounter with Jackson on the beach the previous night, when he'd been stumbling along, red eyed, angry and desperate to get away from me.

CHAPTER SIXTEEN

Waking in darkness, I tried to work out what had interrupted my much-needed sleep.

Fragments from the previous day crowded in on my bleary early morning mind. Jackson draped in seaweed, making all the kids scream and laugh – had that really been less than twenty-four hours ago? The sight of Catriona Mackay, disorientated and distraught, holding a wailing toddler. Eilidh hugging me, police cars and sniffer dogs, TV crews jamming the tiny main street of the village.

I wondered if it was their bright lights which had woken me but when I peered through my curtains, there was just darkness.

Competing with those remembered images was the one nagging at my mind, that of Jackson, hurrying in darkness along the beach away from the village.

Then I heard it – a soft "tap, tap, tap" on the bottom of my bedroom window. My heart contracted and I froze for a moment, before trying to calm myself down. The noise stopped, and I thought I might have imagined it, but then it came again, more insistently this time.

Murdo I thought - although plainly that was ridiculous. If he'd been hiding out in the village all day, why on earth would he come tapping at my window? Trying to breathe normally, I pulled the corner of the curtain back, and opened the window a crack.

"Claire, it's me. Can you let me in?"

"Jackson? What on earth…?"

"Just let me in. I'm coming round the back."

I pushed the window back down and grabbed my dressing gown from the hook on the bedroom door. Not wanting to admit to myself that I was frightened, I nevertheless paused for a moment before making my way through the bathroom to the little lean-to utility room at the back of the house.

The door was rarely used and was stiff and unyielding at first, but when Jackson leaned on it from the other side it gave way, and he tumbled into the room. I shot backwards, tripping over the laundry basket and banging my ankle on the corner of the washing machine.

Jackson put a hand out to steady me, but I backed away, rubbing my ankle.

"Claire, don't be silly. Come here; let me look at your ankle."

I shook my head, aware that tears were warming my cheeks.

"I'm….fine…." I stuttered. "Why are you here?"

By now I was convinced that Jackson was about to confess to some terrible crime.

"Claire. Please look at me?"

I looked up, still wary.

"I know I've been pretty useless as a friend, but I'm hoping you can forgive me because I really need to speak to you. I need to hear a kind voice in my ear, to convince me I'm not going mad. Please?"

"How do I know if you're mad or not, Jackson? You never tell me anything. And how do I know anything, any more, after what's happened in the past couple of days?"

"Because you know me, Claire. In here, where it counts." He took my hand and placed it across his heart, and locked his eyes onto mine. I shook my head, and pulled my hand away, but I had no reserves left to fight him with.

"Come through to the bedroom," I said. "It's the only vaguely warm room in the house."

"Thank you," he said, following me back through the bathroom towards the sliver of light spilling from my bedroom door. It was noticeably cosier once we were in the bedroom with the door closed.

"I'm getting back into bed," I told Jackson. "You can sit in that chair and tell me whatever it is you want to tell me. And then you can leave."

"Of course." Jackson sat down on the chair in the corner of the room and stretched his legs out in front of him.

"I have an awful feeling about Murdo," he began. "I think something has happened to him."

I didn't reply but waited for him to continue.

"I've….seen missing children cases before and usually they turn up within a few hours. When they don't, it's nearly always bad news."

He sighed heavily, a sigh that became a groan. I decided to speak.

"What do you mean, you've seen them before?"

"On the news, of course. You'll have seen them too, in your line of work, maybe even worked on them?"

"One or two, yes."

"So you'll know what I mean then, when I say that the longer it goes without a sighting, the worse the outlook."

I nodded, my mind filling up with images of school photographs, children frozen in time, preserved as children forever more.

"Strictly between the two of us, Iain Cameron is of the same opinion."

"So what do you think has happened to him? What does Iain think?"

Jackson shook his head. "He has no idea, or if he does, he's not saying anything. They can't rule out the fact that he could have been abducted, but they'll be questioning everybody tomorrow, establishing where people were at the time the boy disappeared, that kind of thing."

Here, he stopped and looked at me, as though prompting a response. When I stayed silent, he carried on.

"I can't actually tell you where I was on Tuesday night, Claire, even though I wish I could. Please believe me when I say that if I was going to confide in anybody then it would be you. You have to trust me when I say that I've done nothing wrong."

I paused before speaking again.

"I'm trying to understand, Jackson, really I am. But you don't make it easy. One minute I'm your friend, the next you're ignoring me, or worse, shouting at me to go away and leave you alone. I come across you staggering along the beach, clearly upset, but you won't tell me where you've been or why. Is that really how friends are supposed to behave? Would I treat you in the same way? I don't think so."

Jackson didn't answer me, but looked down as if studying the carpet in great detail. Then a strange sound like a discordant musical instrument escaped across the room, carried through the air between the two of us. It took me a moment to realise that it was the sound of weeping.

I sat up rigidly, staring at the distraught figure in the chair in front of me. He was bent forwards, his face in his hands now, his breathing coming in gasps. As he showed no signs of stopping, I climbed out of my bed and went over to him.

I knelt on the floor in front of him and took hold of both his hands in mine.

"Jackson," I whispered. "Please stop it."

"I can't bear it," he sobbed. "I was so desperate to find him. I looked and I shouted and I scoured the harbour and every one of those boats. And I was so certain I'd find him. Where is he, Claire?"

At this, he raised his face to the ceiling.

I struggled to think of something to say. Unable to find any words of comfort, I just held his hands in mine, and let him cry. Through his sobs, he was mumbling to himself, but I couldn't make out his words.

As I held his hands, I became aware of the unexpected softness of Jackson's palms beneath my thumbs. I began to stroke, ever so gently, and after a while the sobbing slowed, then ceased altogether, and the pressure in my hands was reciprocated.

An almost eerie silence descended. I closed my eyes and allowed myself to enjoy the feeling of being touched. I felt a hand move up to my face, didn't dare to open my eyes as Jackson's other hand found its way around the back of my head and began to stroke my hair, ever so gently, as though I might bolt at any moment.

But there was no question of that. This was what I'd wanted ever since that day in November when I'd first seen Jackson on the beach, seemingly spirited in from who knew where.

I moved my face instinctively towards his, and my lips brushed the soft fuzz of his beard. We kissed properly then, a lingering, soft kiss. Close up, he smelled of peat fires and tasted of sea salt.

Jackson pulled slightly away, although he continued to stroke my hair.

"Claire."

Reluctantly I opened my eyes.

"Are you – are you sure you are okay with this?"

I nodded and allowed him to help me to my feet and lead me back to bed. And then I allowed him to undress me and we tumbled clumsily under the sheets together. I clung to him, revelling in the feeling of his skin upon mine, and not thinking any more. For once, I was entirely in the moment.

*

I woke as the first tentative slivers of daylight crept into the sky, stirred perhaps by the cooling of the vacant space beside me in the bed. I hadn't heard Jackson get up and leave, but had a feeling that it couldn't have been very long ago.

I eased my legs out of bed, wincing as the cold air hit my bare thighs and grabbing for my dressing gown, which was crumpled in a heap at the foot of the bed. Stumbling through to the bathroom, I peered at myself in the mirror over the sink. The same old Claire stared back – except for a definite hint of smugness around the lips, and a gleam of pleasure in the eyes.

Then I remembered the enormity of what had happened to bring Jackson to me in the dead of night.

CHAPTER SEVENTEEN

Even though it wasn't yet 7am, the school was already a hive of activity when I got there. There was an eerie difference to a normal school-day though. Instead of children being dropped off by parents, the playground area was full of police officers, dogs, photographers and journalists. Just inside the entrance hall, a woman was dispensing polystyrene cups of tea and coffee.

My body gave an involuntary shiver when I saw, just behind her, Jackson. Spotting me, he picked up two cups and headed towards me.

"You might need one of these, since you're in so bright and early."

I wondered at his ability to act as though nothing had happened. My face was so hot you could have fried eggs on it.

"Thank you."

We both sipped our coffee, seemingly at a loss as to what to say next. Maybe Jackson wasn't quite as cool as he was pretending to be.

We were saved by a new wave of people coming into the school, sounding like a swarm of agitated bees as they pushed through the double doors.

"You should fetch your camera, Claire," Jackson prompted me. "You can't stop filming now."

"I know. But I hate stuff like this. I feel like such a ghoul, preying on someone else's misfortune and that's not what I wanted to do with this film."

He smiled, sympathetically.

"Believe me, this wasn't part of the plan for me either."

Reluctantly, I fetched my camera and fired off a few shots of the activity around the school. I shot mostly from the ground looking up, to give a sinister feel to the pictures of these intruders silhouetted against the vast, empty sky. As the crowds of people swelled, I went up into the sand dunes to capture them scouring the silver sand. From up here they looked like lines of soldier ants searching for a new colony.

When I saw the police divers arriving, I headed back down to the beach to get pictures of this new, sinister development and then, feeling faintly disgusted with myself I put away the camera and went to ask if there was anything I could do to help.

It turned out that the police had called a press conference in the school hall, so I sidled in at the last minute, standing at the back as though the physical distance could somehow remove me from the nightmare unfolding around the village.

A table had been set up in front of one of the huge Sea Life murals that Jackson had spent weeks working on with the children. "The things we find on our beach!" was its title. That this happy work would be the backdrop to a grim press conference seemed wrong but there was no way of stopping it from happening – already the noise in the hall had dropped, as Iain Cameron entered the hall by the door at the top end. He was followed by Janey Macleod, who had her arm around Murdo's mother, Catriona, and finally a tall, grey-haired man in police uniform, who I presumed must be the Chief Inspector from Inverness.

Like most people, I'd witnessed far too many of these events on TV. Unlike many people, I'd also been present at a few of them in the past. I could scarcely bear to watch as Catriona stammered her way through a few words. Although she'd been less than friendly towards me, I had no reason to bear her a grudge – part of me agreed with her that having a TV camera stuck in your face is an invasion of the worst kind. That was why I preferred to be behind mine.

"Please come home, Murdo, you're not in trouble, I just want to give you a big hug," she managed, before dissolving into sobs.

The grey-haired man introduced himself as DCI Dingwall Brown and read out a statement relating what was known about Murdo's disappearance and appealing for people to use social media to spread the word.

"At present, this is still a Missing Persons investigation," he announced, his dry, clipped Highland voice at odds with the emotion all around him in the hall. "We have no reason to believe that the boy has been taken away from the area. However, we do ask that his photograph be circulated far and wide, to give us the best possible chance of returning the wee lad to his family."

At this, Catriona's sobbing increased in its intensity, and he stopped and whispered something to Janey, who stood up and led her from the hall.

Once they'd gone, pursued by an obscene number of camera flashes, DCI Brown resumed.

"Any questions?"

A forest of hands shot up.

Where was the boy's father? Returning from Singapore, where he'd been working on an oil rig for the past fortnight.

Why had the divers been called in? Routine, in any location where water was a possible factor.

Wasn't searching the ocean akin to looking for a needle in a haystack? Was there anything specific to suggest that the boy had drowned?

Here, DCI Brown lost his mask of patience, and snapped back:

"Are you suggesting that we just presume the boy is not in the water? Kindly allow us to do our jobs, and we will endeavour to help you do yours."

There were a few more questions, and then he put up a hand.

"Thank you for your time, ladies and gentlemen. One to one interviews will be available in thirty minutes time, outside the main entrance, after I have given my team an update."

He swept rather grandly from the hall, leaving Iain Cameron to fend off the reporters who were already swarming around the table.

"I don't know about you, but I need another coffee," said a voice in my ear.

I turned, relieved to see Jackson despite the circumstances.

"I didn't see you come in."

"I sneaked in even later than you did. I've been showing one of the police teams around my humble abode. They seemed to take an unnecessary amount of interest; in fact I've left them to it. Although I did tell them in no uncertain terms not to disturb my highly effective but completely personalised book-cataloguing system."

"I didn't know you catalogued your books," I said, thinking of the piles of novels, poetry pamphlets and non-fiction volumes that I'd so admired.

"I don't. But I thought it would stop them from creating havoc in there."

"Don't they need a warrant to look through your things?"

"Technically speaking, yes they do. But if you've nothing to hide, why stand in their way? I told them they were wasting their time, but they're the local guys from Ullapool, so I reckon they want to impress the boss. Come on, let's get that drink."

Instead of going to the urn at the front of the school, with its long queue, we made our way through to the kitchen, where Eilidh was sitting chatting with a couple of the other mothers. They went silent as we approached. I smiled at Eilidh, who smiled back at me, but the other two women remained stony-faced.

"I see they're searching your van, Jackson," said one of them, her tightly drawn-back ponytail swinging angrily as she spoke. It was Kelly MacIver.

"They are indeed," replied Jackson calmly "although I have already assured them that they will find nothing of interest, unless they are partial to 20th Century literary fiction."

The other woman scowled.

"Fine time it is to be making jokes," she snapped.

"Exactly," muttered Kelly MacIver.

"No, you're right to be angry. I apologise." Jackson looked stricken. "Humour is my fall-back position you see. I always think that there's no situation that can't be improved by a touch of levity, at least in preference to deep sorrow. I meant no offence by it."

I thought back to the early hours of the morning, when I'd been witness to Jackson's distress over the missing boy.

111

"Jackson cares as much about Murdo as anybody," I burst out. "He cares about all of the children here. He'd do anything he can to help find him."

"Nobody's interested in your opinion," retorted Kelly. I still think it's interesting that they're searching his stuff before anyone else's. Maybe the police know something we don't, eh?"

"Leave it, Kelly." It was Eilidh who spoke this time, her voice sharp. She rolled her eyes in my direction. "Nobody knows anything, do they? Or they'd have told us by now."

"Believe me, if I thought that there was anything I could do to help, I would have done it already," said Jackson emphatically. "I can see why people might want to find a scapegoat, but until we find Murdo we should resist speculation. It's better for everybody if people just stick to known facts."

Eilidh made us coffee in polystyrene cups whilst the other two women kept a stubborn silence, glaring at Jackson until we left the room with our drinks.

As we headed through the entrance hall, Iain Cameron appeared.

"Ah – just the man I wanted to see. Jackson – could I have a word?"

"Certainly."

He might have seemed relaxed to an outside observer, but I thought I sensed an undercurrent of resignation in his voice.

"Miss Armstrong, I would also like to talk to you in a wee while. Could you come back here in about half an hour, do you think?"

"Of course."

Watching the two of them head back into the school, I observed that Iain Cameron wore his police garb as comfortably as an old dressing gown.

*

To pass the time, I headed back up to the dunes, where I sipped my coffee and took my mobile phone from the pocket of my gilet. It had been switched off ever since the search yesterday morning – the signal was so patchy in Kylecraig that I never relied on it. Besides, I'd been too preoccupied to remember to turn it on.

Now it came alive in my hand, buzzing and vibrating for a good minute or two before it finally quietened down. I read the display screen - twelve new text messages, of which six were pointing me in the direction of my voicemail.

I listened to those first – Mum, twice, sounding considerably more worried the second time. Leonie, who seemed to have taken a while to realise why the name "Kylecraig" on the national news was so significant. "I've only just realised, oh my god, that's where you are! Jeez! Are you okay? Ring me!" My brother, jokingly asking if this was my idea of how to get the ratings up for my documentary, before realising what bad taste this was in and apologising. "Call me," he urged, as did my former news editor, and my current boss.

The texts were largely repetitions of the voicemail messages, but there was an extra one.

Seeing Tom's name flash up on my phone screen jolted me – I knew I should have deleted him.

I opened the message anyway.

Saw the back of your head on Sky News last night. Hope you're okay up there. Looks like a weird and windswept place. Stay safe. T x

How dare he, I thought, how dare he put an x at the end. I deleted his message with a shaking hand, and then erased his contact details as well.

Glancing at my watch, I saw that I still had twenty minutes before Iain Cameron wanted to talk to me, so I texted Mum, Leonie and Alex the same words: *Thanks for your message; all a bit weird up here, I'm fine but very busy. Will call later, love C xx*

Then I texted my former news editor a similar version, without the love and xx's at the end.

My current boss deserved a phone call. Even so, I hesitated before dialling his number. He picked up before I'd even heard it ring out, and the urgent buzz of an office in Salford filled my right ear.

"Claire. What on earth's going on?"

"It's nothing to do with me, Paul, I can assure you."

"How are you? It must be pretty hellish up there?"

"I'm okay. I can't stay on the phone for long; the police want to talk to me."

"Shit. Claire, I'm really sorry. Do you want me to come up? Or one of the other members of the team? Give you a bit of support?"

No, I thought, panicking, no no no.

"Thanks Paul, that's really kind of you. I think it's probably better if you leave it though. The place is already over-run with journalists and TV cameras."

"I'm sure. Are you – god, I hate to ask, but are you still filming stuff?"

I gave a bitter little laugh.

"Of course I am. Not the news conferences or interviews, there's no point. I'm trying to make it different, to get the story from the angle of how it's affecting the school and the village. It's so weird though. I still can't quite believe any of this is happening."

"I know. I saw the news conference earlier, that poor woman. You're sure you're okay though?"

"Paul, I appreciate your concern, really I do. But I'm fine. And hey, look on the bright side. Everyone's heard of Kylecraig now."

My feeble attempt at a joke fell rather flat.

"I know I'm always concerned about ratings but even I'm not that cynical." He sounded wounded. "I just wanted to check that you're coping."

"I am. I am coping. But I just want Murdo to come back and everybody else to go away. I'm pissed off that the world and his wife have landed up on my doorstep"

"I'm sure Murdo's parents would agree with you," said Paul, slowly. "After all, they have considerably more reason to be upset than you do."

"Fine, yes, thanks Paul. Got to go, I'll call you soon."

I pressed the red "end call" button and let out a huge breath. Bloody hell, I thought crossly, shaking my head to try and hold my tears at bay. This was not how it was meant to be.

*

Iain Cameron told me that he was trying to build up as full a picture as possible of events in the village in the hours before and after Murdo's absence had been noticed.

"I just need you to tell me where you were and what you did that day and night," he said.

I began by telling him about my landlord's knock on the door, whilst I was trying to eat my late lunch, and I saw his face change immediately.

"Who is your landlord?"

I gave him the details, including a landline and mobile number which were written down in my Moleskine diary.

"Two ticks, Claire – I'm just going to pass these on to the team."

He all but ran from the room, and I kicked myself for not having thought of telling somebody earlier about Mr Frazer's visit.

"It probably won't amount to anything, but we must leave no stone unturned," he told me a minute later, slightly out of breath as he sat back down.

"I know, I'm sorry I didn't say anything earlier. I honestly didn't think of it."

"Never mind that now. What happened after that?"

I recounted the drive up to look at the horrible caravan (already checked out, Iain assured me) and the rather more successful viewing of Billy Mackenzie's cottage.

"Then the landlord left. He offered me a lift but I chatted to Billy for a bit and then walked back along the beach."

Iain Cameron looked up from his notebook. "What time would this have been?"

I thought hard. "I'm not too sure. Around six? It was almost dark but not totally."

"I see. And did you see anybody on your walk home?"

"Yes," I told him. "I saw Jackson, just before I got to the far end of the bay."

"And did you talk?"

"We did." I was becoming more and more aware of how my voice sounded. It seemed to be getting posher and quieter with every answer. "But not for long."

"Can you remember what you said to one another?"

"Yes." This came out as a squeaky little whisper.

"I'm sorry; could you speak up please Miss Armstrong?" He smiled encouragingly.

"Yes. I told him about going to see Billy's cottage and that I was going to be moving in there."

"I see. And did Jackson contribute to this conversation?"

"Well you must know he did," I said, stalling. "You've already spoken to him."

"Yes, but I need to hear both sides of the conversation," said Iain Cameron patiently. "To make sure that everybody remembers it the same way."

I sighed.

"He wasn't really in a mood for talking much."

"Please, Miss Armstrong, if you could just answer the question…."

"Yes, sorry. He told me to go home."

"And he didn't tell you where he had been?"

"No. I presumed he'd just been for a walk. He likes walking."

"Do you think that he might have been to visit somebody in the village?"

I paused, trying to make my mind come up with a suitable answer.

"He told me afterwards that he had been to see somebody, but that he couldn't tell me any more than that. Or at least, he told me that he couldn't tell me where he had been. He did apologise for that."

Iain Cameron's face remained inscrutable.

"And how did he seem to you? How was his mood?"

I hesitated again, and then decided that I would have to be honest. My statement was irrelevant anyway, since Jackson would already have told Iain all of this.

"He seemed upset. He got a bit angry with me, but I think it was because I was being annoying."

Iain Cameron had the good grace to smile slightly.

"And then you went home and stayed there for the rest of the evening?"

I nodded, relieved that we'd moved on.

"I did. I had an early night."

"Okay. One final question. How did Jackson appear the following morning, when you saw him in school?"

I thought back to that lovely limbo, as it now seemed, before we knew that Murdo was missing. I pictured Jackson cavorting on the beach, draped in seaweed, and I smiled.

"He was on good form. He was cheerful, lively, the centre of attention. The children always cheer him up."

Iain Cameron wrote some more and then looked up again from his notebook.

"Thank you, Miss Armstrong. You've been very helpful. Good luck with your film."

"Thank you."

I got up and walked from the room in a trance. There was a strange ringing in my ears which seemed to be magnifying noises, so that the gentle everyday sound of the door shutting behind me was more like the clanking closure of a prison gate.

CHAPTER EIGHTEEN

"I'm coming up there."

I'd finally called Mum back later that night. It had been another terrible day of police divers scouring the bay, search parties combing the beach, and even more members of the media descending on the village. The name "Kylecraig" was now plastered across newspapers and TV studio backdrops, and was in danger of joining those other places tainted forever by one awful event.

I'd only been half thinking as I dialled mum's number, responding to the half a dozen messages she'd left on my mobile. Now, though, I was on full alert.

"What?"

"I said I'm coming up there. You need somebody to look after you, Claire, it's not right that you're dealing with this all on your own."

"I'm not on my own, Mum; there are more people here than I can even begin to count."

"That's not what I mean and you know it. I bet you're not eating properly, are you?"

I thought back over what I'd eaten that day – coffee for breakfast, coffee for lunch, and a hastily microwaved jacket potato with beans for supper, which I'd wolfed down about ten minutes ago. Still, I protested.

"The place is packed to bursting, Mum, and honestly, it's really not very nice being here just now."

"Even more reason why you could do with somebody looking after you," she said firmly. "Please don't argue with me, Claire – I want to make sure you're alright."

At this, I caved in. The idea was actually rather tempting. Mum would cook me nice food and talk sense – or nonsense - to me, which was just what I needed.

"You couldn't be here by Saturday, could you?" It was Tuesday night. "I have to move out of this place and into Billy Mackenzie's cottage. I don't have much stuff, but it would still be really great to have an extra pair of hands."

"I'll look at the options and call you back," said Mum, clearly delighted to have a mission to get stuck into.

"Things might have changed by the weekend anyway," I said. "Murdo might turn up."

We both went silent then, knowing that the chances of that happening were looking increasingly remote.

*

Within half an hour, plans were in place. Mum was booked onto the Friday night sleeper from Crewe to Inverness and had hired a car.

"I would offer to come and get you, but I don't really want to leave here at the moment, just in case," I apologised.

"Quite right too. I'll do a big shop when I arrive. Is there a Waitrose in Inverness?"

I laughed.

"Not reached this far north yet, no. There is a decent M&S with a food hall though. Right next to the station, you can't miss it."

"That will be fine. Email me any special requests, won't you?"

As I put down the phone, I already felt better at the thought of having her with me.

*

A dreadful kind of hush seemed to envelop the village over the next forty-eight hours, as the police, the press and the local people stepped around each other. It was as if we were all engaged in some awful stage performance which nobody knew how to bring to an end. The usual human traits of courtesy and kindness were just a heartbeat away from suspicion and hatred, and the air was brittle with tension.

It didn't help that the weather had decided that it was time to put on a show. A warm sun dusted the beach and ocean with sparkles of silver and gold, and the marram grass at the edge of the dunes brushed spikily against the scattering of pretty little coloured flowers which formed the early spring machair. On crofts around the edges of the beach, feeble-legged lambs wobbled on unsteady legs and called reedily for their mothers. It was idyllic and it was horrific, and I felt as though I was slowly suffocating.

More than anything, I wanted to talk to Jackson – but whenever I tried to find him he was closeted away in some room or another, speaking endlessly to the police.

*

When I did finally see him, early on Friday morning, I was shocked by his appearance. He was walking across the school hall, deep in conversation with Janey Macleod, and he was wearing a short-sleeved shirt. The sight of his bare arms, pale and freckled, made him seem younger and somehow vulnerable – I realised afterwards that like the rest of us he'd just shed

121

several layers of winter clothing, but my first impression was that he'd shed several pounds as well.

I'd come into the hall to fetch my camera kit from the cupboard and was hidden by the half-closed door. I was so relieved to see Jackson that I almost stepped straight out to greet them but then Janey raised her voice and I caught a scrap of their conversation.

"…and this was always going to be a terrible idea. It was all from the governors you know, you being here. I was quite happy to do the teaching myself, until this wretched thing came along. Then I was steamrollered into having you to fill in the gap. And now look what's happened. How can I ever recover from this, let alone save the school?"

She sounded angry, but also close to tears.

"Come on, Janey, you know that's not fair. The events are completely unrelated."

He sounded exhausted.

"Oh Jackson, stop it. Surely you can understand how I'm feeling? My first duty is to the children and I just wish to God I'd never laid eyes on you."

I couldn't see them by this time, but there was no mistaking the fury in her voice, and the next thing I heard was the sound of her high-heels clipping hard and fast across the floor away from me, back towards the door.

"Janey!" Jackson's voice called out, then stopped as the door slammed shut.

I realised I was holding my breath and let it out as slowly and as quietly as I could. I wanted desperately to go to Jackson, but realised he could well be furious that I'd been hiding in the cupboard - and been a witness to what had just happened.

Whatever it was.

I decided to stay where I was and within a minute or two, I heard Jackson's footsteps heading in the same direction as Janey's. The door closed again, more quietly this time, but I waited for a long time before stepping out into the empty hall.

*

At a lunchtime press conference, the police announced that any more such events would be held in the village hall, "in order that school life can resume with as much normality as possible, for the final two weeks of term." There would be a trained counsellor present at the school from Monday morning onwards, who would be able to help the children to talk about what had happened, if they wanted to. Other than that, all entry to the school would be forbidden after tonight, other than for parents, teachers and other members of staff. I presumed this would include me.

It felt like a particularly grim landmark day in the week, as Murdo's father Lachlan had finally arrived back from the South China Sea and was sitting at the top table with Catriona on one side and DCI Dingwall Brown on the other. I felt particularly sorry for Lachlan Mackay – returning from a month on an oil rig must have been disorientating at the best of times. Coming back to Kylecraig in these circumstances was truly horrifying, and now he had cameras zooming in on his face as he joined his wife in another emotional appeal.

Jackson and Janey Macleod were both conspicuous by their absence from the hall. And as the press conference closed and everybody filed sombrely out of there, fragments of that overheard conversation kept spilling into my head. I was torn between wishing I'd heard more and angry that I'd heard any of it. Especially since I was making up the bits in between what I'd actually heard.

The more I thought about it, the more convinced I became that Janey had a thing about Jackson. Why would she not? He was handsome; she was as single and as available as I was. Taller and slimmer than me too. Maybe they'd even had a bit of a fling, for all I knew. I was angry with both of them; and angrier with myself for caring.

*

I spent the early part of the evening packing, ready for the house move the next day. I then connected my hard drive to the laptop and made back-up copies of all of my more recent material. Finally, I decided to catch up on my emails, but when I opened my inbox I chickened out. There were hundreds of unread messages in there.

I started deleting the emails, one at a time to begin with and then a page at a time. Then, realising that this was going to take forever, I lost patience and cleared the lot. If anyone really needed to get in touch, they could call me. And if they didn't have my number, then they didn't know me well enough to be in touch in the first place.

Pleased with this reasoning, I finally had the satisfaction of an empty void staring back at me in place of the overflowing inbox. I closed the lid of my laptop and packed it into a box, throwing a couple of blankets over the top to protect it, before continuing to scour the cottage for any of my belongings that I might have missed.

At about 9pm, my packing was interrupted by a loud knock at the door, which made me jump. Heart thumping, I went to answer it, hoping - as always - that it would be Jackson. But to my surprise, it was Eilidh Ross.

"Can I come in for a moment?" She sounded stressed, which was not like her.

"Sure, come on in." I opened the door fully and showed her into the living room.

"Sorry about the mess," I said, moving a few boxes out of her way. "I'm moving out tomorrow."

I expected her to be surprised by this news but of course she already knew.

"You'll be a lot more comfortable in Billy's cottage. This old place is a bit of a dump. Bloody absentee landlords."

"I won't be sorry to leave it," I admitted. "Can I get you a cup of tea? Glass of wine?"

Eilidh shook her head, then caught my eye and smiled wanly.

"Do you know, I think I will have a glass of wine, if you're having one yourself? We've cancelled the minibus tomorrow, so I can relax a bit. At least not have to worry about having a drink anyway."

I poured two large glasses of white wine, and we sat at the kitchen table – although it was barely big enough for two, there was marginally more space there than in the box-strewn living room.

"How are you doing, Claire?" Eilidh asked me. "It must be really weird for you being in the middle of all of this?"

"It's nowhere near as hard for me, since I don't really know the people involved. I can't begin to imagine how awful it is for everybody who lives here."

"It's horrendous. And if it was one of my children who'd gone missing I don't know how I'd cope. Thank god, I don't have to, it doesn't bear thinking about. But I just wanted to say that I feel bad about what's happened with Jackson."

"You mean those women who were having a go the other day?"

I noticed now that Eilidh looked uncomfortable.

"Well that, aye, of course. And – with what happened earlier."

Before I could query this, she hurried on.

"I'm just hoping you know that nobody feels the same way about you."

"What are you telling me? What's happened tonight?

"Eh? You mean you don't know? I thought you'd have heard already. Lachlan Mackay – him and Jimmy's dad, Donnie, they were after him."

"What?"

Eilidh looked embarrassed.

"I was sure you'd know, with the two of you being so close. Anyway, now that he's leaving, I guess it doesn't matter. I just wanted you to know that........."

I could see that her lips were still moving and was vaguely aware that words were still coming out, words that were being directed at me, but I was no longer listening to any of them.

"Leaving? What do you mean, Jackson's leaving?"

Eilidh looked at me strangely.

"You didn't know?"

"No."

My hand was shaking so much that I had to put down my wine glass, and my voice came out loud and angry.

"How do YOU know?"

"Claire, I'm really sorry – I just presumed you must have heard. Janey emailed all the parents about three hours ago."

She fished her phone out of her pocket, pressed a couple of buttons and then passed it over to me.

"I wish to inform you that Jackson will be leaving the school with immediate effect," I read. "Classes will be shared between myself and Marnie, from Monday morning until the Easter break. We will of course endeavour to find a new teacher but I do not anticipate that this will happen before the new school year begins in August. Thank you all for your patience and understanding at this most difficult of times."

It was signed by Janey Macleod.

Knocking over my wine glass, I threw Eilidh's phone back at her, rushing from the kitchen onto the dark street outside. I heard her call my name but by then I was already running down the road, past the TV trucks and vans with their arc lights shining towards the dark and silent beach.

As I headed for the far end of the bay, I tried to recall whether I'd seen Janey's name on any of the emails I'd deleted. I was pretty certain that I hadn't – but I'd been so keen to erase them all that I could have missed it. Or maybe she'd chosen to keep me in the dark.

Which I now was, quite literally, and I cursed my stupidity for charging out in such a hurry that I hadn't picked up my torch.

Picking my way across the sand dunes, I peered into the gloom, willing my eyes to adjust to some kind of useful degree, or to pick out a welcoming glow of light from Jackson's van.

But I already had a horrible feeling that I was too late. And when I saw a dark, oblong shape looming up at me in the gloom,

I knew that I was right. I called his name, hammering on the door of the van; in reply, I heard only the eerie rattling sound of the wind playing with the loose catches around the windows.

The padlock was hanging free from the door handle. Feeling my way into the van, my hands found only emptiness – empty seats, empty table, empty shelves where his books had been.

"Jackson!" I shouted loudly, my voice cracking as it bounced back off the flimsy walls.

The realisation that he must have been planning to leave for a while sent an additional shiver through me. For there was no way he could have packed up all his belongings in the few hours since I'd last seen him. Lachlan and Donnie coming after him must have been the final tipping point.

Had he known even before he spent the night with me? I couldn't bear to think of it, but there was a new coldness gnawing in my gut, a mixture of rage and indignation that convinced me that he had.

I staggered out of the van, knelt down in the cold, damp sand, rubbing the individual grains against my wrist where once he'd grabbed me and hurt me. That had been nothing, compared to the pain I was feeling now.

"Jackson!" I shouted, an angry sob escaping and choking in my throat.

But there was nothing but the wind and the waves, the waves and the wind, and the cavernous silence of the void where a man had vanished into a ghost of himself.

CHAPTER NINETEEN

My poor mother couldn't have predicted the sorry mess that would greet her in Kylecraig. After yet another night of little sleep, I'd made a futile attempt to disguise my puffy, exhausted features with make-up, but the "rosy-glow" blusher and tinted lip-gloss seemed only to accentuate the shaky state I was in.

She pulled up in a bright red Fiat 500 at lunchtime on Saturday and I was genuinely overjoyed to see her – she too had a huge smile on her face as she climbed out of the car, but it disappeared pretty quickly when she saw me.

"Don't say anything," I said. "I'll tell you later."

She hugged me, fiercely, and I had to fight hard to stop the tears from welling up again.

"Shall we move first, or have lunch?" she asked, tactfully ignoring my appearance.

"We'd better move. Believe it or not, there are holidaymakers arriving today, so there's a cleaner coming at two to get it ready for them."

I'd finished packing, so it was just a case of loading up the two cars and driving them from one end of the village to the other. I pointed out to Mum that a larger hire car might have been more helpful.

"Yes, but not nearly as much fun, dear."

Finally I was able to lock the door at Ceol na Mara and leave the key under the mat. I turned away regretfully - much as I'd been lonely and cold in there at times, it was also the place where Jackson and I had…..but no. Better to forget about that. The memory of our only night together now just made me feel hollowed out and foolish

*

Over crusty French bread, cheese, and a bottle of wine (which caused Mum to raise an eyebrow), I updated her on the events of the past few months, and, crucially, the twenty-four hours leading up to her arrival.

Practical as ever, her first reaction was to reassure me that Jackson couldn't possibly have just disappeared into thin air.

"The police must know where he is. Until they work out what's happened to that poor boy, they're not just going to let people vanish."

"I know, I'm sure you're right. But I can hardly go and ask the police to give me a forwarding address, can I?"

"I can't help thinking that he has behaved very badly," said my Mother. "If the two of you are such good friends, why didn't he let you know what was happening?"

Ignoring the fact that she'd be a damn sight ruder about him if she was in possession of all the facts, I pointed out that the past few days had driven everybody in the village to breaking point.

"He's always been very private, but I know he was ever so fond of Murdo, and to be accused of having something to do with what's happened….I can only imagine how that must have made him feel. But then nobody's been acting rationally."

There was silence for a while, and then she spoke again.

"You must remember that I only ever have your best interests at heart. At the moment, all I can see is somebody who's taken you in and then hurt you. But you're right – these are hardly normal circumstances. You'll see him again, if he's worth seeing and if he's not, then you're better off without him."

I did my best to smile, and finished off the wine in my glass. I was reaching for the bottle to pour another, but she put her hand firmly over mine.

"I suggest we clear away these lunch things and go for a walk along the beach. We can sort out the boxes later but it's too nice a day to be sitting indoors, not to mention the fact that I've spent most of the past twenty-four hours travelling. I could really do with some of this famous fresh air that you've been going on about."

*

As we walked between the dunes onto the beach, the first thing we saw was Billy Mackenzie standing outside Jackson's van, his hands on his hips.

"Hey," I called, running over to him.

As I got closer I caught a glimpse of something that seemed to have been daubed crudely onto the side of the van.

"What's that? Let me see."

"Oh, it's nothing Claire, just stuff and nonsense".

I looked past him, to see what they'd painted on the flimsy walls of Jackson's home.

Paedo? Child-killer? This wasn't Jackson.

"Who did this, Billy? Who would do such a thing?"

"I don't know. But I can't think that anybody from around here would have had anything to do with it."

The uncomfortable expression on his face told a different story, however.

"Was it Lachlan? Was it, Billy?"

He shook his head, certain now.

"He would never do such a thing, not even in the state he's in. But there are others who aren't so reasonable. Just idiots, Miss, but emotions are running high."

I rubbed at my face. A horrible mixture of guilt and helplessness was clawing at my insides.

"What will you do with it?"

Billy looked embarrassed.

"He said I could keep it. Might be able to tart it up a bit, sell it on. Failing that, I can always use the extra storage. Aye, it'll come in handy, right enough."

He was, by now, looking over my shoulder rather than at me, so I presumed Mum had reached us, but I was more interested in finding out about Jackson than making formal introductions.

"When was this? When did you see him?"

"I didn't actually see him myself. He stuck a note through the door."

"Do you have it?"

"Claire."

Mum's voice came from behind me, its warning tone telling me that I was out of order, but I didn't care.

"Do you Billy? I'd really like to see it if you do, it's important."

He fumbled in his pockets and pulled out a crumpled piece of paper which I recognised as coming from one of the school's notebooks. It was all I could do to curb my impatience long enough to stop myself from snatching it off him, as he smoothed it out. Finally, he handed it over to me and I scanned it quickly.

"*Billy,*" the note began. "*Many thanks for your kindness over the past few months. I'd like to make you a gift of the van. It's still in decent condition and I would like to think that it could be of some use to you. That way, I feel less guilty about leaving without a proper goodbye. Yours, Jackson.*"

I read it several times, barely aware of Mum and Billy saying hello to one another.

"Did he leave before they did this to his van then? It doesn't make sense. And anyway, why would he leave you a note and not leave me one?"

"Really, Claire," said Mum, sounding quite angry now. "I must apologise, Mr Mackenzie – I can assure you that I did not bring my daughter up to be so rude."

"I'm sorry. I don't mean to be rude. But we were friends. I can't believe he would just leave without a word."

Billy was clearly desperate to get away from the middle of a mother-daughter tussle over manners. "Have you checked your mailbox?"

Mum and I had walked past the small metal box, which was nailed to the gatepost, several times; but I hadn't thought to look inside.

"Don't get your hopes up, Claire," she said, but I was already running back to the cottage, before realising that I had no idea where the key for the mailbox was kept. I turned around and Billy called out to me.

"It's hanging inside the meter cupboard. Just inside the front door."

"Thank you, Billy!" I shouted back, vaguely aware of Mum shaking his hand.

By the time she'd reached the gate, I was back outside with the key.

"What has got into you? You're behaving like a teenager, Claire."

"Don't care," I muttered, proving her right as I fumbled with the little key. The door of the box opened easily and a mini tsunami of junk mail poured out onto the road.

I leafed through adverts for window blinds, the Co-op, Sky TV and other assorted nonsense until I glimpsed, wedged into a brochure for the Hardware Store in Ullapool, a piece of lined school notepaper, carrying Jackson's unmistakable hand-writing.

"*Claire*" I read.

"*I am ashamed to say that this is goodbye. Too much has crowded in on me over the past few days, and I'm unable to face the inevitable trauma of a face to face farewell. I am aware that this is a coward's way out. I am also aware that it is unreasonable to ask that you remember me as a genuine friend and confidante.*

But please recall the happier times we spent together with fondness rather than anger. Whatever you may hear about me, I am a decent man who just wants to make everything right.

One day, maybe, I will be able to do that.

Until that day I remain very much

Yours,

Jackson."

"What does it say?" Mum had tactfully kept her distance but couldn't curtail her curiosity any longer. I passed her the note and watched her face carefully as she read it, but she showed no reaction as she handed it back to me.

"Let's go for that walk, shall we?"

Without waiting for an answer, she took my hand and squeezed it tightly, and we headed back towards the beach.

CHAPTER TWENTY

With Jackson gone, I carried on as though in a trance and had cause to be grateful to my Mother on a daily basis. On Monday she drove me up to the school. I couldn't face the walk along the beach which I still thought of as Jackson's domain, or past the sullen press photographers, who'd taken up residence at the school gates now that they weren't allowed inside.

In the afternoon she picked me up and we drove out of the village. Over the next few days, we explored some of the other beaches and beauty spots in the area before returning to Kylecraig in the early evenings. I think she felt more at home in my new cottage than I did, humming away to Radio 2 in the kitchen whilst I tried to return my focus to the small matter of making a film.

We avoided watching news bulletins on TV, since there was less to report with every day that passed. And with the focus of my documentary firmly on the school, I had no reason to attend press conferences once they'd been moved to the village hall.

Instead I filmed the children's return to their classrooms on Monday morning, and the resumption of lessons. It had been deemed important to carry on with these for the final couple of weeks before the Easter break. Marnie was warm and compassionate with the children, but it seemed that a wall had gone up between me and her.

Jackson's absence was barely commented upon, although one of the younger pupils, Cat, said solemnly to me: "Nothing is fun now he's gone."

Afterwards, I reflected that she could have meant Murdo, but I was certain at the time that she'd been referring to Jackson.

It wasn't even as though everything had just returned to normal. Normal was now a remote and longed for state, and the air of sadness inside the school was palpable.

Janey Macleod was unreachable, locked in her office with the counsellor and a never ending stream of parents, children and other visitors. I filmed the outside of her office door but what went on inside was strictly out of bounds to my camera.

By the final Monday of term, Murdo had been missing for two weeks, and the police had failed to turn up a single clue as to his disappearance. They stopped holding daily press conferences and most of the TV crews who'd stayed now pulled out of the story. By the end of the week, only a handful of police officers, journalists and photographers remained.

But now came a new wave of visitors.

Undeterred by Kylecraig's infamy, holidaymakers had started to arrive for the Easter holiday season. According to Billy Mackenzie some people had cancelled their visits, but others had booked at the last minute – either because they were curious, or because they'd seen from the pictures on their TV screens how idyllic the village was.

The invasion was obvious as Mum and I arrived back from a shopping trip to Ullapool one Saturday afternoon. It was the first day of the Easter holidays, and also the first day of April, and the sun was still high in a perfect blue sky. From the road above the village we could see brightly coloured windbreaks, canoes and kites decorating the silver sands like scattered jewels. What should have been a joyful sight only made me shudder.

"Ah well. Life goes on," said Mum, negotiating her way around a uniformly blonde-haired, Boden-clad family who were almost completely blocking the narrow lane as they loaded up their shiny 4X4 with beach paraphernalia.

"For some people it does. But how can they just behave as though nothing's happened here?"

"It didn't happen to them. And they've been looking forward to their Easter break too much to let anything interrupt the flow."

As Mum unloaded the car, I went to check the mailbox – and found a postcard.

It bore a picture of a turquoise lake circled by high mountains – "Duck Lake, The High Sierras," I read when I turned it over. The postmark was just a grey-black blur, but I recognised Jackson's handwriting straightaway. There wasn't much, so I read it and re-read it.

Wish you were here? Me too. Wish we were both here. Sadly, I'm not – and since you're reading this, neither are you. You're probably standing by your mailbox opposite the beach. And just picturing that makes me feel a little bit happy. J

When I showed her the postcard, Mum was rather less than impressed.

"He's toying with you, Claire, and I don't like it. No address, no clue as to his whereabouts. No suggestion that he's even remotely bothered about how you might be feeling. I call that very selfish."

I didn't reply. Jackson was in touch – and, for the time being, that was all that mattered.

*

The postcards came regularly after that, almost every other day in fact. Having felt excited by the first one, I soon became frustrated that they said so little, and didn't even bear a legible postmark, just a generic digital stamp. With no way of responding, I tried to curb my impatience but part of me was furious.

Having always given Jackson the benefit of the doubt, it was becoming harder to hold on to my conviction with my mother arguing the case for the prosecution.

Meanwhile, after almost a month in Kylecraig, she was starting to make noises about going home.

"It's not that I don't want to be with you, dear. I just don't think you need me any more. And my garden does – I dread to think what it must be looking like by now. You're so wrapped up in your life again that you probably won't even notice I've gone."

The thought of being alone sent me into a panic. It had taken Mum being here to make me realise how close to the edge I'd been before she'd come.

"Stay another couple of weeks? Please? The kids go back to school tomorrow and I'll be able to get into some kind of routine again."

She peered at me over the top of her glasses, clearly puzzled.

"Of course I will, if you want me too. But in that case, I'm going to call Audrey and see if she can find somebody to go in and tidy up my garden."

After we'd eaten she busied herself with a phone call to her neighbour and I returned to my laptop, supposedly to work.

Instead, I found myself watching one of the sequences I'd filmed with Jackson and the children on the beach, over and over again. There was Murdo, just a cheeky little boy before he was lost, using a piece of driftwood as a sword and chasing the other children. Jackson was keeping a watchful eye on him, making sure that he didn't curtail his fun whilst ensuring that things didn't get out of hand.

"If only you'd known what was going to happen here," I said, addressing his image, which I'd frozen on my screen. "What would we have done differently?"

But it was too late for that.

*

I was sitting on the grass eating a sandwich the following lunchtime, the first day of the new term, when I saw Iain Cameron and Janey Macleod leaving the school by the main entrance. To my surprise, they headed in my direction. I jumped up, alarmed – both of them were grim-faced.

"Have you got a minute, Claire?" asked Iain.

"Of course. What's happened?"

"Just come inside and we'll have a chat," he replied, which did nothing to put my mind at rest.

I followed the two of them into Janey's office and she closed the door.

"The police would like to see your footage," said Janey. "They want to go over it all to see if there are any clues in there."

I wasn't surprised by the request, more by the fact that it had been so long in coming. Although I hadn't offered up my footage at the start, I'd expected somebody to ask for it, but nobody had. Still, I protested.

"There is a huge amount of it, hours and hours' worth I mean."

"Is it catalogued?" she asked.

"Up to a point. But I work alone, so I have my own system."

"That's fine. Obviously, we can discount anything you've filmed since Murdo went missing." She paused, and then gave me a sly look. "And the police don't need to see anything from before Jackson arrived."

"What? Hey, hang on." I looked from one of them to the other. Iain Cameron was looking down at his shoes, but Janey appraised me, coolly.

"We just need the footage that shows Jackson with the children."

I thought back to the lovely, innocent pictures I'd been viewing the night before, and lost my temper.

"What are you trying to do, prove some kind of horrible link between him arriving and Murdo going missing? That's a terrible thing to do to him. Jackson wouldn't hurt anybody, you know that, Janey."

"And what do you know, Claire?" she fired back at me. "What do you actually know about Jackson? Do you even know where he is, right now?"

Iain Cameron sighed aloud and spoke for the first time.

"I am in touch with Jackson," he said, calmly. "And he has never been anything other than co-operative."

"So does he know you want to see my footage?"

Iain paused.

"I – this is a new request. However, I can't imagine that he would have a problem with us viewing it."

"Of course he wouldn't, since he has nothing to hide," I snapped.

I suddenly felt very tired, and very tearful. But I didn't want to break down in front of Janey Macleod.

"If I give you my stuff, can you tell me where he is?"

Iain Cameron smiled but shook his head.

"I'm sorry, Claire, but it doesn't work like that. In fact, I can probably force you to hand over the footage if I have to, but I'd rather you gave it willingly."

"I'll need to speak to my boss," I said. Janey MacLeod started to protest, but I ignored her. "The footage is the property of the organisation."

"It was filmed in my school," said Janey coldly. "And it is my pupil who has gone missing. A ten-year-old boy, Claire. I can't believe you want to impede the police in this way."

"And I can't believe you are making the police try and frame Jackson," I retorted, glancing at Iain, who seemed to be finding some source of fascination in his shoes again. He allowed Janey to continue, rather than speaking himself.

"Don't be so ridiculous," she said. "This request didn't come from me."

"So who did it come from then? And how come Jackson seems to be the only suspect here?"

"It was Lachlan Mackay, if you must know," she snapped. "Murdo's father."

I looked at her, but her eyes slid away from mine, and I suspected that she wasn't telling the whole truth. Even if it was Lachlan who'd asked the police to look at my footage, somebody had put that idea in his head.

"I'll call my boss now, Iain," I said, and he finally looked up at me. "Just to keep him informed. Then I suppose you'd better come down to the cottage with me.

"Thank you. I'm sure somebody is going to spend the next few days watching your pictures and still find absolutely nothing of use in them, but we have to follow up on this. We owe it to Murdo's parents. And even if we do feel as though they're clutching at straws by now, well we can hardly blame them for that."

No, I thought, I know exactly who to blame for this, and she's sitting about ten feet away from you.

*

Mum was out when Iain and I got back to the cottage.

"Nice for you to have your mum staying," said Iain, kindly. "I expect it's been tough on you these past few weeks, trying to do your job in the face of all this."

I could tell that there was genuine sympathy behind his words and I told him so.

"Aye, well, the police are hardly flavour of the month in Kylecraig right now either, although it's hardly our fault the missing boy hasn't turned up. We're not magicians. It's hit me hard, not being able to help but that's just how it goes sometimes."

I resisted the temptation to remind him that they'd never found out who took my car either, and handed over a box of neatly labelled disks, containing all the footage I'd shot between November and Murdo's disappearance in March.

"This will keep somebody busy," said Iain. "Glad it's not me. No offence."

I managed a smile.

"None taken. But please look after it."

"It's all backed up I take it?"

"Yes, it's backed up, but I'd still like it all returned - and in the same order."

Iain promised me that he would take personal responsibility for my material, and then popped the box into his car. He offered me a lift back up to the school but I declined, and as soon as he was out of view, I went to my mailbox. I had a strange feeling that there would be something from Jackson, as though the events of the morning could have somehow produced a response.

There were no postcards but there was a smooth, rather old-fashioned cream vellum envelope, containing a single, folded piece of paper, on which was written, in elaborate calligraphy, a poem, entitled "Adrift":

Beneath it, Jackson had added a line of explanation.

"Not mine, I'm afraid - I wish it was. Norman McCaig wrote the above – but it sums up how I'm feeling at the moment."

I looked down at the smooth paper, tried to read between the oh-so-carefully handwritten lines, wished that I was strong enough to crumple those words between my fingers.

Instead, I looked around to check that nobody was watching, then sneaked a gulp of whisky from the small bottle I'd stashed inside the mailbox. Within moments I could feel the tension starting to ease from my shoulders.

CHAPTER TWENTY ONE

Mum was due to leave after the May Bank Holiday weekend, and we'd decided to treat ourselves to a champagne tea at a posh hotel on the Monday. As with most things in the Highlands this had taken quite a bit of planning. We intended to leave a car there and collect it the following morning, so we'd booked the local taxi (there was only one) to bring us back to Kylecraig.

We'd been looking forward to our treat, so it was a shame we never got to enjoy it.

Just before we were due to go out, I became aware of the buzz of a helicopter circling the bay. This was unusual enough to drive me outdoors, and Mum followed when I called her. It was the distinctive yellow coastguard's chopper and it was flying low, following the coastline of the island of Greagha before heading out to sea, and then coming back in to retrace its previous route.

I climbed the dunes in front of the cottage for a better view and saw a cluster of people standing at the edge of the sea, watching. At that point, the mobile phone in my pocket began to vibrate – gaining just a bit of height had been enough to find a signal. Glancing down, I saw that it was a voicemail, but had no chance to listen to the message, as Billy Mackenzie had appeared on the road outside the cottage.

"You might want to get down there with your camera," he shouted up at me. "I hear they've found something on the island."

"Let's take your car," said Mum as I skidded back down the sand dune.

My camera was already in the boot of the car, so we lost no time in getting to the other end of the village. However, I lost my nerve when I saw that Catriona and Lachlan Mackay were amongst the people who had gathered at the end of the beach.

"I can't get my camera out," I hissed at Mum. "Everybody will hate me."

"No, they won't. Just keep your distance. You're the only one here with a camera, just think of the kudos."

But I cared less about the prospect of getting exclusive pictures than I did about being run out of the village. Having seen how Jackson had fared from being on the wrong side of some of the locals, I had no desire to emulate him.

I was still wrestling with my conscience when Eilidh Ross appeared. Seeing me, and clearly desperate to talk, she headed straight over.

"Have you heard? They think they've found a body."

Her voice was a curious mixture of awe and horror and, as usual, her capacity to be several steps ahead of the game amazed me.

"Who did? Where?"

"Some holidaymakers. Kayakers. They went for a paddle over to Greagha and pulled in at some remote little beach. Went for a wee potter about and found something they weren't expecting."

"How did you hear about it?"

"Alasdair was down on the croft with Graham." Graham was the local coastguard. "They were painting the new sheds when the call came through."

We watched for a while as the helicopter flew low in another pass between the beach and the island. As the news spread, more and more people were arriving on the beach, but a curious hush had descended. The only sounds were the crude noise of the helicopter's rotor blades and then, as it flew away, the baleful sighing of the waves sliding along the sand.

"You should get your camera out. Get some pictures before the world and his wife are back to spy on us again."

I explained my dilemma to Eilidh, who surprised me once again.

"Pish. You're doing your job, aren't you? You'll be out of here in a couple of months anyway, so let them talk about you if they want to. Anyway, isn't it better for you to be filming this than someone who's just been flown in from London for a bit of glory?"

I wasn't entirely convinced that anyone else would see it that way, but knew it was only a matter of time before the media descended en-masse again. So I set up the camera on the tripod and filmed as discreetly as I could from the back of the beach.

I was grateful that I'd insisted on a camera with a far more powerful zoom lens than the one I usually used - although looking at the distraught, tear-streaked face of Catriona Mackay, I could have done without that zoom. Once I had her framed and focused in the centre of the shot I had to look away, while the camera kept on rolling, recording every second of her pain.

*

Within hours the police were back in Kylecraig, and a rather ineffectual cordon had been set up around the village, so that only locals, accredited media and genuine holidaymakers would be allowed in. It wasn't working particularly well, since anybody who said they were staying in the village was being let through. Clearly the concept of dishonesty hadn't occurred to those who'd thought to set it up.

Because the holiday season was now underway, there was very little spare accommodation in the area, and holidaymakers suddenly found themselves being offered large sums of money to rent out spare beds to journalists and TV crews, which was leading to rows between visitors and locals.

In the midst of all the bickering and nastiness were the rumours – still unconfirmed - that a body had been found. The police had called a press conference in the village hall for 9pm but were remaining tight-lipped until then.

In the meantime, I had checked the voicemail on my mobile phone, with a wild fantasy that somehow Jackson must have heard about what had happened and called me. But it turned out that it was just the local taxi driver wanting to confirm our booking. I hoped he wasn't still sitting outside the hotel waiting for us.

Having handed over a copy of my footage - or at least, some edited highlights - to a grateful BBC News crew who'd been sent from Inverness, I felt that I'd done more than enough for one day. Much to Mum's disappointment, I decided that I didn't want to go to the press conference. It seemed that she had assumed we'd be going together.

"You wouldn't get in anyway," I told her incredulously. "It's accredited press only."

"I could be your sound-woman. Or your assistant."

"No, you couldn't. Iain Cameron knows exactly who you are. Anyway, I've done enough nosing around in this for one day. I vote we go back to the cottage, make some pasta, and watch the press conference on TV."

So we turned our backs on the media scrum at one end of the village and headed to the other. It may only have been a mile or so away, but the emptiness and silence served as a surreal and welcome contrast. To get away from the news-hungry crowd was to shake off some of the stresses of the day, like removing a too heavy coat.

At 9pm we were on the sofa with bowls of spaghetti carbonara on our laps, watching the live News Channel broadcast an event which was happening just up the road.

The presenter in the studio was clearly filling time, as the shot of empty chairs behind him showed that the press conference had yet to begin.

"We will be going to Kylecraig just as soon as that press conference gets underway," he said, smoothly. "And we are expecting that we will have some kind of conclusion to this tragic story which has, of course, gripped the nation."

He disappeared from view and the screen filled with that all-too familiar photograph of Murdo, cheeky grin in place, hair all over the place.

"Murdo Mackay disappeared from his home almost two months ago, in the middle of March. In spite of an extensive police investigation, no trace of the ten-year-old boy has been found. Although we think that may be about to change….." there was a pause here and he then re-appeared in vision……" yes, it looks as though we are now able to join our team live in Kylecraig for the press conference."

The trestle table had been set up at the end of the village hall where Jackson and I had sat at the ceilidh – I recognised the mural on the wall. Making their way to the chairs behind the table were DCI Brown from Inverness, a young couple wearing casual outdoor gear who I presumed must be the kayakers, and Iain Cameron. There was no sign of Lachlan and Catriona Mackay or Janey Macleod.

The Chief Inspector kicked off the press conference in a barrage of flashlights, confirming that human remains had been found washed up in a remote cove on Greagha. As yet, the identity was unknown, but the body had now been recovered and removed to a forensic laboratory for testing. There had also been some fragments of clothes adhering to the body which would help to speed up the identification process.

"Until we have the results of those tests, we are unable to say for certain whose remains these are. However, given the location in which they were found, we cannot rule out the possibility that this could be the missing boy, Murdo Mackay. We would ask that the privacy of the parents and other family members be respected at this most difficult time."

He looked down at his hands, as though reluctant to continue, and then up at the camera.

"I will now take questions from the floor. Please bear in mind, however, that I am unable to tell you very much more than I have already."

As questions poured in from the floor, I wondered where Jackson was right now. Was he sitting, like us, glued to the TV? I found it very hard to imagine that he would be. The desire to see him, mixed up with the usual anger and guilt pierced me with a searing pain, until I became aware that Mum was waving a hand at me.

"Are you listening? Did you hear that?"

"Sorry, I was miles away. Hear what?"

"That know-it-all journalist, giving the police a hard time for failing to find the body."

"Shows how little they know. With the weather and the tides we get here it's amazing anything's turned up at all. Did you know the coastline of Scotland is ten thousand miles long, when you include the islands?"

"Is it really?"

Mum was clearly impressed by this fact, which I'd found equally astounding when I'd heard Jackson imparting it to his class.

Back on the TV, DCI Brown was assuring the media that the coastline had been searched, and that teams of specialist police divers had combed the area around the beach and the harbour, but that searching the ocean for a body was somewhat akin to looking for the proverbial needle in a haystack.

"In fact, if it wasn't for these two," he indicated the kayakers, "then it is quite possible that we could have been left none the wiser. As you know, Greagha is uninhabited, and the tides mean that many of the beaches on the island are underwater for much of the day."

The female kayaker looked as though she'd rather be anywhere else. Her head was bowed and her hands clenched. It was her partner who spoke next.

"We're just glad if we've been able to help," he said. "Obviously it was pretty distressing to find something like that, but if it means there's a conclusion – some kind of closure – then that can only be a positive thing, going forward."

"Why does everybody speak like that now?" Mum grumbled. "Closure. A positive. Going forward. What happened to good old-fashioned English?"

In spite of the gravity of the subject, I couldn't help grinning – the mangling of the English language was a pet hate that we shared.

"Jackson would agree with you there. He took great pains to correct the kids when they lapsed into that way of speaking."

"Well, he's just gone up a notch in my estimation then."

We returned our attention to the TV.

"Were you aware of the missing boy?" shouted someone from the floor at the press conference, addressing the kayakers.

"Of course," the man replied. "Who could have missed it?"

"But you didn't think to cancel your holiday, go somewhere else instead?" persisted the same journalist.

"We thought about it, but we love it up here," replied the kayaker. His girlfriend nodded mutely. "We'd already paid for the caravan as well. Besides, it'd be awful if the village was abandoned by the people who spend their money here, that's not going to help anyone."

The conference went on but there was really nothing more to be said, and after a while we switched off the TV.

"Are you still leaving tomorrow?" I asked Mum.

"I can stay if you'd like me to."

I cast around in my mind for some kind of indication as to how I might feel if left alone, but it was hard to gauge. Over the past few weeks and months, I felt like I'd been stripped red raw like a blister, and every time the skin had begun to heal, something had happened to open up the wound again. Having Mum around had certainly helped to get me through the weeks since Jackson left, but I couldn't help feeling it was time I stood on my own two feet again.

With the help of a bottle or two.

"I'll be fine," I said, my voice carrying a confident note that I was far from feeling. "I will find a state of Zen. All is well, and all will be well in the world."

"Misquoted but understood," said Mum, with obvious relief. "It would be good to get home, if you're sure you don't mind? And I'm sorry I have to go so early in the morning, but my train leaves Inverness at 0755. I will come back if you're struggling though; you only have to say the word."

"I think I'll be okay. I'm going to call Leonie and get her up here since she owes me a visit, and I've only got a couple of months left in Kylecraig now."

"It'll fly past," said Mum, giving me a hug. "Try and make the most of it. Remember that you're here to do a job, and just do that to the best of your ability. The rest can always be sorted out later."

CHAPTER TWENTY TWO

A fter I'd waved Mum off at the hideous hour of 4am the next day, I tried going back to bed but found that I was too restless to sleep. I got back up, paced from room to room, turned the radio on because it was too quiet, then turned it off again because I couldn't bear the inconsequential noise. Although the cottage was small, I'd got used to sharing the space with her.

Having stripped the beds and put the sheets in the washing machine, I noticed that the sky was starting to lighten, and decided to go for a walk down to the other end of the village. I stayed on the road for the first bit, only cutting down onto the beach once I was safely past the spot which spoke far too profoundly to me of Jackson's absence, and wondered for the thousandth time how Murdo's parents were dealing with their loss. Even in my lowest moments, I had to remind myself that at least my story had the glimmer of a chance of a happy ending.

It was shaping up to be another glorious late spring day of pale blue skies, laconically drifting clouds and flat, lazy surf. I thought back, fleetingly, to the last holiday I'd shared with Tom – a week on a beach in Crete last summer, which had done nothing but emphasise how unhappy we'd become together. And that was before I knew about the affairs.

"Better to be alone than suffer the loneliness of a rubbish relationship," I reminded myself now. It was the mantra that Leonie and I had come up with over a teary, boozy night out, after that holiday had effectively ended my five years of torment.

Had I moved on in the months since then? I'd moved away, yes; and maybe the decision to come up to the Highlands had been taken too lightly. I couldn't help reflecting that Leonie had been right in so many ways. By burying myself in work in such an isolated location, I'd run away from my problems, rather than facing up to them. All that had happened was that I now had a whole new set of problems to deal with – not least of which was having fallen, once again, for the wrong man.

No doubt Leonie would love to hear me admitting that she'd been right. And since she was my very best friend, I wouldn't even mind giving her that pleasure. I vowed to call her later on and get a firm date for a visit into the diary.

Feeling a bit chirpier at this thought, I quickened my pace and was soon at the far end of the bay. A couple of TV News crews were already set-up outside the school gates, with smartly dressed presenters delivering reports for the Breakfast TV audiences. I wondered what they could possibly find to say.

Heading from the beach back up onto the road, I caught sight of Iain Cameron talking to Kelly MacIver. I hesitated, but Iain raised a hand in greeting when he saw me.

I took this as an invitation and walked over. Kelly couldn't even bring herself to give me a smile. Reminding myself that Jimmy was one of Murdo's best friends, I once again felt my dual status as outsider and non-parent picking me out like a runner wearing a luminous jacket. Look at me - I'm not one of you - Beware!

"Hello, Claire," said Iain Cameron. "That's your mother away then?"

Once again, I marvelled at the way everyone knew everything in this village.

"I saw her drive past a few hours ago in that wee red car," he explained. "I'm having trouble sleeping at the moment. You'll miss her, I expect?"

"Yes, it's been really nice having her here. I've eaten a lot better, that's for sure."

Kelly spoke now, clearly desperate to get away.

"That reminds me, I'd best go get the kids their breakfast."

Iain and I watched her go.

"This is so hard for everybody. How do you try and explain what's happened to a ten- year-old? That they're not going to see their wee pal again?" He shook his head. "It's the worst thing I've dealt with in my time with the police, that's for certain."

"What's the latest?" I asked. "Off the record I mean, not as a journalist. I'm not digging I promise you."

"Don't worry, I'm not one of these anti-media types and even if I was, I wouldn't be counting you as one of them. There's nothing much to say in any case. Inspector left late last night, and most of the press will probably be heading off this morning. The remains are already away to forensics for testing and they're unlikely to know much in the next few days or maybe even weeks. If it does turn out to be the boy, then let's hope they can tell us what happened to him. Until then, life returns to normal. At least, that's the theory."

"What do you think?" I asked him. "I mean, what's your gut instinct?"

"Officially, no comment. Unofficially, he was a tricky wee bugger was Murdo. Tell him not to do something and he'd be twice as likely to go ahead and do it. Reckon he could have gone out, in a huff like, and had an accident. It wasn't a night to be mucking about outside, especially if he was anywhere near the harbour."

"So you don't think there's anything suspicious about it?"

I was fishing, and Iain knew it.

"I've heard the rumours as well as you have Claire, and I know there are some folk who were all too keen to point the finger at someone they don't know. And until we have the results from those tests, I'd be unwilling to rule out anything or anybody."

He looked at me then, sighed and carried on.

"But – if you're asking me for my opinion as a villager, and not as a policeman – I'd put money on it being an accident. It would certainly be preferable to any other alternative. "

I smiled then, the tension in my jaw releasing itself into a smile. Iain gave me a warning look and then spoke again.

"That's just my personal wish. And it remains strictly between the two of us."

"Iain – is there no way you can give me Jackson's address? Please?

He was shaking his head now. "I can't, Claire. I'm sorry."

"But you said to Janey and me that you were in touch."

"We're in touch, yes".

"Then if it turned out….If it turned out that…."

I stopped. I couldn't bring myself to finish the sentence, to say, "…that he had something to do with Murdo's disappearance?"

Iain seemed to know what I wanted to hear though.

"You'll just have to trust me when I say that I do not consider him to be a suspect."

"Do you have a phone number for him?"

Iain looked a bit uncomfortable now.

"Listen to me. We're in contact with him, but that's all I can say. And I know that if we need to speak to him in person, then he'll make the journey back here immediately."

"So when did you last speak to him? Have you been in touch since the kayakers found the....what they found on the beach?"

I was aware that I'd raised my voice, but Iain Cameron was smiling at me, his grey eyes sad and tired.

"Yes, we've spoken, briefly. I told him that we hoped to have the full picture within the next few weeks. He was relieved to hear that, although he was understandably upset at the thought of what might have become of Murdo."

Iain then made a show of looking at his watch.

"I really should be getting on. I've a mountain of paperwork to deal with and this isn't getting any of it done. I'm sorry I can't be any more help to you, but I've already said far more than I should have done. You will keep this conversation to yourself?"

"Of course," I promised.

*

That evening, I was having another difficult conversation, this time with Leonie. I was trying to persuade her to come up and visit me, and she was pleading work commitments, family plans – anything, it seemed, rather than fulfil a promise to a friend. After a few minutes of increasingly heated conversation, I slammed down the phone, expecting her to ring back and apologise. It was only when she hadn't done so within five minutes that I realised she didn't know my new number.

Angrily, I called her again. She picked up straight away.

"I've been calling your mobile," she said.

"No signal. That's why I'm using the landline. Anyway, I can't believe you aren't going to come and see me....."

"Calm down, dear," she said, interrupting me. "I think I've found a window. How about two weeks' on Friday?"

"Fine. Any time is fine. My diary is empty."

Leonie laughed.

"I'm sorry, I don't mean to laugh, only you just sound so sorry for yourself."

"I am. Strange though this may seem, I miss my friend."

"Oh Claire, truly, I am sorry. I'll make it up to you. I'll bring food and wine, and all the latest gossip mags of course. Oh, and my best sparkly night-clubbing shoes."

"Walking boots would be better," I said. She could always make me smile, in the end.

*

Having persuaded Leonie to visit, I felt as though I'd entered some kind of alternative universe where things were gradually getting slower and slower. It wouldn't have surprised me if the hands on my watch had begun to go backwards. "If only that were possible," I couldn't help thinking, "if only."

The ludicrously bright May mornings now woke me up at about 5am – and since it wasn't dark until almost 10pm, there seemed to be too many hours in the day. I went through the motions of filming in the school, but in spite of having promised Mum that I'd throw myself into work, my heart really wasn't in it.

It wasn't just me though. There was a strange atmosphere in the classrooms and corridors. The children were subdued and fractious a lot of the time, and the teaching, now that Jackson had left, seemed lacklustre. Janey Macleod was even more evasive than usual – she would barely greet me, when our paths crossed, and never made conversation. Once, I asked her if I should stop filming, but she seemed nonplussed by the suggestion.

"Don't be silly, we all know you're just doing your job. Of course you must continue."

As she walked away I was tempted to run after her and beg her to tell me what had happened between her and Jackson.

"She's glad he's gone," I thought, bitterly. "She didn't want him here. So why did he come in the first place?"

It was still a mystery, but one which I was determined to get to the bottom of.

In the meantime, I recorded the life of the school as it struggled to return to the happy, carefree place that it had been before Murdo went missing.

And so, minute by minute, hour by hour, day by day, we passed the time, the people of Kylecraig and me.

CHAPTER TWENTY THREE

K eeping me going during these peculiar weeks were my written messages from Jackson.

These were arriving every two or three days now, usually consisting of a couple of enigmatic lines scrawled on postcards which he seemed to have been collecting over many years, judging by the variety of locations. All were scenes of mountains and lakes, places which he'd clearly loved - and knew that I would too. I kept them in an old shoe box I'd found in a cupboard – except for the poem, which I'd stowed in its vellum envelope in the drawer beside my bed.

I'd bought a copy of Norman McCaig's Complete Works from the bookshop in Ullapool and had been reading a few poems each day. As I read, I could feel the eerily beautiful West Highland landscapes crawling under my skin.

I could see why Jackson had pointed me in this direction – it was his subtle way of telling me that I should make more of an effort to engage with the Highlands whilst I still had the chance. But the truth was, without him, it just wasn't the same. To my shame, now that he was gone, I was beginning to count the days until I would be able to leave Kylecraig.

*

Leonie was clearly delighted to hear this. She arrived at Inverness airport on a drizzly Friday afternoon, and I was there to greet her. All the way back to Kylecraig – a drive of over three hours – she alternated exclamations over the beauty of the landscape with comments about the dreadfulness of the weather, and how "amazing" I'd been to "stick it out" up here.

"I had no choice," I reminded her. "I've been working, remember?"

"Oh, I know but Claire, nobody would have blamed you if you'd come running home after a few months. I mean just look at it."

She swept out a hand, dramatically, as we came around a bend in the road to be greeted by yet another epic vista of sun slanting through low black clouds, illuminating moorland, sheep and mountains.

"Yes, who on earth would want to live amongst such beauty, when you could be tramping the filthy pavements of the big city?"

"Very funny. I'm not denying it's beautiful, but there's nothing to do here. I mean, I like hills. Well, I don't mind the odd weekend in the Lake District."

"As long as there's a gastropub and a decent spa involved."

"Well yes, obviously those help to enhance the loveliness factor."

Even without looking at her, I could hear that Leonie was grinning, and I smiled as well.

"But seriously, even someone who loves the hills as much as you do must have got a bit sick of them by now?"

I thought for a moment before replying.

"Not exactly. I mean, I still love the scenery, it's just so much nicer when you've got somebody to share it with. Even better when it's someone who can make you appreciate it more by talking about the geology, the birdlife…."

I didn't get any further.

"Jeez, Claire. Just listen to yourself. The sooner we get you back to Manchester the better. You've turned into a twitcher."

I laughed aloud. It felt so good to be sharing a joke again that I didn't even mind it being at my own expense.

*

We were treated, as we approached the turn-off to Kylecraig, to one of the most spectacular sunsets I'd had the pleasure of seeing in my nine months there.

"Wow," said Leonie. "I take it all back. I'd swap this for the Trafford Centre any day of the week."

"I haven't got my camera with me. Typical! That would have made for some fantastic pictures."

I parked up in the layby above the village and we watched in awe as the vast sun sunk into a reflection of itself before sliding languidly into the horizon.

"Talk about the Golden Globes," said Leonie as I started up the engine. "That was stunning."

"Glad you came?"

She touched my arm. "Of course I am. I'm sorry I've been a crap friend."

"So have I. It takes two to keep in touch and neither of us has been much good. I've been caught up with all of the madness over the past few weeks...."

"...and I've been doing the old nine-to-five treadmill at work and then the five–to-nine treadmill of trying to be a good wife. I sometimes wonder if feminism ever happened. You're better off without a man, Claire – sooner or later they all turn into someone who just wants a hot meal on the table and a hot woman in the bed."

I smiled at her. I knew that she and David were blissfully happy, but it was good of her to try and make me feel better about being alone.

"Come on," I said, as we pulled up outside the cottage. "Let's get drunk."

We fell easily into an evening of food, wine, and gossip. Now that he was gone, I felt able to tell Leonie about Jackson. But when I mentioned how much I'd enjoyed spending our weekends hill-walking, she jumped up from her chair and dragged me from mine, pulling me towards the front door.

"We need to get you out of here! Emergency! 'The Ramblers' have stolen my friend!"

"Get off me," I protested, laughing. "You're such a bully."

She managed to drag me as far as the front door before we both collapsed in fits of drunken giggles.

"Oh dear." I wiped my eyes as we both sat back down. "More wine?"

"Absolutely. The more wine we drink, the more my old friend comes back to me."

"That's a bit of a sad indictment."

"But it also happens to be true."

Leonie refilled our glasses and we chinked them together which, inevitably, reminded me of Jackson. It was an instantly sobering thought.

"What is it?" Leonie asked me. "You've gone suspiciously quiet. You're thinking about him again, aren't you?"

I nodded. I wanted to show her the postcards, but I was afraid she'd diminish their importance to me by laughing at them.

"Promise me you won't take the piss? He's been in touch with me, ever since he left."

"Really?" She leaned forward, and I decided.

"Wait there. I'll show you."

I went to my bedroom and picked up the box of postcards, although I left the poem in its place by my bed. That, I felt, was the closest thing I had to a love letter, and I wasn't going to share it with anyone.

Leonie looked through the postcards without comment. There were over thirty of them now, all of them saying something but nothing, as though Jackson was leading me on by touching my fingertips without ever grasping me firmly by the hand.

"Was your Mum still here when these started arriving?" Leonie asked finally, putting down the box on the table.

"She was."

"And what did she think?"

"She thought he was messing me around. She was quite cross about it actually."

"Far be it from me to agree with your mother. Or to say something that you don't want to hear. But do you think she may have a point?

I picked the box up, angrily, and returned it to the bedroom.

"Claire," shouted Leonie. "We're only trying to protect you."

"Protect me from what?"

"Well – he probably left because he's waiting for all the fuss and hoo-ha to die down. He is still a suspect, after all."

"Really. And where did you get that piece of crappy information from?"

"The papers." She at least had the decency to look a bit shame-faced. "I know you'll tell me that it was only in the tabloids, but he was definitely named and shamed, Claire. No wonder he's keeping his distance."

"I can't believe you still read those trashy websites" I fumed. "Yes of course I've seen what they said about him and it's all rubbish. Whatever happened to innocent till proven guilty?"

"Come on - you said yourself that you saw him on the night the lad vanished. And you said he looked upset."

"Not THAT kind of upset. I reckon he and Janey Macleod had had some kind of bust up about something. If only I could get to the bottom of all that."

"Some things are easier to get to the bottom of than others" smiled Leonie, waving the half-empty wine bottle at me. "So come on, help me out here."

*

In spite of the drunken Friday night, we were determined to make the best of our weekend together. Leonie had taken my advice and brought a pair of decent walking shoes, and I'd decided to take her up to the Black Loch and then to the hidden whisky bar in the cliffs.

The path up the hill was dry underfoot, small birds flew up as we brushed through the heather, and the gentlest of breezes stopped us from getting too hot and sweaty. I felt like a proud parent showing off a child's achievements as the dappled landscape unfolded before us. We didn't see a soul on the way up, and, when we reached the Loch, we had it all to ourselves.

"This is pretty special," said Leonie. "I can't believe there's nobody here."

"I know – if this place was in the Lakes it'd be mobbed."

"Somebody's been here though – look."

She pointed to a pile of cigarette stubs, glaringly white against the peat.

I looked at it for a moment, and my mind flashed back to the mystery smoker who'd scared me that night at Ceol na Mara.

"Probably the owner of the boat" I said. "I've still no idea how they got that up here."

"Sherpas? Anyway, it's stunning. I'm so pleased you made me come up here, Claire. And I'm sorry I wasn't here sooner." Leonie gave me a tight hug.

"I don't blame you for waiting until spring," I replied, once she'd let go. "When I came up here with Jackson we got cold and soaked. This is definitely the best time to visit."

We lay back on the springy heather, enjoying the feeling of the sun on our faces. The only sounds were birdsong and a gentle lapping of the loch waters. I felt myself drifting off…it was one of those moments that you want to preserve, to be brought out when you're cold, tired or stressed. I decided that I must have been mad to be missing Manchester, and to want to swap all of this for the big city.

"What are you thinking?" asked Leonie after a while. "As if I didn't know."

"Actually, I wasn't thinking about Jackson."

"Well, that makes a change."

I sat up and leant back on my elbows, and she did the same. We pulled a face at one another – one of those spontaneous gestures between friends – and then I continued.

"I was thinking about how much I'll miss the fresh air and the big skies up here, when I move back to the city."

"I know what you mean. It's tough getting the balance right, isn't it? I hadn't honestly realised how much I needed this. You get so swept up into the day to day busy stuff that you forget how to take a breather."

"I'm not sure I could live here permanently though. There must be a happy medium somewhere."

"Well, when you find this Utopia, do let me know. Especially if you also find a job there, oh, and an affordable place to live. Hey, talking of places to live, where ARE you going to live? When you come back I mean?"

"I'm not sure yet. Mum has a spare room."

Leonie looked horrified.

"You can't move back in with your mother at your age!"

"Actually, I think I could. We just spent a few weeks together and we got on fine."

"Yes, but she was on holiday. And it wasn't her house."

But the more I thought about it, the more it seemed like a good idea.

*

Although she wasn't a whisky drinker, I was sure that Leonie would love The Craggan – but when we got there, the wooden door was chained and bolted on the outside.

"How weird." I stood back, staring up at the outside of the building. Above the door was a window, opaque with dust and age.

"It looks like nobody's been here for years," said Leonie.

"But I came here just a few months ago."

I walked back to the door, rattled the chain and gave the wood a good thump, but all that achieved was to send a flock of gulls skywards from the roof.

"Maybe the old woman died."

"What old woman?"

"The old woman who served us, when I came here with Jackson.

"Ah. Did you think it would make you feel closer to him, coming here?"

"I was probably hoping that it would. But now I'm just wondering if I dreamt the whole thing."

"Maybe you did."

"Ha ha. Maybe that's why Jackson was always telling me to be in the moment," I mused. "Maybe he knew that the moment wasn't going to last."

"It never does. Things always move on, and that's how it should be. At least you didn't sleep with him before he did a runner."

I felt the colour flood my face and was powerless to stop it. I saw from the expression on her face that Leonie had seen it too.

"Oh my god. You did. When?"

"The day that Murdo went missing. Well, that night."

"And?"

I scowled at her.

"And nothing. He came round to see me, he was in a state. It seemed like a good idea at the time."

"Claire, jeez. I can't believe you didn't tell me this before."

"I didn't want to spoil it."

"What, by me pointing out to you that "shag and run" is not a particularly attractive character trait?"

I took a deep breath.

"That's not how it was."

"Really? He spends the night with you and then vanishes into thin air. What am I supposed to think?"

"I know it doesn't look good...."

"Look good? It looks appalling. Why aren't you furious, Claire? I would be. I am, on your behalf."

I shrugged, at a loss, unable to find any words that would account for my feelings. Staring up at the clouded glass above the door of the Craggan Bar, I was sure that if I could only see through to the other side, I might have some kind of hint as to what the hell was going on.

CHAPTER TWENTY FOUR

W e were about three miles from Kylecraig when the car radio surged loudly into life, as reception returned. We'd been so busy talking that I hadn't even noticed the lack of background music or noise, but as the pips of a news bulletin interrupted our chatter we both went quiet.

"Police in Inverness say that they have identified the remains found on a remote island as those of the missing boy, Murdo Mackay."

I swerved.

"Pull over," said Leonie sharply, and I swung the car into a Passing Place.

"More now from our Scotland Correspondent," continued the newsreader.

My hands were shaking but Leonie took them in her own and held on tight.

"The story of the missing Kylecraig boy has captured the public imagination in a way not seen since the disappearance of Madeleine McCann" said the disembodied female voice on the radio. "However, when human remains were found on the remote island of Greagha just under three weeks ago, it seemed likely that they were, tragically, connected with the case. That has now been confirmed by police here in Inverness. They issued a press release late this afternoon, saying that forensic tests have established the identity of the body as that of ten-year-old Murdo Mackay. Detective Chief Inspector Dingwall

Brown has been leading the investigation and I was able to speak to him just a few moments ago."

Another voice came on, instantly recognisable as that of the tall, patrician DCI from Inverness.

"I can now officially confirm that the human remains found on Greagha Island are those of Murdo Mackay. Further tests are ongoing, to see if a cause of death can be established. In the meantime, we will make no further comment, and we ask that the family and the wider community be left in peace to come to terms with their loss."

Leonie and I looked at one another.

"So they still don't know how he died," she said. "Not sure I want to go back to the village now."

"Don't be so daft. It's just a normal place where a terrible accident happened. The problem is, people wanted to make it more than that."

"Who says it was an accident? That's not what the police are saying."

"They aren't saying anything."

"I bet they would, if they thought it was just an accident," Leonie persisted.

"You're just speculating. Trying to read between the lines."

"Yup, just like the media do, all the time."

"Not just the media. We reflect the public opinion, we don't create it."

It was an old argument that we'd had many times before, but this time it was far too personal.

*

As we turned off the main road into the village, I caught sight of Billy Mackenzie. He was leaning on a fence, chatting to one of the older crofters but they both stopped talking when I halted the car beside them and wound down the window.

"You'll have heard the news then, Claire?" Billy asked me.

"Yes, we just heard it on the radio."

He nodded, slowly.

"What do you think, Billy? Do you think it was an accident?"

"I don't think it's my place to say anything, Miss. With respect."

"Of course. I'm sorry."

I paused, and there was an awkward moment whilst we all gazed around, without any of us making eye contact. Then I carried on. "I don't suppose you know what's happened to The Craggan?"

The two men exchanged a glance, but still, neither of them spoke.

"You DO know. Did the old lady die?"

"Die? Old Evie? She'll die in prison, that one." This was the other man, who looked amused; but Billy wasn't laughing.

"I'm not sure when you were there, Miss, or why, but it's not somewhere I've ever visited. And now, if you'll excuse me, I've work to be getting on with."

This seemed to be unlikely; but our presence, it was clear, would be tolerated no longer. I said goodbye, wound up the window, and we drove the rest of the way in silence.

*

"Let's go for a walk along the beach."

This suggestion, from Leonie, came around an hour later. We'd tried Googling "The Craggan," but drawn a blank. We'd also read everything we could find online about Murdo's body being identified, but nobody knew any more than we did. In

173

spite of the dark events of the day, the evening sun was now dancing through the windows, as enticing and beguiling as a handsome but unsuitable man.

We set off along the road, until, around half a mile from my cottage, the dunes tapered away, leaving just the short-cropped machair between us and the flat white sand. A couple of fat lambs ignored us as we walked past, intent as they were on munching through the grass. Apart from a young couple walking a dog, the beach was deserted.

Leonie took an exaggerated breath of air.

"Do you think too much fresh air could actually be bad for you? Send you into shock if you come from the city? I reckon my body would only last a few days here before it started craving petrol fumes and greasy fast-food aromas."

As we reached the end of the beach nearest to the school, four figures appeared at the edge of the sand and, as we came closer, I recognised Eilidh Ross and her three children. When she saw us, she put up a hand, then bent and spoke to Kirsty, the oldest child, who took the others away towards the sea.

"Claire, how are you doing? It's been a while since I've seen you properly."

"Yes, I've been thinking the same. This is my friend, Leonie. Leonie, Eilidh."

The two of them exchanged smiles, but I could feel Lee's disappointment – she'd been hoping for a chance encounter with Janey Macleod, I was certain, after hearing me go on about her so much.

"I'm just going to explore a bit more, get the most of this whilst I can. Nice to meet you, Eilidh."

Watching her go, I felt myself wobble a bit. My two worlds had bumped together, merged then separated; and I felt like I'd been left behind in the wrong one. Eilidh's soft voice broke the peace.

"You've heard the news, I presume?"

"Yes. But only what's been made public. Do you know any more?"

I looked at Eilidh, and saw a strange expression pass over her face, like a shadow. I realised that she was fighting back tears.

"I can't say."

"You don't have to tell me anything. I'm sorry, I shouldn't have asked."

"I trust you Claire, I do. It's not that. It's just – it's more that I don't want to tell you something and then find out that I was wrong. And I really hope I AM wrong, because I just can't believe it of…..can't believe that…."

She stopped, and rubbed at the tears as they came.

I waited, as the screeching of gulls filled my ears, louder and louder, and I focused on the turquoise water coming and going behind Eilidh's face, so that I wouldn't have to see her lips when she said his name.

"I think there's been a terrible mistake," was what she said next.

"If somebody's saying awful things about Jackson again…….."

It was my turn to stop, mid-sentence, but my words had had a strange effect on Eilidh.

"Jackson? Who said anything about Jackson?"

"Well, I just assumed…..from what you were saying…"

I stopped, again, looked at her for help, but she was shaking her head now.

"I thought you were his friend?"

"I am. I was. I honestly don't know what I am to him, anymore."

"To be quite honest with you Claire, I don't think any of us knows much anymore. This whole thing has just – I don't know, I can't find the words for it. Come on you're the clever one, find some words for me."

I thought back to the day that I'd first met Jackson, right here on the beach, and I felt a stab of pain come at me from deep inside. The relative simplicity of those ice-sharp days of winter seemed like something out of a fairy-tale.

I gazed at Eilidh, dumbly, unable to put into words what either of was feeling. But I knew that, in spite of our many differences, we both shared feelings that only come when your world and your certainties are ripped apart.

*

Much of Sunday was spent in the car, thanks to the six-hour return trip to drop Leonie at the airport, and so I was exhausted on Monday morning. Still, I somehow managed to respond to my 6am alarm. I was determined to get into school early enough to catch Janey Macleod before anybody else arrived.

As I'd suspected, she was already in when I got there just after 7. She looked as exhausted as I was, and not at all pleased to see me, but I had come prepared.

"Can we have a chat?" I asked. Before she had time to turn me down, I carried on, smiling with more conviction than I felt. "I've got proper coffee here – and breakfast."

I produced my trump card from my rucksack – a packet of luxury *Pains au Chocolat.*

To my amazement, the ploy worked. It seemed that Janey Macleod, like most other people I knew, was defenceless in the face of the finest produce M&S could offer. She even managed a weary smile, saying: "Oh, how lovely. Thanks."

In the kitchen, preparing coffee and heating up the pastries, I told myself that it was ridiculous to feel nervous. It had taken Leonie to remind me that Janey and I had got on just fine – until Jackson had arrived. Now that he was gone, surely there was no reason why the two of us couldn't be allies once again.

I returned to her office with a tray containing a full cafetière of lusciously scented coffee, two pretty flowered china cups which I'd brought from my own kitchen, and four warm *Pains au Chocolat.*

Janey was replying to emails when I walked in, but she waved at me to sit down.

"Give me two minutes. I have to do this now or I'll lose my thread."

I poured out the coffees and placed one, along with two pastries, in front of her. When she finished typing, she glanced at them and then looked at me.

"So what's brought this on?"

"It's a peace offering. I'm tired of feeling like the two of us are at loggerheads over something. I'm only here for another few weeks, and I hate working in a bad atmosphere. Aren't things bad enough, without adding extra stress into the situation?"

Janey took a bite out of one of the pastries, and a large slug of coffee before replying.

"Did Jackson put you up to this?"

"I haven't spoken to Jackson since he left the village," I replied, as calmly as I could. "I just want to do my job."

Janey carried on eating and drinking, looking at me intently as though trying to work something out. The longer the silence went on, the more tempted I was to fill it, but I dug my nails into my palm to stop myself, telling myself that she was just playing games with me.

Finally, she spoke again.

"I don't have any problem with you being here, Claire. I know you find that hard to believe, but it's the truth. Any….issues that there may have been between us were to do with Jackson, not to do with you."

I nodded, unsure what to say next. Janey seemed disinclined to add anything else to the conversation, although she was clearly enjoying the breakfast I'd provided. Trying to remain calm, and before the silence became unbearable, I spoke.

"When I first came up here, you said you only agreed to the film being made because we got on so well". I blushed, aware that I was practically begging her to be my friend again, like a schoolgirl with a soppy crush on a prettier, cleverer, sportier one. "I still have to finish my film, in spite of everything else that's happened," I finished, speaking as firmly as I could.

Janey nodded. "I suppose you do."

"And I want you to know that the film will be exactly as we talked about it. Obviously, it will have to include the…events of the past few weeks. But really, this is a portrait of a school at the centre of a community. I don't think that my film will harm the school, not at all. I think it will show everybody what a special place this is."

"You might truly believe that, Claire. But we both know that people are going to watch your film precisely because of what's happened here."

"In that case, I need you and everybody else here to show the outside world what kind of a place this is. We've got a few short weeks of term left to move things on."

"Rousing words, Claire. I wish I had your faith in human nature."

"But you did." Aware that I had raised my voice, I now lowered it again. "You still do, I'm sure of it. You believe in this school, and in the teachers and the children."

"I'm not sure what I believe any more. *We've* all been through hell in the past few weeks, and I don't even feel I can trust people I thought I knew well – let alone people who I don't."

I couldn't very well miss the loaded way she'd said "we."

"But what happened to Murdo had nothing to do with you, or me, or any of us. He wasn't even at school when it happened."

"Who said I was talking about Murdo?" Janey looked at me mutinously.

I stayed silent, until she spoke again.

"Have you really not heard from Jackson?"

She spoke his name as though in inverted commas. And now I was in a dilemma. I decided to come clean.

"I've heard from him. But we haven't spoken, and I have no idea where he is now."

She smiled.

"Let me guess – he's written to you?"

I'm sure the look on my face must have answered this question but she waited for me to confirm it anyway.

"Yes."

Janey actually laughed aloud.

"Of course. Typical Jackson."

She opened up a drawer beneath her desk and pulled out a familiar looking envelope. Thick, cream, expensive vellum. From within it, she pulled out a letter. She didn't pass it over to me, but showed me just enough of it to see that the writing was the same as the handwriting on the letter and cards I'd received.

"I mean really, who writes letters nowadays? Most of us have moved onto emails and social media," she continued. "Not Jackson though, oh no, he thinks he's so much better than the rest of us."

She stuffed the letter back into the envelope and tossed it back into the drawer.

I could think of nothing to say. I just stared at her, uncomprehendingly, until a knock at the door startled us both.

CHAPTER TWENTY FIVE

A s Marnie came into the office, I almost knocked her over as I hurried through the door, desperate to be out of there. The look on Janey's face seemed to follow me out – it had been a mixture of anger and pity and something else that I couldn't quite fathom.

I rushed past some of the children who'd started to arrive, ignoring a shout from Eilidh Ross, and just kept on going until I reached the beach. The blood seemed to be fizzing in my veins; I couldn't face the thought of standing still, so I headed to the water. Unlike me, the waves were calm, and I tried to slow my breathing down to match their unhurried, repetitive motion.

Why had Jackson written to Janey? I tried to gather my thoughts, still wanting to give him the benefit of the doubt. Leonie and my mother had both been certain that he was manipulating me and playing with my emotions – but neither of them had met him. He wasn't like that; I knew it with as much certainty as I knew that Tom was.

I kicked pointlessly at the sand, sending flurries of grains and spray into the air, muttering under my breath. Idiot woman – me – for letting him get under my skin. Horrible woman – Janey – for getting in the way, not just letting us be. And stupid, careless boy – Murdo – for pushing us all to the edge.

This thought at least shamed me into remembering that what I was going through was inconsequential. I ceased my kicking and muttering, and had a tussle with my conscience instead. What I wanted to do was go to the cottage, climb into bed, and pull the covers over my head. What I needed to do was to hold my head up high and get back to work.

Trudging towards the school, I awarded myself a mental pat on the back. I was barely through the school gates before Eilidh, hard at work cleaning the school minibus, pounced.

"You okay, Claire?"

I forced a smile.

"Just about. Had - a bit of bad news - from home."

The look of concern on her face chastened me into continuing, hurriedly;

"That is to say I thought it was bad news but it turned out to be....erm, nothing, really."

A hopeless explanation, I thought, but her mind was clearly on several other things.

"Thank goodness for that. There's been enough bad news around here lately."

I thought about confiding in her, but she was already reaching back into her bucket of soapy water and so the moment passed.

I didn't see anything more of Janey that day. Maybe after all that early drama she'd decided to lock herself into the office. It was a relief not to run into her again but although I tried to do some filming, I was too preoccupied to gather anything of much value. I was going to have to pull myself together soon, or my film would be in danger of falling apart.

*

Arriving back at the cottage and desperate to talk to somebody about my day, I realised that there was nobody I could call. Leonie and Mum would both feel that their misgivings about Jackson had been confirmed by what had happened. My brother (who was often surprisingly helpful when talking about my disastrous love life) was going through a particularly tough time with his ex-wife Sally, according to Mum, and I didn't want to trouble him with my relatively trivial pursuits.

Looking out of the window, I saw that the rain clouds were clearing, with the promise of a golden evening. It was just the excuse I needed. Collecting my camera and tripod from the boot of my car, I made my way onto the beach and spent three hours shooting a time-lapse sequence.

When speeded up, the shafts of sunlight would appear to pierce the racing clouds like fast-flung arrows, producing a beautiful and dramatic effect. It would, if I was lucky, last for twenty seconds or so.

If only I could do a time-lapse on myself, I thought, and whizz through the next few weeks. Then I could get on with the rest of my life.

*

As part of my film, I needed to do some lengthy interviews. A few parents had already pulled out of filming, worried that I would ask them about Murdo, in spite of my assurances that I wouldn't. Nothing I could do or say would persuade them to change their minds, but luckily I still had a few people to talk to. I suspected that Janey may have talked some of them into doing it, since my programme remained the best chance she had of keeping her school open.

I set up chairs and a basic lighting rig in one corner of the main hall, and people trooped in to talk to me. After the turbulence of the past few months, it was amazing how good it felt to be back in control.

Even when working in a busy newsroom, turning stories round as quickly as possible, I'd always tried to be a sympathetic listener. Now, with time on my side, I found myself enjoying the process of getting the best out of people, and watching them relax into a situation which they had initially found unsettling.

I'd been worried that the awful events of the spring and early summer would cast a pall over everything, but my interviewees talked with pride and passion about their village school. It helped that Murdo's family were still away, staying with relatives in Inverness. Nobody even mentioned them, and I certainly wasn't going to risk it.

With the children, it was a different story. I talked to them in pairs, since this was the best way to get answers that were longer than a syllable, and it worked a treat – I often found myself just laughing along as they engaged in giggling banter.

As with the adults, I didn't mention Murdo at all, but some of the children brought it up spontaneously. Calum, who'd been close friends with Murdo, talked solemnly about the need to respect the sea. He clarified this by adding:

"But Murdo never listened about any of that safety stuff. I wish he had of done."

I kept the camera rolling.

"Jackson told him, he was always telling him about it. I remember him being really cross one day when he thought Murdo was mucking about by the sea. His mum was always telling him as well, but he just laughed, even when she said he'd get what was coming to him."

He looked at me, then at his sister, Jessie, sitting beside him.

"Have we said enough now? I'm hungry."

"Me too," said Jessie . She'd said little else but she was only five. I smiled at them.

"Yes. You've both been brilliant, thank you. Go and tell Eilidh I've said to give you an extra-specially big lunch."

"Thanks, Claire!"

They jumped up and wheeled noisily from the room like a pair of grouse startled from the heather. I pulled the disk from my camera, labelled it, and filed it in a box with all the others.

I had only one more interview to do – with Janey Macleod – but not today. With sports day looming and the weather settled and fair, I'd decided that I would set her interview apart from the others by doing it in the school's garden, which overlooked the beach.

It wasn't the stunning backdrop that was the reason though – more the fact that I couldn't bear the thought of being face to face in a room with her again.

CHAPTER TWENTY SIX

I spent the next few evenings watching the interview footage back and logging it, but Jackson was never far from my thoughts – although the postcards had stopped coming a while ago.

Sometimes I dreamt of him. I awoke from these dreams in the hazy half-light of the summer dawn wondering whether the whole thing had, in fact, been nothing but a dream. Was he a man I'd imagined, a placebo partner?

Even my favourite words from him were false – or rather, they were not his words. The Norman McCaig poem, which I'd framed because I loved it so much, now just seemed to mock me, to tell me that I'd been taken for a fool.

In a fit of anger, I chucked it into a drawer in the kitchen, where it was soon buried under a swirl of books and bookmarks, paper clips and sellotape, earplugs and wet-wipes and magazines.

And then everything changed.

*

It was the day before sports' day – traditionally the last event of the school year before the long summer break. It would be my last day at Kylecraig School and that realisation had hit me quite suddenly, as though I couldn't have seen it coming.

I'd spent the day filming preparations – the hard-boiling of eggs for the egg and spoon race, the frenzied baking of cakes in the school's kitchen and the careful pasting-up of children's artworks upon walls. One of the dads had also spent much of the afternoon painting rather crooked white lines along the grass.

"Although that's a waste of time" Eilidh Ross had told me, "since they always end up holding all the races on the beach anyway, and they just draw the lines in the sand."

We'd chatted on together as I filmed her putting out rows of cups and saucers next to an urn borrowed from the village hall.

"Do you really need this many?"

"Well, it's quite the big event around here you see – it's not just the children and their mums and dad who come along – it's a proper village affair."

Jackson should have been here too. What might have happened, had he stayed? Would he be looking forward to a summer break, planning to return for the new school year? Or had he meant it when he told me he'd only ever planned to be a short-term teacher, filling in a gap? Would we…..?

I shook myself out of that half-thought, sensing Eilidh looking at me as she put the last few cups on the table.

"Heading straight back to Manchester are you, once this is done?"

"Not quite, Mum's coming up with my brother and nieces. We thought we'd have a week's holiday together, say goodbye to the place properly. I'd have liked them to come for the sports day, but the girls are still at school in Edinburgh. They'll all be here on Saturday."

"Nice for you to have your family here. Shame they couldn't come tomorrow though, it should be a nice day. Especially after everything else that's gone on this year."

"Will the Mackays be coming, do you think?"

I'd spoken without thinking, and caught what looked like a flash of disbelief in Eilidh's eyes before she spoke.

"Oh, I very much doubt it."

"I'm sorry – stupid of me to ask. Have you spoken to Catriona?"

Lachlan and Catriona were still in Inverness, with Murdo's little sister Maggie. I assumed that they couldn't face the thought of returning to Kylecraig until they knew what had happened to their son.

Eilidh was shaking her head.

"Nobody has, as far as I'm aware. I daresay they'll come back when they're ready, and not before. Besides….."

She looked at me, and a strange expression crossed her face. She was clearly wrestling with something.

"Is there something you want to tell me Eilidh? I'll be out of here tomorrow, after all. You can tell me and know that you'll probably never see me again."

"Aye, but you're a journalist. Telling you'd be like telling the whole world."

I pinched the skin on the inside of my arm hard, to stop an angry outburst.

"On the contrary, if you tell me something off the record, I would never tell another soul."

She still looked dubious, so I carried on.

"Most journalists abide by very rigid standards. Like doctors. Or like priests, hearing confession. And anyway, as a friend, I wouldn't betray a secret."

That seemed to decide her.

"It's hardly a secret, half the village is talking about it. I'd have dismissed it as idle gossip, except I've seen evidence of it with my own eyes. Catriona Mackay was carrying on with Donnie MacIver."

She stopped, but I said nothing. I'd been hoping for something more interesting than an affair.

"Of course, the whole Murdo thing's put a stop to it, and I don't see how Kelly can say anything now, since you wouldn't wish that on your worst enemy. But I can't see Lachie and Catriona hurrying back here either, not any time soon."

"No, I can see that would give them another pretty good reason to stay away. I guess it's not so surprising, with the men here away from home for so long at a time."

Too late, I remembered that Eilidh's husband, Alasdair, was one of them.

"Most of us are too busy with the lives we've got, let alone adding in extra complications," Eilidh said. "But Catriona's never been that independent. She's always been one who needed a man about the place, to get things done. Reckon one thing's just led to another; the longer Lachie's been away, the more she's got used to Donnie doing jobs for her."

"I can sympathise with that," I said, thinking back to when I'd first arrived in Kyecraig. I'd struggled to even light a decent fire, let alone haul logs and coal, feed sheep and cattle and look after young children.

"Aye, well. You've done alright, in the end. Hopefully you'll find it's been good for you, spending time in a place like this. Anyway, I'd best get on home – dinner won't put itself on the table."

She was back to her usual, almost brusque self, either relieved to have confided in me or wishing she hadn't, I couldn't tell which.

189

We said our goodbyes and I stayed for another half hour or so filming the empty hall, the deserted garden – the calm before the storm of the final day. Then I packed up my camera and walked home slowly along the beach, cutting in through the dunes at the usual place.

*

When I reached my front door, I was thinking back over what Eilidh had said, trying to recollect what I knew about Donnie MacIver. Given that he had forbidden me to film his son, and was at least partially responsible for hounding Jackson out of Kylecraig, I harboured no warm feelings towards him; in fact I couldn't even picture him.

But as I headed into the kitchen, all thoughts of Donnie and Catriona vanished.

Sitting at the table, looking straight at me, was Jackson.

CHAPTER TWENTY SEVEN

"I'm sorry."

I stared at him, shook my head.

"Is that it? After all this time, after everything that's happened – you're sorry?"

Jackson shrugged, a gesture which I found even more irritating than the apology. I turned my back on him, went to the fridge, and poured myself a large glass of wine.

"I'm going to need a whole lot more than that, Jackson. A hell of a lot more. How did you even get in here, for a start?"

I sat down opposite him, took a glug of wine, and waited.

"Oh that was easy. But let me start with the apology. And – and I'm afraid that's about all I can give you, for the time being. But I need you to ask you to trust me."

"Maybe you could tell me why I should?"

Jackson sighed. I felt my hands trembling, and tucked them under my legs on the wooden seat of the chair.

"The more I tell you, the worse it will be. You've only got a few days left here, Claire. I think the best thing you can do is to finish your film and then get the hell out of here."

"That sounds like some kind of threat. Would you mind just telling me what the hell is going on?"

Jackson stood up, went to the door and closed it, then to the window and pulled down the blind. Whilst his back was turned, I took another large gulp of wine.

Then I felt his hand on my shoulder, and his voice was in my ear.

"Listen. When I told you to steer clear of me, I had very good reasons. I ignored my own advice, I know, and that was stupid of me. The more I tell you, the worse I'm going to make it. I had to get out of here, and you need to do the same, as soon as you can. I've been watching you for the past few days, to make sure everything's alright......"

I shook his hand from my shoulder and pushed back my chair, facing him.

"You've been watching me? What do you mean by that? How?"

"It doesn't matter how. I came back a few days ago, but I couldn't tell anybody. I just needed to reassure myself that you were alright."

"Oh I'm fine, Jackson. Staying with Janey Macleod, were you?"

I watched his face closely, saw the look of apparently genuine confusion come across it.

"Why on earth would you think that?"

"I know you've been writing to her too......."

Jackson grabbed my wrists in his hands, and I couldn't break free. "Listen to me. I'm only thinking of your safety. Just – just keep your head down, do your job, and then leave this place as soon as you can."

"So you don't deny writing to Janey?"

"No of course I don't. Why would I deny it? I may not like the woman but she was my boss, and I owed her an apology too."

"So that's all it was then? An apology for leaving?"

"Yes, Claire, that's all it was."

"No – no poems?"

I saw a flicker of something in his eyes then, and his grip on my wrist tightened, then he released me abruptly, and I fell back down into my chair.

"Me and my stupid sentimental streak. I'm not cut out for this." He seemed to be talking to himself now, rather than addressing me. "Listen, would you just do me a favour and do as you're told, for once. Finish the film. Leave Kylecraig. Get on with your life."

He headed towards the window, lifted a corner of the blind and looked out. Then, before I'd realised what was happening, he'd pulled up the sash window, and jumped through it. As I reached it, I could see him running across the garden towards the sea, and as I tried to clamber out through the open window, I heard a motorbike engine starting, and then receding at speed.

By the time I reached the road, the bike – and Jackson – were already nothing but a dark blur.

As I turned to go back to the house, I thought I caught a sight of movement in the dunes, and my stomach heaved. Then a ewe and her lamb came trotting out from behind the marram grass, and I tipped forward, put my palms on my knees and tried to breathe slowly, to calm the hammering inside my ribcage.

*

The weather for the school's sports day was dry, fine and sunny – in direct contrast to my mind, which was definitely cloudy and overcast. I'd spent the evening re-running Jackson's words inside my head and puzzling over what he'd told me, drinking the dregs of a bottle of whisky in the process.

I'd dressed as though sleep-walking and was barely aware of leaving the house, walking along the beach and arriving at the

193

school. Somehow it appeared I'd made these things happen since, by 8am, I was sitting on the grass outside the main doors setting up my camera as though on auto-pilot. Jackson's words flooded my mind as I tried to focus, both literally and metaphorically, on the job in hand.

I dutifully filmed the events of the day, feeling a strange detachment as I did so. Like the events surrounding Murdo's disappearance, what was going on in front of my lens seemed to have little to do with me – I knew things were happening and I was able to frame them so that they looked good but without really seeing anything. It was like applying make-up in a vintage mirror which has lost its lustre – when you've done it so many times before that you can make a good stab at it, even though it's all a bit hazy.

It was good to just keep moving about and thinking in terms of filming sequences. Close-up, wide, cutaway. Close-up, wide, cutaway. Such was my mantra, and it got me through the day. I even had a few conversations with people although what they were about I had no idea afterwards.

And then it was over. The last race had been run, the final medal awarded, and nothing remained on the trestle tables but crumbs and piles of dirty mugs. My encounter with Janey Macleod could be put off no longer.

As though our minds were in sync she appeared in front of me and spoke without smiling or any other kind of pretence that we liked one another.

"Right then. Shall we get this over with? In my office, yes?"

"I was hoping we could do it in the garden, overlooking the beach."

"No. I want to be sitting down, indoors. I suggest you follow me."

My anger rose as bile inside me. This was my film, not hers. On the other hand, I would have no film, if I didn't get this interview. Squashing my feelings down, I smiled as convincingly as I could, and followed her down the corridor and into her space. I began setting up, and was about to take audio levels, when the old-fashioned phone on her desk rang.

"I'd better take this. Excuse me."

I half-suspected her of arranging the call, but as I watched her face, every feature seemed to tighten, and it was clear that she had not.

"What? That's – that's not possible. Are you sure? No, of course. Yes, right away."

She replaced the receiver as though it was made of fine bone china. I noticed that her hand was shaking.

"Bad news?"

She looked at me and seemed to be on the verge of saying something, before changing her mind and nodding. I watched, intrigued and fearful, as a single tear fell from the tip of her nose onto the wooden desktop.

"Can I – do anything?"

Still she didn't speak, just shook her head. Her knuckles, gripping the arms of her chair, had drained of colour. We stayed like this for a minute or two, hunter and prey. Finally, she took a deep breath and spoke.

"If that camera is rolling, I want the footage erased."

I looked at the camera in my hands. It was so much a part of me that I wasn't even aware I'd been holding it.

"We hadn't started. I was just about to turn it on when the phone rang."

"You'd better be telling me the truth. Right now, I have enough to deal with."

She pushed herself away from the desk, rose up out of her chair, and was out of the door before I could speak again. I watched it swing shut behind her, and looked down at my camera, where a little red light was glowing at the back. I thought I'd spoken honestly to her; but it turned out I'd been filming the whole time.

*

By the time I'd packed my kit away and followed Janey outside, the school was deserted. But as I walked out through the gates, I became aware of a cluster of people standing outside the village hall. As I got closer, I saw that many of them were parents who had refused to talk to me for my film, so I was glad to see Eilidh Ross in amongst the crowd. When she looked up and saw me, she made a motion with her hand for me to stay back. I hovered, uncertainly, at the bottom of the path, until I saw her break away.

"Come on, get yourself away from here with that camera, or there'll be trouble," she muttered, drawing close to me.

We walked, briskly, until we were out of sight of the others, at the back of the beach.

"What is it Eilidh? What's happened?"

"The worst thing possible. The rumours I'd heard – it seems they were true. I still can't believe it."

I thought back to the conversation we'd had the day before.

"I thought everybody knew already, about Catriona and Donnie."

"What? God no, that's not what I'm talking about. That doesn't even seem to matter now."

"So what is it?"

"We've just heard from Iain Cameron that Catriona Mackay's been accused of murder. Of killing her own wee boy."

CHAPTER TWENTY EIGHT

C onsidering all the scenarios that my brain had scanned since reading Jackson's letter, this one came at me like a fast car in my blind spot. I couldn't think of anything to say and stood staring, stupidly, at Eilidh until she spoke again.

"There was no way I could tell you, you do understand? That's why I just gave you the old news, about the affair. I mean, everybody else knew that already, so I thought it wouldn't matter if you didn't keep your word."

I nodded, still trying to let the facts sink in. Finally, I managed to formulate half a sentence.

"Are they sure?"

"I hardly think they'd say anything unless they were. Iain said it's taken so long because of the state of the evidence, but there were a couple of other factors, which he couldn't go into with us."

"As you know, I'm not a mother" I began cautiously. Eilidh took over.

"But even so, you can't imagine how any woman could kill her own child? Me neither. Strictly between you and me, Catriona has had – issues in the past, a few problems with her mental health. But hey – who hasn't, right? And I thought she'd put all that behind her years ago."

I was about to question her further, but a sudden loud shout made us both start, and we stared back up the path towards the hall where an argument had ignited.

"I'd best go – take care, Claire."

Eilidh left me standing at the bottom of the path, where I hovered, for a while, until one of the other women saw me. I realised, with a start, that it was Kelly MacIver.

"What the hell are you looking at?" she shouted. "Go on; piss off, you and your bloody camera. Get out of here."

I took her advice and headed on shaky legs for the cottage.

As I got near, I heard footsteps, running, coming closer. I whipped round, prepared to defend myself, but relaxed when I saw Iain Cameron.

"Claire. Glad I caught you. I've got something for you."

I saw that he had a large brown envelope in his hand.

"What is it?"

"It's your material. We've made copies of what we needed, but the originals are all in here."

He handed it to me and as I took it, I peered inside, as though any clues or answers to such a tragedy could possibly be contained within two thin sheets of paper.

"Thank you for your co-operation, Claire. I'm only sorry that your programme will be affected by this."

"What do you mean?"

"Well – whilst there is an ongoing court case, it can't possibly go on air."

How monumentally stupid of me. I hadn't even considered this.

"But my programme isn't about Murdo."

Even as I said it, I knew that it would make no difference. Iain's face told me that.

"How long?" I asked.

"Difficult to say, a few months probably. I really am sorry Claire; I know how much you've invested in this project. Now I must go, I've got a pile of work to get on with."

By now, I just wanted to get back to the house, pour myself a large glass of wine and collapse onto the sofa. But as I approached, I lost any thoughts I might have entertained about a peaceful evening.

The glossy white stonework on the front aspect of the building had been defaced, a stark message scrawled in ugly black spray paint. I drew level with the porch, and read:

"WE WILL GET YOU FOR THIS."

I looked around, quickly, as though who ever had perpetrated the vandalism might have hung around to witness my reaction, but there was nobody in sight. I dropped the key three times before I finally managed to make it connect with the lock, and I went straight to the phone, where I made my trembling fingers hit 999.

After hanging up, the house felt ominously quiet. Glancing outside, I saw that a soft rain was falling, fat droplets of water sliding down the windows guiltily, like shamed outsiders who know just how unwelcome they are.

CHAPTER TWENTY NINE

For the second time in less than an hour, I found myself alongside Iain Cameron, only this time we were standing outside my cottage. After studying the graffiti for a while, Iain took a phone from his pocket and took some photos.

"I'm afraid Billy's on his way down" he said. "And he's pretty unhappy, to put it mildly."

I stared at him.

"Is that all you can say? I've had my home violated – yes, I know it's Billy's house, but I'm living here – and a threat made against me. Does that not mean anything to you?"

"I don't think that threat is really aimed at you, Claire."

"Who then? Nobody else is here?" I hadn't mentioned Jackson's visit, wanting to hear it from Iain's mouth instead, but he was looking beyond me, seemingly in relief. Turning, I saw the fast approaching figure of Billy Mackenzie. When he reached us, he didn't even look at me, but spoke directly to Iain.

"What the devil is all this about? As if I didn't know."

"Well, I'm not sure we do know, Billy. And it's nothing that a bit of fresh white paint won't sort out."

Billy snorted.

"Offering to get up there on a step-ladder and do it yourself Iain? No, I thought not. And as for you…."

He turned to face me, and I shrunk back behind Iain.

"I want you out. Tonight. I should have had nothing to do with either of you."

He seemed to be waiting for a reply, but when I stayed silent, unable to think of anything to say to him, he simply turned around and headed back up the lane towards his croft house.

"Right" said Iain, with a sigh. "Let's go inside. I could do with a cup of tea."

*

"Do you think that message is aimed at Jackson?"

We were sitting at the kitchen table with mugs of tea, and I'd even managed to find some biscuits, which neither of us had touched.

"Without wishing to go into specifics, Claire, all I can say is that I'm certain that it is not aimed at you."

"But he's not here". I was determined to continue with my pretence. "Everybody knows that he left weeks ago."

"Hmmm." His face was impassive.

"So you DO think this has something to do with him then?"

For somebody who'd always played things straight with me, Iain's manner had altered, and he was no longer looking me in the eye.

"Iain, I really don't need any more mystery in my life right now. Do you know who did this?"

He put his mug down on the table, heavily, and let out a deep breath.

"I'm not certain. But I do have a hunch. And it has nothing to do with you."

"You're talking in riddles now."

"I'm aware of that, Claire, and I do apologise. But I'm unable to say any more."

We sat in silence then, sipping our tea, looking out of the window at the encroaching darkness. Finally, Iain drained his mug, and stood up.

"It's been a hell of a day, so if you'll excuse me, I need to get back home. I've still got a whole pile of paperwork to do, and now I've got a whole load more. Not that it's your fault."

"But what am I supposed to do? Billy said he wanted me out of here."

"He's just all fired up. Don't worry about that, I'll call in on him on my way home and tell him to let you be. You just try and get a decent night's sleep."

I laughed.

"Really? With a threat to my life on the wall outside my bedroom window?"

Iain looked at me properly now, for the first time since we'd come inside.

"Your life is not in danger, Claire. On that, you have my word."

How does he know? I wondered. How can he know?

But before I could ask him, he was already out of the door, and I was left alone once more with Radio 4 and an increasing sense of dread.

*

Iain had obviously managed to talk Billy round, since nobody arrived to evict me, and I finally fell into my bed sometime after midnight. I lay there, eyes screwed shut, watching dark green shapes slide and meld across the insides of my eyelids, willing myself to lose consciousness, wanting more than anything for this night to be over.

I must have dozed for a while, until strange slap-slap noises outside my window had me almost falling out of bed in panic, unsure whether to hide or flee.

Gradually, I worked out that it was morning; 7am, according to my watch, and that daylight was working its way in through a loose flap in the curtains. Gathering my courage, I stepped up to the window, and pulled them back, only to come face to face with Billy Mackenzie. I stifled a scream, and then a giggle, as his ladder wobbled. When we'd both regained our composure, I opened the window a crack.

"Cup of tea, Billy?"

"That's the least you can do," he replied, gruffly, which I took as an apology.

When I took it outside to him, I saw that he'd already managed to obliterate most of the black paint.

"Needed a fresh coat anyway," he told me, climbing down the ladder to accept tea and biscuits.

"It does look better," I said. "And I'm sorry you had to do this Billy, but I've no idea why it happened. I promise you, it has nothing to do with me, I've only ever wanted to come here, do my job, and then leave."

"Aye well. Things around here have changed, forever. Best you finish up what you need to do, and then get out, if you ask me. Leave folks to heal their wounds without that blasted camera of yours getting in the way."

"Believe me Billy, as soon as I've got my interview with Janey Macleod, I'll have everything I need."

He nodded, passed me back the mug, and made as though he was about to climb back up his ladder, but then he stopped.

"Did you not say you had family coming up for a holiday?"

"I can cancel them. It doesn't feel right, having a holiday here, not now."

"Shame for them to miss out though. I know a lady with a new place, just done up like, down in Ullapool. Want me to ask her if it's available from tomorrow? I'm pretty sure it will be."

As evictions go, it was subtle; I had to give him that.

*

By 8am, I was in school. Although term had now finished, I was hoping to find Janey in her office, so that we could get the interview done, once and for all. Sure enough, the main door was open, and so was her office door, and although there was nobody in sight, a waft of Chanel No 5 told me that she wasn't far away.

Loitering in the doorway, uncertain whether to wait or to go and search the school for her, I caught sight of a local newspaper on her desk. The main headline was about Murdo and accompanied by THAT school photo. I glanced along the corridor, but there was no sign of Janey, so I edged around to the back of the desk and looked more closely.

DID MOTHER KILL HER SON?

I scanned the story, but it said no more than what Eilidh Ross had already told me the previous night. I was about to put the paper back, when a second front page headline caught my eye.

DRUGS GANG TRACED TO HIGHLAND HIDEOUT
Craggan Inn revealed as den for illicit activity

"Are you looking for me?"

I dropped the newspaper, as Janey materialised in the doorway, like a vengeful spirit.

"Yes. I was. I was hoping we could do the interview now."

"Do we have to? Iain Cameron tells me there's no chance of this programme airing now."

I bristled.

"It will be airing. I haven't just spent a year of my life here for nothing. It might just have to wait until after the court case is over."

"Can't you come back and do the interview then? Surely that would make more sense?"

Annoyingly, she had a point. Still, I was reluctant to concede, worried that if I didn't get something down, she would somehow evade me. So, I stood my ground.

"I'd like to do one now, just about the school. No mention of Murdo. I'll need you talking about life here as the head, which means I can at least crack on with my edit. Maybe after the court case, I'll come back and we can tie up the loose ends."

To my surprise, Janey put up no further argument, and I wondered if she'd just been testing me. At least I'd proved that I wasn't going to let her trample all over me any more. I took out my camera, wired her up with a microphone, and conducted possibly the blandest, most tippy-toed interview of my life.

*

As soon as I got back to the cottage, I opened my laptop, and did a search for the Craggan Inn story. It flashed up as headline news on the local BBC website, knocking even poor Murdo into second spot.

"Police discovered more than six kilos of cocaine at the Craggan Inn, after spending more than 24 hours searching the property," I read. "Two drug dealers are now awaiting their fate, after the remote Highland pub was revealed as a distribution den. The cocaine onsite was worth over £390,000, and was found by Highland Police officers acting on intelligence. It's the biggest ever haul of drugs seen in this region of Scotland, and it's thought that the Inn could have been used for several months, after being rented out from a landlord based near Inverness."

I stopped reading, thinking back to my first visit to the pub – with Jackson. What was it he'd said about the place?

"I doubt it will be open for much longer."

He'd been right about that.

For a man who openly called himself an outsider, Jackson had garnered an impressive amount of local knowledge during the few months he'd spent in Kylecraig.

And he seemed to have made an impressive number of enemies as well.

CHAPTER THIRTY

After another fitful night, filled with nightmares of drowned bodies and sinister shadows at cloudy windows, I gave up on sleep at 5am.

Billy had popped a note through the door the previous night, with the address of a holiday cottage in Ullapool. "Free of charge to you and your Mum."

Money was hardly the issue here, I thought, still sulking at my unjust and untimely removal; but as I started packing, I felt nothing but relief at the thought of getting out of Kylecraig.

I'd arrived in the village with just a couple of suitcases, but seemed to be leaving with a whole lot more. Apart from my camera kit and laptop, I had my precious box of labelled SD cards and the back-ups, on an additional hard-drive, not to mention another box full of letters and postcards from Jackson. Then there were the vast number of books and DVDs I'd bought to keep me going through the winter, as well as all the extra emergency warm clothing I'd purchased online.

My instructions from Billy were to leave the cottage unlocked and the keys on the kitchen table so, having filled every crevice in the car with stuff and done a final sweep of the house, I simply walked out and pulled the door to behind me.

A year ago, I'd have been uncomfortable about this arrangement but now it seemed normal. God knows how I was going to adapt to life back in the real world.

Driving away felt surreal – there really should have been a soundtrack, like the glorious welling of Mark Knopfler's *Local*

Hero score. Instead, I wound down the window and tried to catch the sound of the waves; but all I could hear was the noise of the engine, as the car struggled up the hill to the main road. My last glance of the village was a brief glint of silvery sea in the wing mirror. Then I rounded a corner, and Kylecraig disappeared.

*

I'd been hoping for some time to myself in the holiday cottage but as I drew up outside the little house on the seafront, I saw my brother's shiny black Range Rover cruising along the road towards me. Pulling alongside, he wound his window down, and I caught a blast of the Frozen soundtrack (the twins' favourite film) before he muted it.

"Good morning, sis. Is this it? Looks great. I'll just let this lot out, and then I'll park up."

The girls were already halfway out of the back door, and came barrelling up to me, almost sending me flying. My mother seemed to be having a bit more difficulty extricating herself from the lofty heights of the passenger seat, but finally managed it.

"You're here early," I said, rummaging underneath the doormat for the key.

"We stayed in Inverness last night. And the twins have been awake for hours."

"Me too."

I found the key, slotted it in, and stood back as the girls ran past me into the house, screaming the over-excited screams of children on the first day of their summer holidays. My heart flooded with a sudden sharp pain for Murdo, who should have been enjoying the same feeling, and I watched the twins opening doors with a new appreciation of the preciousness of childhood.

"They've been so excited about coming up here," Mum said, her voice filled with warmth that caught me in the back of the throat all over again. "It's so lovely that we can all be together like this."

As Alex came through the front door, whistling and jangling his car keys, I vowed to try and make myself relax, and enjoy a week of normality. A week not dominated by thoughts of dead children, mysterious strangers and drug dens.

*

But pretending to be happy and relaxed, whilst constantly worrying about where my life was heading, meant that I was on edge and slightly nauseous the whole time, even when we were on boat trips to see the seals, or eating fish and chips sitting by the harbour in the sunshine.

Then, on the last night of our family holiday, I got an email, from an anonymous looking Gmail account:

"Claire it's me, Jackson. Fancy meeting up for a walk tomorrow, on your way to Southport? I thought it might break up your journey. I'll be waiting here at midday."

There followed a grid reference, somewhere in the northern Lake District.

When I tried to reply to the email, my message bounced back.

Typical bloody Jackson, I thought. But before I closed my lap-top I wrote down the grid reference and worked out how long the journey would take me.

Just in case I decided to go.

After the twins had gone to bed, the rest of us stayed up and laid waste to a bottle of wine with indecent haste, and then opened a second. I'd intended to keep my problems to myself but it's amazing how too much wine can make a dent in even the most steadfast resolution and it all came pouring out almost as quickly as that first bottle of red had done.

Mum and Alex listened in silence, as I spoke. They'd been following the news about Murdo of course, but it seemed that the "Craggan Inn Drugs Raid" story had failed to make much of a dent in the nation's consciousness outside the Highlands. I left out the bit about graffiti on the wall of the cottage, figuring that it would only alarm my mother, who looked quite shocked enough at the thought that Jackson had taken me for a drink in a notorious drugs den.

"I do hope you're not going to contact him again. It will only end in tears. And before you say anything, I know you don't agree with me, but I am your mother and I want what's best for you."

I looked helplessly at Alex, who shrugged.

"I'm sure he didn't know it was a drugs den, that's hardly where you'd take someone to impress them. For what it's worth, I think he at least deserves a chance to explain himself. Who are we to judge, when we've never even met the man? If Claire thinks this bloke's genuine well, maybe he is."

"That's hardly the issue here. You have a stressful few months ahead of you – not just making your film, and trying to get it on air, but moving back home as well, at your age – not that you're not very welcome of course, you know you are, but surely you should be thinking about buying a home of your own, and what's going to happen to your career? And what about your relationships, and starting a family? Those are the things a thirty-five-year-old woman should be worrying about, not agonising over a man who seems to waft about like some kind of – gypsy or something."

There was silence. Finally, Alex spoke.

"Blimey Mum. Say how you feel, why don't you?"

"Well I'm sorry, Alex, and I'm sure I don't need to point this out, but Claire is my only daughter. And I'd quite like some more grandchildren, preferably before I'm too old to pick them up."

Out of the corner of my eye, I could see Alex shaking his head. I toyed with the idea of getting angry, but the thought was way too exhausting. Anyway, I'd already decided on a plan of action.

"Here's how it's going to be. I'm not due in the office until Monday. So tomorrow, when we all leave here, I'm going to head for the Lakes and talk to Jackson. And until I've done that, the subject will be closed. I wish I hadn't brought it up at all, but at least you're both fully aware of how things are now. Okay?"

Alex grinned, and topped up my wine glass.

"Go for it, sis."

"Mum?"

"If that's what you feel you need to do then I'm not going to stop you. I just worry that I'm going to be the one mopping up the pieces. Again."

"Ouch. You won't Mum, I promise. I'm feeling strong about all of this. And anyway - that's Leonie's job."

*

The confidence in my voice belied how I was really feeling. Lying in bed that night, unable to sleep, I wondered if I had a migraine coming on. My head was fuzzy with wine and my insides were churning, a jumbled-up mess of fear, excitement and a kind of nervous anticipation more akin to nausea.

At least I had a plan. As a compulsive organiser who'd had her life turned upside down over the past twelve months, it felt good to be back in control of making some decisions again. Even if they were the wrong ones, at least I could say they were my own.

I realised that it was only the thought of seeing Jackson again that was making me feel this way. Like a migraine, that man had a nasty habit of twisting and skewing my vision, so that I couldn't see things clearly any more.

CHAPTER THIRTY ONE

The journey to Swindale felt like the longest drive of my life. After leaving Ullapool at 6am, stopping only to pee and fill the car up with fuel, I finally crawled along a single track road to a sign that read "No Parking beyond this Point."

There was one other vehicle in the small lay-by at the foot of the hill – a motorbike – but no sign of anybody. But, as I turned the car to reverse in beside it, I caught a glimpse in my wing mirror of a figure descending the hill.

Jackson raised his hand, then carried on coming towards me, and I was able to watch him as he approached in a way that I'd been unable to during that short visit to Kylecraig. He'd lost weight, but he looked well. The beard was back, but neatly clipped, as were the sometimes unruly curls of hair. There was a glow of health to his skin that I hadn't seen before – it was clear that he'd been out in the sun. He was wearing clothes I'd not seen before – a blue shirt, grey shorts and trekking sandals. He looked like a holidaymaker, a hillwalker without a care in the world.

I applied some lip gloss and pushed my shades onto my head just as he reached the car door and opened it.

"Well – here I am," I said hurriedly, my cheeks warming in a way that had nothing to do with the July sunshine. His hand reached for mine and then he was half-helping, half-pulling me out of the car.

Barely was I on both feet before I was smothered in a hug which smelt of wood smoke and soap and cut grass. I gulped back tears and pushed Jackson away.

"Hey. What makes you think I came here to be molested?"

"Thank god you got away from there. And thank you for coming here."

"It's on my way. Pretty much"

"I know, that's why I suggested it."

"Do I get an explanation now? Or are you just going to carry on messing with my head? Running away from Kylecraig with no explanation – not once, but twice – not to mention all that flirting with Janey…."

"Claire, you can accuse me of anything but that. The relationship with Janey was entirely in your own head."

"I don't think so. She was certainly flirting with you, even if you didn't notice."

"There was nothing going on between us, unless it was in *her* head."

"Let's not start off with an argument. We've plenty of time for those later on."

"A walk, then? I'd imagine you'll be needing to stretch your legs."

"Good idea. I'll put my boots on," I said. "And then you can tell me what the hell's been going on."

Just for a second, his eyes slid away from mine. Oh god, I thought. He's not going to tell me anything. I'm going to be given the run-around, again.

We were both silent as I laced up my boots, and set off along the lane. It was such a beautiful afternoon, that it seemed a shame to disrupt the birdsong and the bleating of sheep.

And yet….

I took a deep breath, trying to ignore the pounding inside my ribcage, and asked;

"So what did you think when you heard the news about Catriona Mackay?"

"Honestly? Very sad, but not altogether surprised. Murdo always had the air of a boy who had a desperate need to be loved, and no good mother would ever allow their child to feel that way. How about you, what did you think?"

I'd forgotten Jackson's habit of turning things around.

"Me? I was shocked, to be honest. I was hoping it was just an accident. I may not be maternal, but I can't imagine what would make any mother kill her child."

I waited for a response, but there was none, so I carried on.

"Eilidh Ross mentioned something to me though, something I wasn't aware of."

"Oh yes?"

His voice was polite, rather than inquisitive. He could have been enquiring as to the next day's weather forecast. I'd been going to mention the affair with Donnie MacIver, but I changed my mind. Instead, I carried on.

"She said that there was some kind of history of mental health problems. That Catriona was known to be a bit unstable."

"There you are then. It doesn't surprise me."

"Doesn't it?"

"Not really, no. I just wish I'd done something."

For the first time in the conversation, some emotion crept into Jackson's voice, and I stayed silent.

"If only I'd followed up on my hunch that there were....issues at home, then I could have saved him. I failed Murdo there. I was his teacher; I should have questioned him more closely."

"If the people who were close to her didn't suspect anything, then why would you, a total stranger?"

Silence, again. By now, we were heading steeply uphill, on a path ominously signposted as "The Coffin Road." I resolved to save the rest of my questions until the ground had levelled off a bit. Half an hour later, sitting by the cairn at the top of the hill, I took my chance.

"That whisky bar in the cliffs that you took me to one time, the Craggan Inn – why did we go there?"

Jackson was so close that I could hear his heartbeat, and I could swear I felt it speed up, ever so slightly. But his voice, when he spoke, was perfectly calm and measured.

"I'd been told that it was a unique place to take a dram. And I was right, wasn't I?"

I laughed.

"Unique certainly sums it up. You do know it was the centre of a huge drugs heist?"

"I did hear as much, yes."

Talking to Jackson made obtaining blood from stones seem like a viable prospect. I tried again.

"When we were there, you said you didn't think it would be open much longer. Pretty uncanny observation, don't you think?"

"Not really. You saw how old the woman running the place was."

"So you knew nothing about the place, before we went?"

"Only what I'd been told. But you're right; it was probably an inappropriate venue for a date."

That was putting it mildly, I thought. Aloud, I said;

"When did you hear that it had closed down?"

"I really can't remember. Have your illusions about the Highlands been well and truly shattered, Claire?"

"What do you mean?"

"Well, you went up there to make a charming, whimsical film, and you've ended up with sex, drugs and murder."

I sat up and stared at him, trying to work out whether he was teasing me, but the expression on his supine face was deadly serious.

"I object to your use of the word whimsical. But you're right; it's not quite what I was expecting."

"Which part. The sex?"

Now his mouth was twitching, and before long we were both straddling a line somewhere between laughter and tears, as the tension of the past few days, weeks and months fizzled away like cuckoo spit into the heather.

It was a while before I could get myself in check, but the hysteria had definitely loosened the atmosphere, and I felt brave enough to try and talk about the future.

"What happens next Jackson? I mean, I've got to go to work in Manchester and make some kind of sense out of this film, but what are you going to do?"

"I know what I want to do. Not necessarily the same thing, I know, but what I really want is to get back to being a teacher again. I want to work in a school and teach children about the important things in life – art, poetry, music, nature. That's all I want, Claire."

"Sounds nice, but is it likely?"

"I've seen a job advertised that would be perfect." The grass beside me rustled, and a shadow fell across my face as Jackson sat upright and looked at me.

"It's in the primary school in Kelso, a small town in the Scottish Borders. They want somebody to start at the beginning of the autumn term, which is perfect."

"Well, yes, I suppose so."

"It's as though it's all just meant to be, don't you see?"

"But surely you'll need good references, and that's not going to be easy, after the way things ended...last time."

"Oh, I see how it is. You don't think I'd even get an interview?"

I laid my hand gently on his arm, trying to ignore the pinpricks of desire that even this slight contact sent through my body.

"I believe in you Jackson, that's not what I meant. There has to be a way."

"I admire your conviction Claire. You're not as old and cynical as I am. It's one of the things I like about you. And I have a good feeling about this job." He smiled at me, and I heard myself promising;

"We will find a way to make this happen. You were born to teach, any idiot can see that."

I was about to remove my hand from his arm, but before I could move he placed his other hand on top of mine and held it there, gazing at me until I could feel the colour flooding into my face. He lifted his hand to my face then, pushing a loose strand of hair back behind my ear before tracing the line of my jaw and then my lips oh so gently. Our faces moved closer and closer,

219

until our noses touched. I closed my eyes, breathed in deep – trying to memorise the very scent of him - and then I gently withdrew.

"First things first, Jackson. Let's make sure you at least get an interview for this job. Then we can start to think about what happens next."

*

The rest of the drive to Merseyside gave me ample thinking time. Once I'd set my mind to it, I'd decided, anything was possible – even securing references for Jackson – and it wasn't long before a solution presented itself.

CHAPTER THIRTY TWO

A week later, I was eating a late supper with Mum when the phone rang. As usual, I leapt up to answer it and, this time, was rewarded by Jackson's voice at the other end of the line.

"Well – looks like you did it. But I'd like to know how."

"Who is it?" hissed Mum suspiciously.

I took the phone out of the room to avoid her searching looks.

"I'll ask you again, how did you persuade Janey Macleod to write me a glowing reference?"

I recalled my conversation of six days ago.

"It was a bit awkward really. I called Janey Macleod and I threatened her."

"Threatened her? With what?"

I took a deep breath.

"With a stitch-up job."

"I'm sorry, I'm not following you."

"I told her if she didn't write you a great reference, that I would edit the programme about the school in a certain way. In fact, I may have given the impression that if I didn't get what I wanted from her, then the school would look very bad indeed."

I heard Jackson's intake of breath quite clearly over the muted birdsong and wind noise on the line.

"Claire, that is – extremely unethical."

"Yes, it is rather."

"I know you and she didn't see eye to eye but to threaten her, to jeopardise your own career….."

At this stage, I decided to interrupt.

"Jackson, you surely don't think I would do such a thing?"

"Well – I would certainly hope not…."

"Of course I wouldn't! Good grief, what do you take me for? I would never stitch anybody up in a documentary. Not even her. And the BBC has very high standards, as I'm sure you are aware."

"Of course it does. And quite right too."

"But Janey doesn't know that, does she? She didn't seem outraged, in fact she just agreed, as though she's used to playing games."

"Well, she certainly played around with the two of us."

"Think of this as payback then."

*

After that conversation, things went all quiet on the Jackson front but I tried not to worry about him since, as my mum was fond of pointing out, he was a grown man.

Besides, I had quite enough to occupy my time and my mind.

The commute from Mum's house to Salford took up several hours of each day – I'd forgotten how slow those little Northern Line trains were - which meant that I was permanently exhausted. And then, of course, there was the film itself.

My programme – in its intended form - had originally been given a prime time slot in the week leading up to Christmas. But, even though Murdo would not be the focus of the film, we were now barred from screening anything until after Catriona Mackay's trial. This was due to begin in early December, meaning that it was touch and go whether there would be a verdict in time. Without one, the programme would be shelved until the following year.

I'd intended to crack on anyway, and get the film made. My boss had reluctantly agreed to my request that the essence of the programme should be as I'd originally pitched it to him, with mention of Murdo's disappearance confined to a voiceover at the beginning, and an update at the end.

I'd been happy with this decision, confident that I had the footage to make a powerful and poignant documentary.

But sitting in an edit suite for several hours a day and looking through my footage with a high-end film editor had made me doubt myself.

If I thought the pacing of a particular scene was too fast, the editor disagreed. If I had chosen specific music then the editor didn't like my choice and would suggest an alternative - which I would invariably hate.

Worst of all, when we came to look at the interview with Janey Macleod – the one bit of footage I hadn't been able to bring myself to view – it turned out that there was a fault with the SD card which had corrupted my material. All I had was my earlier close-up shot of her shocked and then angry face, as she took the phone call about Catriona Mackay.

"Looks like you'll have to do that interview again" said the editor, unnecessarily.

"Are you sure there's nothing you can do?" I gazed helplessly at the fuzzed lines and boxes on the screen.

"Not with that, no way. You should have checked it before you left."

I bit my lip, to stop myself from crying. I was beginning to feel as though I had wasted a year of my time and the department's money, and that I'd be lucky to keep my job at the end of it.

I had to email Janey and explain what had happened and fully expected her to refuse to do the interview again. But her terse reply was in the affirmative, which, whilst I was grateful, made me feel even smaller.

All in all, Jackson's career, or lack of it, seemed rather less important than my own.

CHAPTER THIRTY THREE

L uckily, salvation arrived in early August.

Two weeks into the edit, my high-end editor was poached by another department (I suspected he'd begged for release) and I was assigned a new one – a young woman called Mandy, with whom I clicked straight away.

Watching the rushes together, along with the rough edits I'd already done on my laptop, became an enjoyable process rather than a form of purgatory.

"Oh, this is lovely" she sighed at the end of our first day together, as we watched a long, slow sequence of the sun sinking below the horizon. "We can't rush this through, Claire. Go back to your producer and tell him it's a two-parter."

"Two hours? No way. They won't buy it."

"Tell them it's about value for money, since they've got to pay for you to go back up there to interview Janey. You're giving them more than they asked for; I bet they go for it."

Inspired by her positivity, I had another meeting with my boss who, to my delighted horror, took it to the programmers – and they gave the idea the thumbs up.

I suspected this had more to do with the notoriety of Kylecraig rather than a belief in the authenticity of my documentary, but whatever their reasons were, I suddenly found myself trusted with not one, but two hours of prime-time television.

My stress levels went through the roof.

*

A week before I was due to travel back to Kylecraig, Mum and I were watching the latest procession of Hollywood celebs on Graham Norton's sofa. I say we were watching but really, the images were just passing before my eyes, and I was about to call it a night.

Then the phone rang, with the urgent tone that somehow indicated that Jackson was on the other end of the line. I had no idea how he did it, but the sound jolted me out of my stupor, and I was lifting the receiver before Mum even had a chance to say "who on earth could that be at this time of night?"

"Hello?"

I knew straight away that my hunch had been correct.

"Claire?"

It was possible to tell from that one word that Jackson had momentous news.

"I'm sorry to call so late but I've just found out about the job and you had to be the first to know."

"Come off it, Jackson, who finds out about a job at eleven o' clock on a Friday night?"

"I know it's late, I'm sorry. But the head and the deputy both went away on holiday straight after the interview, so there have been conversations going on across multiple time-zones. Anyway, all you need to know is that I got the job!"

In the months that I'd known Jackson, this was the happiest I'd heard him.

"That's fantastic news. Well done."

Mum, by now, was making exaggerated gestures at me from the sofa. I responded by gesturing towards the wine bottle, and she obliged by coming over and topping up my glass.

"Jackson got the job," I hissed, covering the mouthpiece.

"Did he now? Hmmm."

She returned to the sofa and pretended to carry on watching Graham Norton.

"Are you still there?"

"Yes, Jackson, I'm still here. I really am pleased. And relieved, after what I had to do to get you that reference."

Here, Mum dropped all pretence.

"What did you do? Claire?"

"Mum, please! Hang on Jackson – I'm just going to move into the other room."

Glaring across the room, I took my wine glass and the phone and went into the kitchen. Jackson was still talking.

"My main task between now and then is to find a house."

Really, the surprises were coming in thick and fast.

"A house? Jackson, don't tell me you're going all conventional on me?"

"Living in that campervan over the winter nearly did me in. I'm going to have a look at a few places over the weekend. I don't suppose you'd come with me, would you?"

I was about to acquiesce, when I caught sight of my grey, tired face in the mirror, and common sense intervened.

"I can't Jackson, I'm sorry. The commute into Manchester is such a bugger; it's really taking it out of me. I'm fit for nothing else but sleeping and vegging in front of the TV."

"How does the film look?"

I flinched. I knew that we were both now thinking about Murdo, and all of the weirdness of those months in Kylecraig. I was loathe to muddy the conversational waters.

"Yes, it's looking good," I replied, breezily. "I just need to get the interview with Janey done again. Once I'm back, it'll be heads down and cancel everything else for the next couple of months until we're done."

There was silence at the other end for a while. I closed my eyes and felt the warmth of the phone against my cheek.

Eventually, Jackson spoke again.

"I'm sorry that you have to go back there, Claire. But I am so grateful for what you've done for me. If there is anything I can do……"

"You can find yourself a nice cottage; settle down into doing a job that you love and stop beating yourself up. That's what you can do for me at the moment, Jackson."

"When will I see you again?"

"I don't know. I can't think about anything but the film at the moment. I'm not sure I can see you until I've finished it. But in the meantime…."

"Yes?"

"Write to me, Jackson. Don't call me, write to me. I want to hear all about your new life. And when you've found somewhere to live let me have the address so that I can write back."

"Of course I will. I am so glad I still have you to write to."

And it was those words that I carried to bed with me after I put down the phone.

CHAPTER THIRTY FOUR

When an envelope arrived the following morning which was addressed to me, I'd already opened it before realising that it couldn't possibly be from him. A piece of white paper fluttered to the tiled floor of the porch, writing-side down. When I picked it up, cold, bare fear sucked at my insides as I read the short, typed message.

Don't think we have forgotten. We WILL get you for this. And him too.

The paper dropped to the floor once more, as I fumbled with the envelope, trying to figure out the postmark, but it was an illegible smear. My name and address had been typed out in full and I stared out of the window, as though the author of the note could be hiding in the bushes, just waiting to pounce

"Was that the postman, dear?"

Mum's voice, chirpy and efficient, shook me back into suburbia, and I scrabbled to pick up the note, desperate to clear away the evidence.

"Yes – your new Lakeland catalogue's on the side."

As diversionary tactics go, this was brilliant, and I was able to stuff my own, more disconcerting post, into the pocket of my dressing gown without Mum noticing. I had no idea what I could do about the communication, or the threat that it contained, but frightening her wasn't going to help matters; especially since whoever had written it had tracked me down to her home.

I toyed with the idea of calling the police, but what would I say? They'd send somebody round, which would freak my mother out, possibly for no reason.

For the rest of the week, I barely slept. I anaesthetised myself with gin and wine, which, with the help of Classic FM, got me off to sleep. Then I'd wake at 3am, feeling as though my heart might burst through my ribcage in its frenzy. Lying in the uncanny stillness of a suburban cul-de-sac morning, I'd be scared witless by the sudden squealing of starlings wheeling overhead, or the distant, discordant whine of the neighbourhood milk float.

Finally, I'd drop off again, only to be woken at 6am by my alarm. I'd doze on the train, and arrive at work jittery and skittery, spilling drinks and tripping over paving stones, until Mandy, my lovely editor, asked me with genuine concern whether I ought to think about seeing a doctor.

I wanted to confide in somebody, but I was so paranoid that I no longer knew who I could trust. Instead, I told her that I was stressed about my impending visit to Kylecraig.

"Poor you. The sooner that's done, the better," she said, her sympathy making me blush. "And then we just need the court case to proceed quickly and smoothly. It sounds awful, when it's such a sad case, but we need to get this programme on air."

*

I'd been expecting – dreading - more notes, but there was nothing for me at all until Friday morning. The postman arrived just as we were leaving for the airport, and handed me a card with Jackson's handwriting on the envelope. I waited until I was in the passenger seat of mum's Alfa Romeo before opening it, ignoring her irritated glances as we headed out of the driveway.

"Is that from HIM?" she asked, unable to resist.

"Yes, it's a "Change of Address" card. Jackson's moving into a rented cottage tomorrow. It's just outside Kelso. Cherry Tree Cottage – sounds lovely, doesn't it?"

"Mmmm." In profile, I could see the set of Mum's jaw even more clearly, and it said, in no uncertain terms, "We are Not Amused."

"What more does he have to do, Mum? Apart from not existing, I mean? He's got a job, he's got a house, and he's going to have a regular income. What is it, exactly, that is bugging you?"

"I just wish he'd leave you alone, Claire, if you must know, so that you can get your life back on track."

I gazed at her, wanting to say the right thing - but knowing that I wouldn't, because as well as the usual mush of guilt and lust, I was harbouring the cold fear that somebody was watching us, wanting to hurt us, just biding their time until – what? I couldn't trust myself to speak without blurting all of this out, and so I stayed silent.

As we pulled up outside Terminal 3, Mum put a warm hand on my arm, making me jump.

"I'm only concerned for your wellbeing Claire, you do know that don't you? Your taste in men leaves a lot to be desired, and I'm worried about you making decisions that you'll live to regret. But ultimately, you must make your own choices, and I will pick up the pieces. That's what mothers are for."

*

There was something wrong about flying to Inverness. The transition from the crowds, bustle and commerce of Manchester airport to the near-deserted roads of the Highlands was just too abrupt. Within an hour of landing, I was already under the imposing shadow of Ben Wyvis, the vast, flat-topped Munro to the west of the city, and less than an hour after that I was parking outside my hotel in Ullapool.

Walking round the pretty fishing village, thronged with tourists eating ice-creams and islanders waiting for the evening ferry home, I thought back to the time I'd driven here with Jackson, almost nine months ago.

I'd learned nothing about him on that first journey together. Now, it seemed, I knew precious little more - but both of us had moved out and moved on. I was back in Salford, and living with my mother, for crying out loud. Jackson was in a new job and a new home. Somebody was out to get me, or him, or possibly both of us.

And, chillingly, a young boy was dead.

"Top up, dearie?"

I looked up, squinting into the sun, to see an elderly waitress standing over me, wielding a jug of fresh coffee.

"Thanks."

I watched the liquid flow into my green pottery mug in a steady brown stream that reminded me of the peat bogs around the Black Loch, and sighed inwardly. I'd known that coming back would be difficult, had realised that every tiny little thing would remind me of Jackson.

"But you're on your own," I told myself, draining the additional coffee, even though I knew how jittery it would make me. "So best just get on with it and stop feeling sorry for yourself."

I treated myself to an excellent supper of locally landed langoustines followed by an early night. Tomorrow would be my final visit to Kylecraig.

*

The first thing that struck me when I got there was how busy it was. A new sign on the outskirts of the village at least partly explained this:

"The NC500 welcomes you to Kylecraig village" it read.

Clearly somebody had decided that the iconic North Coast 500 road trip was a more appealing reason to call in than a notorious police case, possibly involving child abuse and murder; and you could hardly blame them for that.

I followed a steady stream of campervans down the hill into the village, passing a gang of fit young hikers who looked to be heading for the campsite, and a long line of Japanese tourists wielding selfie-sticks in the layby halfway down.

But as I parked the car outside the entrance to the school, a familiar face appeared at the window.

"Claire!" mouthed Eilidh Ross.

I wound the window down, glad that the first face I recognised was a friendly one

"Eilidh hi – how are you?"

"Ach, you know – busy busy busy!"

I jumped out of the car and gave Eilidh a hug. She returned it, then stood back and appraised me.

"It's good to have you back, Claire."

"I'm not staying. I'm literally here to interview Janey, and then I'll be on my way again."

"Well, you're not leaving until we've had a cup of tea and a blether. And that's an order. Come round to ours after you're done here, and I'll make sure the scones are ready and waiting for you."

She didn't wait for an answer, but strode off in the direction of the village hall. I looked at my watch. It was only 10am. With a bit of luck, I'd still be away by lunchtime.

*

Janey Macleod was waiting for me in her office, with the door open. She didn't look up until I knocked on the door, although she must have heard me coming.

"Claire."

She stood up and came around the desk towards me, her hand out-stretched, and her expression neutral.

"Hello Janey. Thank you for agreeing to do this interview again, I know it's a pain."

She smiled, graciously.

"Well, it can't be helped." Her tone implied that it could have been helped if only I had known how to do my job properly. "It's just a nuisance for you that you had to come all this way to do it again, and on a Saturday as well."

"Yes, well, thank you for coming in."

"Oh I'd have been here anyway – there's so much to do. And I presume that you are happy, now that you've got what you wanted from me?"

I paused, looking down at my feet for a moment before I tilted my chin and met her eye.

"Oh, you mean the reference? You do realise that I would never abuse my position as a documentary maker?"

"Of course I know you wouldn't. You don't think I really believed that whole bluff, did you?"

"If you didn't believe me, why did you bother to send the reference?"

"Oh, I don't know, I think you must have caught me at a weak moment. And I guess everybody deserves a second chance, don't they? There's some small part of me that feels sorry for him. After all, he's a bit of a hopeless case."

I noticed that deliberate omission of Jackson's name and dug my fingernails into my palms.

"It certainly wasn't fair the way people leapt to the wrong conclusions when Murdo went missing," she continued.

You should know, I thought grimly. You were one of them.

"Well – thanks to that reference, he got the job. And he's thrilled about it."

Janey said nothing, but cast a glance at her watch. Her skin was tanned, I noticed, presumably the result of a holiday in the Med rather than a summer in Kylecraig.

"Will this take long? I've a mountain of paperwork to be dealing with."

"It won't take more than twenty minutes. I just need to get a radio mic on you."

I took the kit I needed out of my camera bag and clipped the mic onto the collar of her blouse, asking her to run the wire beneath it. No way was I delving around in there. I hadn't quite finished delving into other things though.

"Listen, even though it's none of my business, I really want to ask you what was in that letter you showed me, from Jackson."

"Why should I tell you that?"

I hesitated. Ever since I'd received the written warning note, I'd wanted to confide in somebody. Janey wouldn't have been my first choice, but given that I'd never see her again….

Decision made, I pulled the envelope out of my bag, and passed it over to her.

"What's this?"

"I don't know. I wondered if you might have any ideas."

She shrugged. "Nutters? There are a lot of them out there."

I finished smoothing the microphone wire and stepped away from her, wondering if it was possible that she'd never heard about the threatening graffiti that had been caused my eviction from Billy Mackenzie's cottage - and decided that it wasn't.

"It's the same message that was painted on my house."

"Is it? Seems like somebody has got it in for you. Or maybe for him."

She couldn't have sounded less interested.

"And you really can't think who that might be?"

"Oh, for god's sake. Why should I know, or care? We've more pressing concerns here at the moment."

"Fine. Let's just get on with this interview then."

"You're lucky you're still getting an interview," snapped Janey. "It's only because of the council funding that I'm talking to you. And THAT is off the record."

"Of course," I replied, smiling inwardly at having retrieved the upper hand.

"I am recording - but the interview begins, officially, now. So if you could tell me, in your own words, what you feel about having the responsibility for a school like Kylecraig."

Janey smiled, and ran a hand through her glossy auburn locks.

"Being the head teacher at Kylecraig is a privilege and an honour. We are at the heart of this community..........."

I nodded, and smiled. And so the dance goes on, I thought, and so the dance goes on.....

*

As the interview drew to a close, I felt a huge release of tension from my muscles, knowing that I would never have to see this woman again. Maybe she felt the same way, since as we wrapped things up and I unclipped the microphone, she was politeness itself. But she still had a surprise in store for me, as she reached down into the drawer of her desk and pulled something out.

"Take it," she said, handing me Jackson's letter. "There's no reason for me to keep it, and clearly it's something you want quite badly."

Before I could reply, she was off, high heels clickety-clicking towards the school hall. I glanced down at the envelope in my hand, saw her name written in Jackson's distinctive hand and let out the last bit of breath I'd been holding. Then I put the letter carefully into my handbag, and - having checked that this interview had recorded without any problems - I packed up my camera gear and walked out of Kylecraig School for the final time.

*

I was greeted at Eilidh's house by the smell of warm home baking and an even warmer hug.

"It's great to see you Claire, I've missed our chats." She paused. "It was good to have an outside perspective on things. Made a nice change, to be honest. Anyway, come on in, there's somebody here who wants to talk to you."

Following her into the immaculate living room, I was shocked to see Iain Cameron. He was standing by the window, looking out, as though unsure about making himself too much at home. But he turned as I walked into the room.

"Hello, Claire."

"Hello, Iain."

My brain was going into overdrive as I tried to work out why he might want to see me. Eilidh had disappeared, and it occurred to me that I'd been set-up.

"What's this about?"

Iain gestured to the sofa.

"Shall we sit down?"

"Okay."

Frantically I tried to remember the last conversation I'd had with Iain Cameron. It had been about the graffiti on my house. Maybe they'd caught whoever did it, or even the people who'd taken my car. I looked at him expectantly, determined not to speak until he did.

Just as he was about to open his mouth, Eilidh came in with a tray of scones and a pot of tea, and we faffed about with that for a few minutes. It was clear – at least to me, if not to her - that Iain didn't want to speak whilst she was still in the room, and finally, she got the hint and left.

"Have you had any more threats, Claire?"

Well, that was straight to the point.

"I have, as a matter of fact." I took the note from my handbag for the second time that day, and passed it over to him.

"And when did you receive this?"

"A week ago. As you can see, they know my mother's address, whoever they are."

Iain nodded, studying the note, and then the outside of the envelope.

"Can I keep this please?"

"Can you tell me what's going on?"

A pained look passed across his face, and I remembered that Iain always made me feel as though I was being unreasonable. But I wanted to hold my ground.

"I think I deserve an explanation. Somebody knows where I live, my mum could be at danger, and I have no idea why."

"I'm trying to think of how much I can tell you Claire, without jeopardising the....operation."

Wow. So I was part of an operation now. This was news to me. I'm sure my face must have conveyed my shock, as Iain hurried on.

"We are very close to identifying a suspect. It's somebody who is connected to an event that happened in this area. We don't think they are a major player, but we think they may have been hired to frighten you. Or rather, Jackson. You've just become embroiled in the whole thing, which is unfortunate."

"You can say that again. Are you saying this could be a hired hitman who's after us?"

It was Iain's turn to look shocked.

"I don't recall using the word hitman, Claire. I have no reason to believe that this will go any further than threats, but I realise how alarming those can seem. And that's why we're doing what we can to track down the perpetrator."

"We?"

"The Force. Police Scotland."

"Oh, okay. Clearly this IS quite a big deal then? Is it something to do with the Craggan Inn?"

As I spoke the last words, Iain's expression altered, very briefly. Then he composed himself.

"Claire, you have to trust me when I say that the less you know, the better. It's for your own good."

"Well, forgive me if I don't believe you."

I stood up and walked over to the window, trying to gather my thoughts.

"If these people are in Scotland, how come they've tracked me down to Southport?

"That's why I don't think you need to worry. You can post a letter anywhere, after all."

"So I can tell my mum that she doesn't need to have any more sleepless nights?"

After all, Iain didn't need to know that I hadn't shared any of this with my mother. Or that she was currently staying in London, with my aunt. I looked him directly in the eye, and he impressed me by steadily holding my gaze.

"Please tell your mother, as a personal message from me, that she has no need to worry. Within a few days, we will have sorted this out once and for all. Both of you can sleep soundly at night."

He looked as though he might be about to say something else, but just then Eilidh came back into the room, waving a sugar bowl which neither of us required, and the moment was gone.

*

Back in my B&B in Ullapool, I dumped my cases on the floor, sat on the bed, and opened Jackson's letter to Janey.

Dear Janey,

I've thought for a long time about whether I should write this letter, but I wanted to apologise to you personally for leaving so abruptly. This was never my intention when I took the job, and I feel terribly guilty for abandoning the children in the middle of the school year. I am well aware that this will have caused you a major headache in the teaching department.

I can tell you no more than this; but I hate to think that you would think badly of me, when I genuinely care so much about the pupils of Kylecraig School.

Yours sincerely,

Jackson

P.S; I apologise for keeping the truth from you, but I have no choice.

I read the letter over a few times. This was clearly a business-like communication, and I felt a smug satisfaction in knowing that Janey was just as in the dark as I was.

Then my mobile rang, and I picked it up without looking to see who it was.

"Hello?"

Silence. All I could hear was static, and my own voice echoing back at me.

"Hello? Is there anybody there?"

The line went dead, and when I tried to redial, an automated message mocked me;

"The caller withheld their number."

Probably somebody trying to sell me PPI, I thought, that's the most likely explanation.

But remembering my earlier meeting with Iain, and his promise to "have things sorted out within a few days," I wondered whether that would be soon enough.

CHAPTER THIRTY FIVE

T he phone call un-nerved me so much so that I was too scared to return to the bungalow on Sunday night, since Mum was still away in London. I didn't want to be alone. So after I'd checked in for my return flight, I called Leonie from Inverness airport, citing an early start as the reason why I wanted to stay with her.

"Of course, come and stay. You know there's always a bed for you here. We can watch crappy reality TV and eat pizza."

Ensconced in her comfortable red-brick terrace in Didsbury, my fears seemed ludicrous – more like one of the alarmist TV dramas she loved so much than anything from our real lives. I said nothing to her about the threats, real or imaginary, and too much red wine with the promised pizza was just what I needed.

But back in the cool, dark sanctuary of the edit suite on Monday morning, Mandy asked me straight away what was wrong. I told her everything, or at least as much as I knew, and she convinced me to talk to Paul, my boss. He was furious.

"Why didn't you say anything before? As soon as that warning appeared on your cottage, you should have told us. There are procedures we have to put in place to protect our staff, Claire."

"I didn't think the message was for me," I explained. "I thought it was a mistake."

"Even so, you should have said something. I need to speak to this police officer chappy, do you have his number?"

"I really don't think it's necessary" I muttered, loath to be giving Iain Cameron any more to deal with.

"You are a member of my department, and I consider it to be essential."

I gave him Iain's number.

Within an hour, I'd received an email from one of the Logistics and Procurement Team, informing me that an apartment had been booked, for myself and Mum, in a block in Salford.

"No arguments, Claire" said Paul, when I called him to protest. "Until I have an official assurance from Police Scotland that you and your mother are safe, I am not taking any risks."

Miserably, I put the phone down. My incompetence had already cost the department the price of an extra trip to the north of Scotland, and now there were more bills to pay. Let alone the fact that I had to try and explain to my mother what was going on.

*

That turned out to be easier than I thought.

I lied.

"Work's really intense at the moment," I said, having called her mobile. I was thankful that that she couldn't see my face. "So they're putting me up in a flat for a few days.....just until the worst of it's over. It's brand new, right on the canal, and there are 2 bedrooms, so I thought you might fancy it for a mini-break.

Mum loved the idea of a few days in Manchester, and I even managed to dissuade her from going home first.

"You've already got a case packed, and there's a washing machine and a tumble dryer in the flat. Anyway," I played my trump card, capitalising on her love of fine dining, "I've booked us in for dinner tonight at that new place by the Lowry Centre."

*

Back in the edit suite, and in my absence, Paul had asked Mandy to show him what we had already done, and had then suggested several changes and what he called improvements.

"That's not the film I want to make," I protested, as she told me what he'd suggested.

"I know. But his point was, you didn't go up there expecting to have a dead child on your hands, did you? Sorry Claire, his words not mine. He does have a point – you've got loads of exclusive material here, and it's significant."

"I agree that it is important. But the film is still about the school."

"Yes, Claire - the film is about the school."

I nearly jolted out of my chair, at the sound of Paul's voice behind me.

"But Murdo was a part of that school. And I'm sorry to say it but we need to think about viewing figures."

I let out a breath I was unaware I'd been holding in, and spun my chair round to face him.

"Okay, I know you're right. I just don't want my whole year of filming to be condensed into some kind of – backdrop."

"And that's why it's so great that you've now got two hours," he beamed, heading for the door. Reaching it, he seemed about to leave, but then he turned and spoke again.

"Hour one can be the film you dreamed about. Then, just as people are starting to get bored, we trail ahead to hour two – which will be the programme that the audience wants."

He left so hastily then that I had no chance to verbalise how affronted I felt.

Mandy smiled sympathetically. "Coffee?"

"I'll get them. I could do with stretching my legs and getting a breath of fresh air."

I hurried towards the coffee shop across the windswept concrete concourse. This area was labelled "The Piazza" on site maps, but had had rather ruder names given to it by those of us who actually had to use the place. In the weeks that I'd been back, I could count on the fingers of one hand the number of times it had been pleasant enough to linger there.

Inclement weather seemed harder to bear in the city than it had been in Kylecraig. Or perhaps my year away from the urban jungle had turned my head forever.

*

Over dinner in the fancy new restaurant that night, I had to think very carefully before opening my mouth, and the more wine I drank, the harder that became.

"Are you alright, dear?" asked Mum, over the cheeseboard. "You seem terribly twitchy."

"It's just nervous energy. I can't stop thinking about how to make the film I want to make AND the film the boss wants."

"Maybe you just need to look at some of your pictures again, only with his head on instead of yours."

It was simple advice – but surprisingly effective, as it turned out.

*

Sitting in the edit suite the following day, watching images of wave-washed sand, I gazed longingly at the wide and wild open spaces. Kylecraig beach seemed as distant as another galaxy. As

Mandy mixed sound effects of gulls and oystercatchers into the waves and the wind, I told her to stop.

"Let's look at some of the footage from the search again. No, not the search. Pull up the rushes from the day the kayakers found the body."

Mandy scrolled through the raw material on her computer until she reached the day in question. I remembered with a shudder how sick I'd felt at having to film, and how relieved that I could hide behind my zoom lens.

There was the shot of Catriona Mackay, her face contorted with grief. I hadn't seen it since the evening of that day, in fact I'd barely looked at it at all – it had seemed too intrusive.

"Freeze-frame there," I ordered Mandy.

I stared at Catriona's face, her reaction captured forever by my camera. Those tears streaking her face, which I'd taken as ones of sorrow for the loss of her son – were they actually for herself? Was that the moment she knew that she'd been caught out?

"What do you think of that?" I asked Mandy.

"I think we'll have to use that shot in the second half of the documentary. Says it all."

"Does it?

Mandy scrolled through the shot, playing around with the mouse, rolling the pictures backwards and forwards.

"There" she said, decisively. "Look at that moment, when her fate is decided. Her eyes are dead. She doesn't look sad, she looks resigned."

"Resigned to the death of her son?"

"Resigned to the fact that she's going to be locked up."

Mandy swung her chair round to face me.

"I'm a mum, and there's no way I'd react like that if I'd just had the news that they'd found my son's body. I'd collapse, pound the floor, scream. She's just too passive."

"Not everybody's the same though."

"True. But just looking at that shot tells me that she's guilty."

"Okay, let's put it in. Let's make the second hour of this film the one that the boss wants to see. It's his money I've been spending, after all."

Then I had an idea. Rummaging around in my box of SD cards, I found the one I was looking for.

"Play this one through Mandy."

She popped it into the slot, and the GVs I'd shot from the hill-path appeared on the screen in front of us.

"We've already used these," she started to say, and then stopped, as the camera swung round, suddenly, to reveal Catriona Mackay. The shot wasn't framed properly – it showed only her midriff, and her chin – but the dialogue was perfectly clear.

"Wow" said Mandy, after a moment. "She really didn't like you being there."

We listened to the confrontation, and watched as the camera carried on rolling, capturing Catriona wandering back down the hill-path.

"She looks drunk," Mandy said.

"She's on a load of medication, apparently. For mental health issues. Woah – hang on a minute. Who's that?"

By now, Catriona was just a dot in the distance, but she'd been joined by somebody else – another dot.

"Can you zoom in on that?"

Mandy put the material onto the timeline, put a re-size on the picture, and we watched it again. I recalled how I'd had a migraine and had slumped down into the heather, unaware that the camera was still recording.

Unaware that it had captured Donnie MacIver, walking up the hill to meet Catriona, and had carried on recording until they disappeared out of view together.

*

Two days later, as I was blown across The Piazza towards the office, my mobile rang. Seeing that there was no Caller ID displayed, I hesitated before answering.

"Hello?"

"Is this Claire Armstrong?" A female voice, Scottish accent, sounding rather bored.

"Who wants to know?"

"I've been requested to contact you by DCI Dingwall Brown. Is this a convenient time?"

By now, I'd reached the shelter of the foyer.

"I guess so, yes."

I tried to find a quiet corner in the echoing, open-plan space.

"Putting you through now."

There was a pause, a click, and then the clipped tones of the Police Chief reached my ear.

"Claire, how are you? I just wanted to call and let you know that we've traced the perpetrator of the incidents against you, and made an arrest. You and your mother are safe to return home."

I got as far as a "who…….," but he ploughed on into another sentence.

"In the other case, I wanted to say a *personal*" (he put a heavy emphasis on the word, as though trying it out for size) thank you for providing material which will be used as evidence in the court case. If you want any more information, I'm going to put you back over to Sheena. Thank you."

The line went dead once more, and then the original voice came back on.

"I'm going to give you a unique caller ID, and a reference number, do you have a pen?"

Fumbling around in my over-sized handbag, I finally found one and scrawled down the numbers she gave me on the back of a Booths receipt. I was about to ask her to repeat them when she wished me a pleasant day and hung up.

Really? Was that it?

Suddenly, my legs buckled underneath me, and I slumped to the cold floor. Dark shapes slid in front of me, like insects crawling across the inside of my eyelids.

Through the mesh of those shapes, and hidden from view by the coffee bar wall, I watched distant feet and legs coming and going about their business through the revolving doors, like an endlessly spooling piece of footage going forwards and backwards, backwards and forwards, relentlessly carrying on, regardless of the chaos in my messed-up little world.

CHAPTER THIRTY-SIX

Mum packed her bag and left the flat the following morning. I waited until she'd gone, and then called Iain Cameron.

"Iain, hello. Apparently, we're safe to go home now, or so I've been told. Can you tell me what happened?"

"I can tell you some of what happened. Not all of it, I'm afraid."

I was getting used to secrets.

"Okay, just tell me what you can."

"The threats were made by a male relative of one of the men we have in custody, over the drugs haul at the Craggan Inn. He has now been arrested as well, and charged with threatening behaviour and possession of illegal firearms."

"Firearms? Do you think he was planning to use those against me?"

"Not as far as we know, Claire, but he threatened the officers who went to arrest him. Fortunately, they were slightly more on the ball than he was."

My head was spinning.

"I still don't understand why they targeted me."

"Ah, well, that's the bit I can't tell you, I'm afraid. Classified information. Now, you'll have heard about Catriona's case being up in court in early December?"

"Yes, I had a call from DCI Brown yesterday."

"That's good, I asked him to call you. He's a busy man though, so you never know."

"Will you be in court?"

"Of course. Not something I'm looking forward to, to be honest. Hard to accept that one of your neighbours is capable of something like that, and I can't help blaming myself for not seeing any signs."

"I don't think anybody could have seen that coming, Iain."

I thought back to the footage that Mandy and I had been editing over the past couple of days. Of course it was all too easy to see signs, with the benefit of hindsight; and super slo-mo; and a bit of re-sizing.

I wondered whether to tell Iain what we'd seen, and decided against it. The police had already had plenty of time to look through my footage, after all.

*

I'd almost made it as far as the edit suite when my phone rang, with Mum's home number displayed. When I answered, I couldn't make sense of what she was saying.

"What? Slow down, I can't hear you. What is it?"

"I said burgled, we've been burgled, Claire."

Nausea rose as bile from my stomach and into my throat, and I grabbed at the wall.

"What do you mean?"

"They've thrown a brick through my bedroom window. I can't believe nobody heard it."

"You're not still in the house are you, Mum?"

"What? No, I'm round at Audrey's. The police are on their way."

"Good. Stay there until they come. I'll try and get home as quickly as I can."

Having explained what was going on to Mandy, I called a cab and asked the driver to take me to Southport. Remembering DCI Brown's smooth assurances that we were safe to go home, I grimly reckoned that I could sue the police for damages. I couldn't believe this burglary was a coincidence – or that it was just a burglary.

Even though I was expecting it, it was a shock to pull into the quiet suburban street and find a police car outside the bungalow. The door was open, and I stepped into the hall to be greeted by a male officer with a notebook. He gestured to the living room, where I found mum sitting on the sofa with a female police officer. Both of them stood up as I entered the room, and I could tell that the officer was about to speak, but Mum got in there first.

"Oh thank goodness you're here Claire. The police seem to think this is more than a simple burglary, I've no idea what's going on."

"If I could have a word with your daughter in private….?" This was the male officer, who'd followed me in.

A quick chat with him, back out in the hallway, established the facts. A brick had indeed been thrown through Mum's bedroom window. There had been a piece of cloth tied around the brick, with the word "WARNING" written on it. Other than that, there was no sign of any further disturbance. Nothing had been stolen, and it didn't appear that anybody had even been inside the house.

"Do you have any idea what this might be about, Miss? Anything at all that you can think of, which might explain what's gone on here."

"Oh yes. There most certainly is."

I told him everything I knew, and gave him the Caller ID and reference number that DCI Brown's secretary had given me the previous afternoon.

"We are conducting enquiries, trying to establish when this could have happened. I believe you and your mum have both been staying away for a few days?"

"That's right. We were told to. But then I was told that it would be safe to come home."

"It could be that this – act – was perpetrated before the arrest was made, in fact it's possible that this is unrelated. But you might want to think about staying elsewhere tonight, until I've been able to talk to our Scottish colleagues and establish what's going on. Do you have somewhere you can go?"

I nodded. I could stay with Leonie – again - and Audrey had already offered Mum her spare room for as long as she wanted it.

As the police were leaving, a white van pulled up outside.

"Don't worry, love" grinned the driver through his open window. "We'll soon have that hole all boarded up for you." Clearly, he thought that I was the homeowner, which was the final insult of the day. Did I really LOOK like someone who would own a retirement bungalow in a cul-de-sac?

Having made sure that Mum was okay, and had everything she needed, I was leaving for the office when a red Post Office van pulled up.

"Everything alright here?" asked the postie, clearly not used to such activity on a dull Wednesday morning.

"Fine, thanks". I'd no intention of getting embroiled for any longer than I had to.

"Only asking. A good postie keeps an eye out for people, that's all."

"Well, perhaps you spotted whoever lobbed a brick through our window then?"

"Really? When did that happen?"

"Well that's a good question. We have no idea; in fact I was rather hoping you might be able to tell me, if you're so good at keeping an eye out."

"Okay love, that's fair enough. But we do what we can. Anyway, this one's for you."

He handed me an envelope with Jackson's familiar handwriting on the outside.

"I'll go and get a cup of coffee with Audrey – she can tell me what's been going on. See you, love."

I put Jackson's letter into my bag, glad that I'd have something to read on the train; which I should just be able to catch if I made a run for the station.

*

Having made it with a couple of minutes to spare, I called Leonie, who was getting used to my last-minute requests for temporary accommodation.

"I told you, you should just move in."

"Be careful what you say, or I might take you up on that."

Then I opened Jackson's letter, which was short and to the point.

Dear Claire,

I now have a telephone. Landline only - luckily there is not much reception around here for mobile phones, which means I don't feel obliged to have one.

There followed a number, and a signature, which seemed even more flamboyant than usual.

There was no point calling him straight away, since he'd be teaching, and, once I reached Salford, I felt compelled to sit with Mandy for the last working hour of the day, though there was little we could achieve in such a short time-frame. When she'd gone, I took advantage of the dark, sound-proofed room, and called Jackson's new number.

Before I'd even heard it ring, he picked up.

"Hello?"

"Jackson it's me, Claire."

"Oh good – you're the very first person to call me on this number."

"Honoured, I'm sure."

"Is something wrong? You sound a little tense."

"You could say that. I've never had threats made against me before, you see. And my mother's never had a brick thrown through her bedroom window, either."

Straining my ears to hear a reaction, I expected a gasp, or, at the very least, a sharp intake of breath, but there was nothing.

"Jackson? Are you still there?"

"Yes, still here. Just trying to formulate an appropriate response to what you've just told me."

"How about a normal one? A bit of shock, or even surprise would probably do the trick."

"Are you both safe? Are the police aware of what's happening?"

"They are, yes, but whether we're safe or not, I have no idea. I've had assurances that we are, but I find it hard to believe any of them."

"I'm sure you will be okay, Claire."

"Oh good. As long as you're sure."

"Please don't be flippant."

"Can you suggest how I should be, then? Should I just shrug off all these frankly rather terrifying things that are happening to me? Oh, and my poor mum. Only it strikes me that it's since I met you that my life has taken a bit of a weird turn. Any idea why that might be, Jackson?"

There was another long silence, and I was on the verge of ending the call, when he spoke again.

"You should not be affected by any of this, Claire. Has Iain Cameron been in touch with you?"

"I've spoken to him, but he wasn't much more helpful than you're being just now. It's all to do with that bloody fake whisky bar we went to. You don't keep very nice company, it seems."

"I should never have taken you there."

"I'm sick of riddles, Jackson. I don't know what's been going on, but I need to try and focus on getting my programme made. Don't expect any more phone calls from me until I've done that. And I'm warning you now, if there are any more strange threats made against me, I'll be giving them your new address and this phone number, and you can sort it out yourself."

Before he could respond, I pressed the End Call button, and then turned the phone off altogether. I'd had enough of Jackson's mysteries. It was about time I started looking after myself, and my immediate future – which was going to be pretty bleak, if I didn't get my programme screened before Christmas.

CHAPTER THIRTY-SEVEN

M oving into Leonie's box-room was a godsend, since it turned my commute from a two-hour hell into an easy twenty-minute bus journey. I stayed in touch with Mum, who seemed quite happy to be shacked up with Audrey, and had even taken the opportunity to get decorators in to give the bungalow an overhaul. She'd always been able to make the best of a bad situation.

I'd expected Jackson to try and contact me, but he didn't, for which I was relieved and annoyed in roughly equal measure. There were no more calls from Police Scotland either, and again, I tried to take this as a positive sign that there was nothing to worry about.

In early October, I called Iain Cameron, who told me that Catriona Mackay had pleaded Not Guilty to the murder of her son. A date of November 27th had been set for her trial. I also asked whether he'd heard any more about the drugs ring, but he reiterated what he'd already told me – there was no need to worry, arrests had been made, and the relevant people were being held whilst awaiting trial.

Nobody, he assured me, was out to get me.

Which was just as well, since the documentary now demanded every ounce of my attention.

Every night, I'd stay in the edit suite later and later, watching back whatever we'd done that day and wondering whether it could be better or wishing that I'd shot something differently. As we got closer to a finished version of the programme, the room got more and more over-crowded and Mandy and I got more and more jumpy.

We were now basing the second part of the film on what we thought would be a "Guilty" verdict in the case against Catriona Mackay (although we were also working on another "Not Guilty" version, so that we could run with either one at short notice).

But working with such sensitive material meant that the lawyers were monitoring everything we did, creating an atmosphere of extreme tension. It didn't help that none of us had more than a rudimentary understanding of the Scottish legal system, so we'd had to draught in extra help from Glasgow to view what we were doing, once the court case finally got underway.

"Too many cooks," muttered Mandy under her breath, as the department head had a terse conversation with the controller of the channel at the back of our edit suite on one particularly stormy Friday afternoon. At such times, it seemed that so many people wanted to have a say in what, up until now, I had considered to be MY film that a consensus would never be reached.

We wasted precious time chopping out footage, only to be told to reinstate it. Meanwhile, our deadline waited, as solid and unmoving as an oil rig, glimpsed on the horizon.

"This had better bloody well happen," threatened somebody from Marketing, who'd popped in to see us one day, shortly after the trial began. "The Christmas *Radio Times* has already gone for printing."

"Our hands are tied," Mandy sighed. "Better call the High Court in Edinburgh, and ask them to hurry that court case along."

*

By early December, with still no more word from Jackson, the past few months had begun to seem like a dream. Each night, lying in bed and scrolling through news websites on my tablet, I caught up properly with events from Edinburgh, where the "Mackay Case" was ongoing, and I watched a procession of familiar faces going in and out of court. There was Iain Cameron, Janey Macleod. One day, to my shock, there was a shot of Jackson going in, almost unrecognisable in suit and tie, with a very neatly trimmed beard.

That almost broke my resolve not to call him, but I'd decided that I would wait until there was a verdict, and I was proud that I managed to restrain myself.

Then, two weeks into the case, on December 11th, Catriona Mackay's counsel changed her plea from not guilty, to guilty, on the condition that the court change the charge against her from one of murder to the lesser charge of culpable homicide.

As usual, the screen in the corner of the edit suite was tuned into the rolling news channel, and its red banner was now screaming,

"BREAKING NEWS…"

"That's it," said our Scottish lawyer, no doubt already thinking about her journey back up to Glasgow. "Guilty. The rest is of it irrelevant really, in terms of your programme anyway."

"Thank god for that," said Paul, possibly thinking of that glittery snowman-covered edition of the *Radio Times*.

I turned up the volume as the reporter outside the court addressed the camera.

"Today's dramatic developments came this afternoon, after the prosecution suggested that Mackay just wanted to teach her son a lesson, rather than kill him. On hearing their suggestion that she'd forced his head underwater, Mackay broke down in court, screaming that it was an accident. The court was told of evidence, found by pathologists, which suggested that his death was not accidental."

"This is a case that has gripped the nation" continued the court reporter, looking a bit too excited for somebody reporting on a case of filicide. "Most interesting of all was the evidence given by the pathologist that although he was found on a beach, and his death was caused by drowning, this little boy didn't drown at sea."

A gasp rippled around the edit suite.

"What's more" continued the reporter, graver now. "Mackay insisted that she was acting under orders, naming a third party as the real murderer."

I felt my stomach lurch.

"Counsel for the Defence argued that this person, who cannot be named for legal reasons, effectively forced Catriona Mackay into killing her own son. The prosecution insisted that this was yet another example of Mackay attempting to manipulate and deceive the jury, to save her own skin."

Mandy and I looked at each other, and I realised she was gripping my hand tightly. I wondered if she was thinking, as I was, about the footage we'd viewed of Donnie MacIver meeting Catriona at the bottom of the hill-path.

I couldn't think why Donnie would have wanted Murdo out of the way, unless he knew something about his mother's affair. I'd stuck stubbornly to my promise to Eilidh, and hadn't told Mandy – or anybody else – about the rumours. Now, I wished I'd confided in her. But in the packed edit suite, it was impossible to say anything; and the TV report was still blaring out.

"Given the lack of evidence to suggest that anybody else was involved, Mackay was deemed to be solely responsible for the death of her son. Although the boy's body was badly decomposed, after seven weeks in the sea, tiny particulates called diatoms were found in Murdo's bone marrow, and it was the discovery of these diatoms which enabled the prosecution team to put its case together."

"Catriona Mackay, a woman with a history of mental instability, wanted to teach her disobedient son a lesson. On the afternoon of Sunday March 12th, he'd been out playing all day, instead of helping her on the croft. When she heard him come home, just after dark, she greeted him in a furious temper and held his head under the water in the bath-tub outside the back door to their house. This was a container most often used for watering the sheep and cattle. But her son stopped breathing. Mackay panicked, and tried to bring him round. Her attempts to do so failed."

The reporter paused to consult notes but in the edit room nobody spoke or even, it seemed to me, breathed.

"It was after hearing this course of events suggested in court that Mackay broke down and changed her plea to guilty, against the advice of her own lawyers. "I only wanted him to behave himself," was her explanation. "I never wanted to hurt him." Mackay admitted that she'd panicked, taken her son's body to the harbour in a wheelbarrow, under cover of darkness, and dumped him into the sea."

I winced at the uncompromising language, and wished that I could crawl away and hide. Silvery light slivers flashed at the edge of my vision, and I groped in my bag for my migraine pills, all the time listening as the news report carried on.

"By this time, the storm was coming in which she hoped would wash the body away. She then had the rest of the night and the following morning to make up her story about Murdo having gone for a sleep-over at a friend's house, a story which she stuck to right up until this afternoon. What she couldn't have known was that because the water which killed him came from a private supply to the croft, it was traceable in her son's bone-marrow."

The reporter paused for breath again, and looked around, wildly, as though hoping somebody would come along and rescue her.

"Amazing" said Paul, who was glued, as we all were, to the TV screen.

"Yes" I murmured.

Back onscreen, the reporter stepped aside, with obvious relief, and I watched as Iain Cameron walked up to the microphone which had been set up on the steps outside the High Court. He was labelled as "Local police officer & family friend."

"This case has shocked our small community and in particular the families and friends of those concerned. Our thoughts are with them at this extremely difficult time, and we ask that they be left in peace now to come to terms with what has happened."

He somehow managed to walk back up the steps to where I could see his wife Kate waiting. Making a huge effort to keep myself from crying, I let out a deep breath.

Then a voice piped up, behind me.

"Terribly sad of course, but hey, great timing. Let's crack on and get this finished. "

I turned around, ready to bite off the head of whoever had just spoken. Then I realised that it was the controller of the channel; and I had to bite my lip instead.

"In fact, I'm thinking, we should strike whilst this particular iron is hot," he continued. "Clear the schedules of something boring, this coming weekend, run the programmes whilst everybody's still talking about this story. We could go with part one on Saturday, and run part two on Sunday."

"But what about the Christmas *Radio Times?*"

The words had come out of my mouth before I could stop them.

"What about it? Can you get this ready to air, or are you saying that's not possible?"

"We can do it," said Mandy, kicking me in the ankle when she realised that I was about to protest.

"Good stuff. I'll talk to the marketing team; get it splashed in the weekend papers. You just wait and see, it'll be worth it for the viewing figures."

*

Somehow, we did it. We cracked on, and we got it finished. And on Thursday afternoon, after three sleepless nights fuelled by coffee and doughnuts, came the moment that I sat down with Mandy, my department boss and the channel controller, to watch the final FINAL version.

Watching the programmes through, I began to feel nauseous. Rather than being the creator - the film-maker - I felt as though the whole process had wrenched these two hours, semi-formed, from my body.

The first hour opened with sombre music and voiceover, reminding everybody that a remote and tiny place like Kylecraig could never have expected to be so firmly – and tragically – placed on the map of the nation's consciousness.

"But the real tragedy is this," continued the serious-voiced narrator, one of Scotland's best-loved actors who came from a similar village, and so had recorded this for a fraction of his usual fee. "At its heart, this small community reminds the rest of us of more relaxed, carefree times. Doors remain unlocked, everybody knows their neighbours, children are allowed to run wild and free. And at the centre of this place, is the village school…….."

From here on in, the first programme was roughly the film I'd had in mind. No more sonorous narration – the children, parents and teachers told their own story. We got to know them through filmed sequences and sound-bites, sometimes pithy, sometimes funny, always (I hoped) engaging.

Part two was not the film I'd intended to make. The images of press conferences, police combing the village, the media presence engulfing the village made it seem like a different programme. But even in the darkness, I could see the channel controller nodding and tapping his fingers on his leg – a sure sign of excitement – when it came to the sequence of shots of

Catriona, which no other broadcaster had had any access to. What felt horribly like prying, to me, was what gave my programme credibility and status in his eyes.

I'd wanted to end the second programme with Scottish folk music, and a montage of my favourite Kylecraig shots. Sunset over Greagha and the children collecting shells on the beach. Eilidh dishing out cups of homemade broth on a bitter cold winter's day when the boiler had packed in, in the days before Jackson arrived.

The montage remained, as did the music, but now it was Janey Macleod who had the final say. Over pictures of a school assembly, accompanied by the joyous (if rather painful) sound of the school band, she did her best to tug at the heartstrings of the nation.

"There are those who say it's not financially viable for a place like this to exist. But I ask you, what kind of a world do we want our children to live in? I believe passionately in this school, and in the people who make up this community. It did not take the tragic death of one boy to bring these people together – because they were already together. And it is because of these people that I will continue to fight for my school."

I'd hated this sound-bite more every time I'd been forced to listen to it, especially given what I knew about the reality of this "close-knit" community. Mandy had over-ruled me, saying that my personal opinion had clouded my professional judgment, and when I saw the controller nodding again, I had to hand it to her – she'd been right.

I did have a small moment of personal pride at seeing the credit "Filmed and Directed by Claire Armstrong." It was no longer the final frame of the programme of course – that was rightly reserved for a photograph of Murdo with a cheeky grin, and the simple epitaph; "For Murdo Mackay – 2006-2017."

The music ended and the screen went black. I pulled my numbed hands out from under my legs – I'd had to sit on them to stop myself biting my nails. There was a moment of silence, and then – not applause, which would have been too much to hope for – but a murmured ripple of appreciation which was reward enough.

"Nicely done, thanks Paul. We'll get the press preview scheduled for tomorrow and then we're airing on Saturday and Sunday, BBC2, 8pm. Let's just hope the viewing figures make it worthwhile – but hey, no pressure!"

This was from the controller, who was already up out of his chair. He shook hands with my boss and then, as if as an afterthought, turned to me.

"What's your next project?"

Before I had a chance to reply, he was reaching for the door handle.

"I'll look forward to seeing it."

He smiled and left, already on his phone before the door had closed behind him.

My boss grinned.

"Take it from me, Claire – coming from him, that counts as effusive praise."

"Thank you."

"Do you have another project in mind?"

I took a deep breath, crossed my fingers behind my back, and spoke.

"As a matter of fact I do….."

I was prepared to continue, but he put up a hand.

"Smart girl. Let's wait until the New Year shall we? I have no doubt these programmes will be well received. At which point – well, let's just say that you will be in a strong position to re-negotiate your contract."

I exhaled and nodded.

He thanked Mandy for all of her work as well, and then, as he turned to go, he put a warm hand on my shoulder.

"Happy Christmas, Claire. Take a couple of weeks off will you? You've earned it."

CHAPTER THIRTY EIGHT

I was spending one more night with Leonie. The two of us had planned to celebrate the completion of the film with a bottle of bubbly and a Chinese takeaway (I still loved the novelty of hot food being delivered to my doorstep), but I was no longer sure I'd be able to stay awake for long enough to enjoy the evening.

I let myself in, calling her name as I did so.

"In here." Her voice came from the small room which doubled up as my bedroom and her study. She was sitting at the computer, but swung round to face me as I came in.

"Hey – you got it done then? Well done".

"Is the Prosecco chilled? I'm in dire need of a drink, Lee."

"I'll go and get you some. But while I'm doing that, just take a read through this, and tell me what you think."

Indicating the screen, she got up and left. I sat on the swivel chair, and looked, confused, at an online tabloid newspaper article on the screen in front of me.

"Undercover policeman married the woman he was sent to spy on."

The story was illustrated with a head and shoulders shot of a decent-looking, dark-haired man, and went on to give details of how he'd been sent to live as an activist, and had immersed himself within a community by lying to everybody he met. He'd finally committed the ultimate betrayal by marrying a woman who had no idea who he was.

"Ring any bells?" Leonie asked, handing me a glass full of bubbles.

I shook my head.

"Never heard of him, or her. Do you know them?"

"That's not the point, not what I'm saying at all. Just forget the photograph, forget the smaller details, and read between the lines. You're a journalist, for god's sake. Does this really not set any alarm bells ringing?"

I swung round on my chair.

"You're not drinking?"

"Never mind that just now. Who do we know who appeared in a small community recently, mysteriously? Who lied, or refused to reveal really simple facts about himself?"

Heat rose inside me, as I realised what she was implying.

"Oh, for god's sake. I know you've never liked him, but are you honestly suggesting that Jackson is an undercover cop, like this bloke? You're too wedded to these gossip sites Lee; you need to get a life."

Leonie remained silent, but gave the slightest shrug of her shoulders.

"Anyway, it's not possible. He was working as a teacher, you know that."

"So they probably trained him as a teacher, to get him into the community. That's what they do, Claire. Jeez, for someone who works in the media you can be pretty naïve at times. And I'm sure you told me that there were rumours sweeping the village about him, that he'd been a copper in a former life. Well – maybe he was. Perhaps he still is, and this whole teaching thing is just a ruse."

I kept quiet, my brain racing to try and make sense of what she was suggesting.

"All I'm saying is that it's worth thinking about. I don't have anything against the bloke; I've never met him, so how could I? But when I read this article this morning, it jumped right out at me. And the more I thought about it, the more it seemed like there could be something to it. At least ask him, Claire? What have you got to lose?"

It was my turn to shrug.

"Come on. Just promise me you'll ask him?"

"Yes, okay, I promise."

I raised my glass in her direction.

"So let's change the subject, for now. Here's to the end of my programme. Are you going to get a glass and join me, or what?"

I watched as a flush spread across my friend's face – and all of a sudden, I got it.

"Oh – you're not drinking for a reason. Lee, are you – I mean, is it what I think it is?"

"'Fraid so. This room's not going to be available after next June. So you'd better get your life back on track before then."

All thoughts of Jackson, undercover cops and criminal gangs flew from my mind, as I leapt up, spilling some precious fizz in the process, and hugged my friend.

"Congratulations! Oh my god, you're going to be a mum, I can't believe it."

"I know, and I'm sorry. I know you don't really like kids."

"I think I'll like yours. At any rate, I like you enough to pretend that I do."

We pulled apart, appraised each other, grinning through our tears.

"And as incentives go, this is a pretty good kick up the backside. You're right; it's about time I got to sorting out my life."

CHAPTER THIRTY NINE

As I sat on the slow train back to Southport the following afternoon, my own reflection, pale and drawn, looked accusingly back at me from the window. My work was done, my programme had been officially signed, sealed and delivered, but doubts still invaded my brain like crows swarming over road kill.

Murdo's death had changed everything and, no matter how often I told myself that I'd just been doing my job, I couldn't get rid of a guilt that twisted my insides until I felt sick.

If I'd made the programme I'd wanted to make, would I still be in a position to re-negotiate my contract, or would it have been a swift handshake, a quick "thanks for all you've done" and a nifty shove in the direction of the back door of the BBC?

And should I have made sure that the police were aware of the footage of Catriona and Donnie? Surely they would have seen it, I told myself - it had been in amongst the footage I'd handed over.

I tried to squash down the nagging thought that Mandy and I had stumbled across those shots almost by accident.

Leonie's news about the baby had stunned me, too. She'd always been more settled and steady than me, but we'd never really talked about whether we'd have children, and I'd assumed she felt the same way about them that I did. I felt like I was losing my only real ally to an alien world of hospital scans and baby showers.

As for Jackson, the more I thought about her theory, the more I wondered whether she might be right. It would certainly explain a lot – the secrecy, the threats, the sudden disappearance, the visit to the Craggan Inn.

What really hurt was the thought that, if he cared about me, how could he have dragged me into that situation, putting me and my mum at risk? And what about the fact that he was now teaching – or "teaching" – in another school. Was that just a cover for another big drugs raid?

To accept that I knew nothing about the man was to accept that I was a fool, and had been duped, just like the woman in the online article.

It wasn't until the lady sitting opposite me offered a tissue that I realised that I was crying.

"It's a stressful time of year, love" she said, indicating the bulging carrier bags piled at her feet.

Christmas shopping! It hadn't even occurred to me to do any.

I tried a smile, but my face felt too wobbly to make a convincing job of it, so I just thanked her and turned my body away from the window, so that I wouldn't have to look myself in the eye.

*

Mum clearly thought I was being melodramatic. Partly my own fault, of course – since, in trying to shield her from the danger we were in, I'd cut off that avenue of communication, and I could hardly backtrack now.

We were sitting at the kitchen table. I'd walked into the house expecting the soothing scents of home-cooked food and the reassuring noise of Radio 2, but both were conspicuous by their absence. Had I been less exhausted, I'd have wondered what was going on. Instead, I babbled on about guilt, Murdo, and what I felt to be the betrayal of my values until Mum interrupted me.

"Look at you," she said, in a tone which felt somewhere between disapproval and sympathy.

"Don't, Mum, please."

"Don't what?" Now she sounded affronted. "Really Claire, I do worry. We're never able to talk properly, and you've clearly been crying, judging by those rings around your eyes. It's about time you joined the rest of us in the real world again. It's been over a year now that this film has taken over your life – and mine, I might add. What with that and the whole business with that wretched man…."

"Jackson…." came my weary intervention, which she ignored.

"I feel that your life has taken on a very strange direction. I only want….."

"…..what's best for me, I know. And I'm sorry. But Mum, really, I'm knackered. All I want to do just now is have a nice cosy evening in front of some mindless crap on the TV with a bottle of wine."

"Well – aside from the fact that I also think you're drinking too much – of course you can spend your evening on the sofa. But I'm going out."

"Out?"

This was odd. Mum never went out in the evening. Especially not in December, when it was dark and cold outside. What was going on?

She stood up and put both hands on my shoulders, forcing me to look up at her.

"I have a date. With John. He's a nice man, who I met on an internet dating site, and I've been seeing him for a couple of months. I'm going to go now, so you can have a bit of time to digest all of that, but there's some M&S lasagne in the freezer. And you know where the wine rack is, of course."

I opened my mouth, but nothing came out. Mum's face softened, and I noticed how pretty she looked. She'd had her hair done and was wearing a dress I'd never seen before.

"I have tried to tell you a couple of times before but you've been so….busy, and wrapped up in things. I am sorry to just blurt it out like that but otherwise you simply wouldn't have heard me."

Outside, a car horn beeped twice, and a look came over Mum's face that I'd never seen before.

"That'll be him."

Still unable to speak, I followed her into the hall, and watched as she grabbed a smart wool coat from the pegs by the door - another new purchase?

Buttoning it up, she apologised for leaving me alone.

"But I didn't know you'd be coming back tonight, dear – you've been at Leonie's for quite a while now, haven't you? Do help yourself to wine – only try not to overdo it. Oh, and don't wait up."

Please don't wink, I found myself thinking and, thank god, she didn't.

The front door slammed and, like a small child excluded from a treat, I ran to the living room and peered through a gap in the curtains, watching as my mother climbed into the passenger seat of a low-slung coupe, which then eased out of the cul-de-sac like a predatory mammal in search of prey.

I stayed there until the tail lights vanished around the corner, and then made my way back into the empty kitchen.

I need wine now, was my first thought.

And I need to call Jackson.

CHAPTER FORTY

J ust over twelve hours later, at 9am on Saturday morning, I was pulling up outside a neat little cottage on the outskirts of Kelso. I'd left a note for Mum on the kitchen table as I sneaked out at dawn. I sat in the car for a while after turning off the engine, staring at the brightly painted garden gate, and trying to imagine the man I knew, contained within such a conventional space.

But then – what did I actually know about Jackson? Not even his surname, presuming that he had one.

Sighing, I looked at my washed-out reflection in the rear-view mirror wishing I had found some time to get my highlights done, since my roots were looking decidedly mousey. I reached into the glove-box and found an ancient mascara. A coating of that, and an extra layer of lip-gloss, was all I could manage in terms of ammunition for now.

Hoping I looked stronger than I felt, I locked the car and headed up the path.

Before I'd made it as far as the front door, Jackson – or whoever he really was – had opened it, and gestured me inside, without so much as a smile or a word of greeting.

"Let's go into the kitchen," he offered, once we were in the hall, the door firmly closed beside us. "I've just made a pot of coffee."

"I hope it's strong."

Inside, the house opened out. Beyond the small frontage, somebody had added a glass-walled extension to the back, which gave a wide view onto hills and moorland. There was a log-burner, and an Aga, both of them chucking out heat into this smart new room.

"Wow. This is a whole lot better than a campervan."

"What a crazy idea that was, thinking that I could pass myself off as some kind of hippie. Even at my age, we live and learn."

"That's good to hear, Jackson, because I'm hoping to learn quite a bit today. And then, if you want me to, I will disappear from your life and never darken your charmingly painted door ever again."

He gave me a rather pained look.

"Claire, I hope you know by now that's not what I want at all."

"Come on then – tell me why I should give you another chance?"

"Can I just pour the coffee first?"

"Yes, by all means, pour the coffee. And then you're going to be doing all the talking, for a change. You are going to tell me everything, and I am just going to listen. Starting with your real name."

Jackson sat down, poured coffee into two pottery mugs, and looked me straight in the eye. "My name is Quentin James Montague Jackson de Clancy."

I almost choked on my coffee.

"You can see why I choose to be known simply as Jackson. And why I was never overly fond of my parents. But please, let's save talking about them for another day."

"It's certainly quite a mouthful. Is that the only reason you choose to be just Jackson? Or is there more to it than that?"

"You're a bright woman, Claire, so I think you already know that there is more to it than that. In fact, it wouldn't surprise me if you already know what you came here today to find out from me."

"That's a neat way of trying to get out of saying it, Jackson."

"Not at all."

"And actually it wasn't me that came up with the – theory. It was my friend Leonie."

"Theory?"

"I'm not saying it. I need to hear you say it. Damn it, Jackson, even after all this time, you still can't be honest with me."

I was shouting by now, and I pushed my chair away from the table and stood up, heading for the kitchen door, frightened of every bit of emotion that this man – this lying, conniving man – still stirred up inside me. I needed to get out of that house, and quickly, before he spun me another line.

But he was too quick and too strong for me. Within seconds he'd jumped up as well, and stood, blocking the doorway, filling the whole frame, holding me by both wrists.

"Let me go."

I lashed out, kicking him in the ankle as hard as I could, but although I saw him wince, his grip held me firmly.

"Jesus, Claire, would you calm down for just a moment and look at me please?"

I shook my head, looked down at the floor. Polished, engineered oak floorboards, I noted. Nice.

There was a moment's silence, and then Jackson spoke.

"Fine. I will come clean, but you need to know that my career, and possibly my freedom, could be on the line if you breathe one word of this to anybody.

I knew, at that moment, that Leonie had hit the nail on the head. Thank goodness for my clever, nosey, gossip-obsessed friend.

"Why should I care one iota about your freedom? You put my life and my mother's at risk, you and your stupid bloody lies."

Jackson's grip slackened, and I watched his bare feet turn and walk away from me across that beautiful floor. This is it, I thought. This is the moment. Everything now hinges on the next words out of his mouth.

"I'm sorry."

Clearly, he knew it.

"I didn't quite catch that, Jackson. Could you repeat what you just said?"

"I can. But only if you come over here, sit down, and look me in the eye."

Was this another trick? Only one way to find out. I crossed the floor swiftly, sat down opposite him, and folded my arms. I looked at him, taking in the creases around his eyes, the so-neatly trimmed as to be almost gone beard, the tamed hair. He looked like a smug housecat, rather than the wild lion of a man I'd met just over a year ago, blown onto a distant shoreline in a swirl of snowflakes.

"I'm sorry, Claire. Truly sorry. I could never have imagined how all of this would – play out."

"So you knew about the drugs dealers then? About the threats. Before I told you, I mean?"

"Yes, I'm afraid so. They're pretty nasty people, and very stupid, but they were only ever trying to frighten you, to get at me, and to make me pay for what I'd done. Only Murdo was the one who ended up paying the price, for all of us. Poor boy."

"What? You've lost me Jackson."

He ignored me, and carried on as though I hadn't spoken.

"Your landlord was the man behind it all, you know. That's strictly off the record, since none of the names are released officially yet."

"Billy Mackenzie?"

"Don't be ridiculous. Frazer."

My mind raced back to that sunny day in August, sixteen months earlier, when I'd picked up the keys to Ceol na Mara, from that huge, ostentatious house on the outskirts of Inverness. And I remembered Eilidh's snide comment about "absentee landlords."

"So that's the real reason why you came to Kylecraig, to try and catch them? You really are an undercover cop, just like Lee suspected?"

"It's not quite like that. I think your friend Leonie needs to broaden her reading and try some of the better quality newspapers, rather than just the ones with the sensationalist headlines. But yes, whilst I was in Kylecraig, I was working for the police – specifically the drugs squad. I was asked to go to the Highlands to investigate the Craggan Inn."

"Did Janey Macleod know this?"

He shook his head.

"It's imperative that nobody knows about these things – or at least, as few people as possible. That's why she was so resentful about me being there. I was put into her school by the head of the board of governors, who also happens to be the only person in Kylecraig who had full access to the facts. Iain Cameron.

Of course. I thought back over all the times that he'd done his best to reassure me, and felt a little guilty that I'd given him such a hard time. Then I remembered something.

"Iain told me that the man who threatened us, one of Frazer's relatives, had access to firearms. He could have killed me, Jackson."

"Many people in that part of the world have firearms, Claire. The guy's a gamekeeper. That was a bit – reckless of Iain, he should never have told you that. I don't suppose he gave you his name, or any more information?"

"He didn't. He said he couldn't. But at least he was looking out for me. You just buggered off and left me there, at the mercy of those men."

"Listen, what can I do, or say to you? Once again, I am so very sorry for putting you in such a risky position."

"What about now? Am I safe now?"

"They're in custody. They're all going to be locked up for quite a while, so yes; I'd say you're pretty safe.

Talking about men with guns, and drugs, and murder all seemed so remote from my safe little world of just a few months ago. I wondered if it was Frazer who'd been hanging around outside my house late at night, smoking his cigraettes, trying to scare me. Then again, I suppose it no longer mattered.

"So who were they then, these men?"

"I can't tell you that Claire."

"Off the record, Jackson, yes you can. My oath is my word, it will go no further than these walls. I think it's the least you can do for me."

Before he even said it, I knew what was coming.

"Donnie MacIver was the local link. There was another guy from outside Inverness, the gamekeeper, but Donnie was the one with the boat. They brought the stuff in by sea, smuggled it into the cove below the Craggan Inn."

My brain tried to catch up with his words.

"Donnie's boat? From the harbour at Kylecraig, where Murdo liked to play around?"

Jackson nodded.

"Jackson, why didn't you say anything at the time?"

"Because I didn't know. Jesus, Claire, do you honestly think I'd have kept quiet about that? I only found most of this out after I'd already left Kylecraig.

"So......so what really happened to Murdo? The unofficial, off the record version, I mean – not the one that I already know.

"I really shouldn't tell you Claire. None of this is sanctioned."

"I've finished with Kylecraig, and my programme. It's all too late now Jackson, don't you see? I want to know how Murdo died. I think you owe me that much."

"You're right, Claire. You, of all people, deserve to know the full details about what happened in that place. I trust you not to breathe a word of this to anybody. Not your mum, or your clever friend Leonie."

"You have my word on that, Jackson. Or whatever your name is."

And so he told me what he knew.

CHAPTER FORTY ONE

"Murdo, as we all knew, could be a little devil. There was nothing sinister in him, he was just a wee boy – naughty, wilful, a bit too curious for his own good. Donnie MacIver had warned him several times to keep away from his boat. His mother had warned him too, she was always telling him that the harbour could be a dangerous place. Anyway – being a boy, he ignored all the warnings."

"Donnie's a local lad – a bit lazy, a bit stupid, and far too willing to make some easy money, as he saw it. Which was why Frazer saw him as the perfect accomplice. He'd been running the drugs ring for a few months when I was called in. I worked out that they were using the Craggan Inn quickly enough, but I couldn't work out where the drugs were coming from.

"It turned out they were being handed over from boat to boat, out at sea. They didn't take them straight to the Craggan though, that was the clever bit. Donnie would take them back into the harbour, where he'd land his catch – a more usual catch. A few days later, he'd go out again – and nobody thought anything of it. Not until Murdo found an unfamiliar stash."

He paused, and then carried on.

"Well – he went and told his mum. He knew what it was alright – you heard me warning the boys often enough about drugs and alcohol, I'm sure?"

I nodded.

"Of course, he didn't know that his mum was embroiled with Donnie. He was just doing the right thing, being a good boy. For once."

I heard the catch in Jackson's voice, and went to reassure him, but he put up a hand.

"No, let me finish. We've only Donnie's word for any of this, remember, so you'll have to make your own mind up. He says he told Catriona to teach her son a lesson – to frighten him, keep his nose out of Donnie's business. She maintains that he told her to get rid of him. She's easily led, and not all there, so it's hard to know the truth."

I was aware that my eyes had filled with tears, and I brushed them with the back of my hand as discreetly as I could.

"All we know, from there on, is what happened. Murdo drowned, and the pair of them covered the whole thing up. She was in love with him, or so she says, and not only that, she was scared of what he might do to her.

"And remember - if those kayakers hadn't found the body, they'd have got away with it. Everybody thinking it was just an accident. Anyway, they're both going to be locked up, in the end, which feels like the right outcome. Once the drugs case comes to court, the whole thing will be out in the open. Which is good – except it doesn't bring Murdo back of course."

I waited a while, but it seemed that Jackson had nothing left to say.

"Thank you, Jackson. Thank you for telling me. I won't breathe a word of it, I promise."

I looked around me, at the velvet hills rolling away beyond the windows, the logs spitting in the wood-burner, and then I noticed, on a coffee table, a copy of the Christmas edition of the *Radio Times*, sparkly snowman beaming inanely on the front cover, and my hands went to my face as my two worlds crashed together once again.

"If you're really a policeman, and not a teacher, then that blows the integrity of my programme right out of the water. Shit, Jackson."

"I did try to tell you that I didn't really want to be in it. Maybe now you can understand why."

My heart racing, I stood up, and paced the room, trying to think.

"It's going out tonight and tomorrow."

"Tonight? But it's in there......"

He strode over to the coffee table, and leafed through the pages of the *Radio Times*. I was touched to see that he'd highlighted both of my programmes with green fluorescent marker pen.

"They've moved it forward."

I told him about the powerful wheels that had been set in motion in order to alter the TV schedules so that my programmes could be shown as soon as possible after the court case. There was no way I was going to call my boss and tell him to pull the plug. If the proverbial hit the fan, then I'd just have to swear that I hadn't known until after the programmes had aired. By which time, it would be too late.

"I still don't understand your role in all of this, Jackson. You were in court, I saw you on the News Channel. Were you in there as a policeman, or as a teacher?"

"As a teacher, of course. And that means that *your* integrity shouldn't be questioned. It just so happens that, whilst I was in

Kylecraig, I was practising a portfolio career. Quite common, in that part of the world."

"You mean, you were both?"

"In a nutshell, yes."

"It's all so dishonest, so shady, this double life of yours. I really don't like it."

I wanted Jackson to agree with me, but he just raised his palms towards me, as if to say "here I am – take me or leave me."

"And are you just a teacher now? Or is this another undercover job?"

"This is the real me, Claire, trying to live the life I've always wanted to. No more lies, no more hiding. I was a really good police officer though. I worked out of Newcastle for a while, which is when I discovered this part of the world."

"Newcastle?" I remembered the train ticket I'd found in his campervan.

"It's a great city; I've still got friends there. I always vowed to come back to the North East, but after my career took off, it took me up to Glasgow. I had a whole new way of policing to learn on the other side of the border, but after a few years I'd had enough of it. I was ready to quit a while ago, until this job came up. The force trained me up, paid for my teaching qualifications. It seemed like the perfect solution, a way to do both teaching and police work."

"Leonie was right. It's almost the same story."

"Hardly. I was doing a serious job, Claire. Two serious jobs, in fact, and I tried, so very hard, never to tell you any lies."

"You never told me anything. That makes it okay does it? I still don't understand how you could live a double life like that. How you could lie – sorry, pretend - to everybody around you?"

Jackson sighed.

"You're right. It's hard, living a double life. I was only able to do it because I could tell myself that I was performing a valuable service to the community, and that there was no other way of doing it. My plan was to pass myself off as a harmless eccentric, a bit of a hippy character, just helping out a school in need for a few months. Nobody applied for that job, you know? That's why Iain was able to put me in place."

"My mum said as much. She fell for the hippy thing too."

"Did she? I'm glad somebody did. I thought I was being clever, not leaving a footprint by not signing a lease on a house, or having a proper name, but it just made everybody curious. Especially the boys. Calum, Jimmy, Rory and Murdo were always popping round to my van, wanting to nosey around."

"Shouldn't the police have found you somewhere to live, given you a new identity?"

"They offered. I'll admit I was cocky, thought I'd be better off inventing my own story. More able to pass it off as the truth. I'm ashamed to admit that I told other people all sorts of lies, Claire. You're the only one I couldn't do that to."

I stared at him, intrigued.

"What did you tell Janey Macleod?"

"She came onto me, flirting I mean, right from the start. I told her I was attracted to her, but that I would never let a professional relationship be ruined by a personal one."

I smiled, in spite of myself. "No wonder she hates me."

"I thought she might respond to flattery, and I wanted to try and soften her up after I took the job. I didn't want to make any more enemies than I needed to."

"I wish you'd told me Jackson. I wouldn't have said anything, you know."

"I couldn't risk it Claire. But I'm sorry I dragged you into this. Do you know how many young people have their lives wrecked by vermin like your landlord?"

I shook my head.

"Frazer and others like him have been operating for years in places like Kylecraig. Bored young teenagers are always an easy target when it comes to shifting coke and heroin. What I do, and others like me, is sometimes the only way of stopping these guys. It's all blown out of the water now, of course, thanks to that one idiot, and his complete lack of morals."

"That idiot, as you call him, is the only reason we are having this conversation now. Leonie read all the articles about him and put two and two together."

"It would have been better if I could have told you in my own time and my own words. And I would have told you Claire, I promise you I would have found a way. But I need you to know one thing. He may have given us all a bad name, and what he did was despicable, but I am not like him."

"Well no – at least you didn't try to marry me."

"Yet."

Ignoring his last comment, I leaned across the table towards Quentin James Montague Jackson de Clancy, over the already obsolete pages of the brand new *Radio Times*.

"One more question. Do I have to call you Quentin from now on?"

"God no." He looked horrified. "I've always hated that name."

"I'm not surprised. And I have to say, Leonie was right about another thing as well. She told me that the Highlands were full of people running away from their lives."

"How about you?"

I paused for a moment, tempted to lie. But there had already been enough lies.

"Yes, I was one of them. And what a mess it's got me into. My next project is going to be something nice and straightforward."

"Like this one was supposed to be, you mean?"

I shot him a look, and he continued, hurriedly.

"And what is this next project of yours?"

I smiled.

"That, Jackson, is my little secret."

EPILOGUE

THREE MONTHS LATER

I was woken up by the sun streaking through a gap in the gingham curtains, which made a pleasant change from the relentless hammering of rain on my metal roof.

Maybe, finally, spring was really here?

A light breeze whispered through the open window and I was smiling to myself as I reached up to the hob and clicked on the gas underneath my bright blue enamel kettle. As I popped a teabag into a mug, there was a sharp rap at the door.

"It's open," I called, reaching for a second mug and teabag.

Jackson entered, stooping to fit inside my space and perching on the bench at the furthest point away from me – which wasn't very far at all.

"It's already glorious out there. And you, festering away indoors….."

"You know me – I'm useless until I've had my cup of tea."

He smiled, the crinkles around his eyes increasing, like channels worn into sand.

"Yes, I'm well aware of that. Will you come out for a walk AFTER your cup of tea?"

The whistling of the kettle screeched over my response; although I'm sure he already knew that it was a yes.

Already, after just a couple of weeks in my new home, I found it hard to imagine returning to bricks and mortar, much to my mother's predictable horror – and Jackson's great amusement.

"I thought *I* was supposed to be the nomad," he'd said, when I'd first announced my intention of living in a campervan.

"Well – let's just say you shouldn't go around putting ideas into people's heads."

*

In spite of my fears, my programmes about Kylecraig had been well reviewed, and I'd had high hopes of moving straight away to start work on the next programme - but I'd reckoned without the vast amount of tedious paperwork that needed to be put in place. Each year, it seemed, programme makers had a harder time just getting programmes made.

I'd kept myself busy over those frustrating weeks of January with my search for a campervan. This was nothing like Jackson's wreck, but a pale blue and cream beauty, sourced on eBay, and paid for with a loan from my long-suffering mother. I'd also been helping Leonie to decorate what had been my bedroom for a short time but was about to become a nursery.

"Definitely time for me to be moving on," I'd told her, when we finally stood back to admire the pale yellow walls and hand-painted teddy bears on the cupboards.

"As long as you come and visit," Leonie had replied, hugging me tight. "You're going to be a brilliant godmother. It will be your job to lead my child astray."

"I'm sure you're quite capable of doing that," I'd replied. "But I'm always happy to help."

Finally, towards the end of February, I'd been given the go-ahead to begin work on my new film. All that remained was to begin my new life as a temporary nomad, starting with the removal of Rosie – my campervan had arrived already christened – from my mother's driveway.

"I'm sorry to see you go," she'd said "but I can't say the same for that thing."

"It's okay, Mum – the neighbourhood is saved. And I'm sure John is waiting just around the corner in his Merc."

"Cheeky madam."

But there had been tears in her eyes as she'd waved me off.

*

Catriona Mackay had been sentenced, in February, to ten years in prison. It seemed too short a sentence, to me and many others, just one year for each of Murdo's. There were petitions, and demonstrations, but the Scottish court system was inclined towards leniency in cases such as hers, where mental health was to blame.

There were others who'd argued that she shouldn't have had to pay at all for committing somebody else's crime. But there was no evidence to link Donnie MacIver to Murdo's murder, and he was now at the start of his own fifteen year sentence for smuggling drugs, something towards which the Scottish courts took a very hard line indeed.

After her sentencing, it emerged in the press that some of the villagers had switched their allegiances as soon as Catriona was accused. As if killing her son wasn't enough, another crime, in their eyes, was that she was a "second generation incomer" – or at least that was how one of them had described her.

Jackson hadn't commented on the sentence – I think he still blamed himself for not sensing that Murdo was in danger.

I'd questioned him about that night though, the one when Murdo went missing and I'd found him stumbling along the beach. It turned out that he'd lost his temper and confronted Frazer, my landlord, when he found him hanging around in the village. They'd almost come to blows – until Jackson had seen sense and turned away. That was why he'd had to leave in such a hurry.

At least, thanks to him, Rory and Calum and the others were less likely to be able to get their hands on Class A Drugs.

*

Jackson and I headed up the steep road to Halterburn, before heading across a small burn and up onto the open hillside.

It was still early but the sun was warm on our faces as we made steady progress up the broad, grassy path. Once we'd left behind the melodic tinkle of the water there was silence, but for the occasional plaintive cry of a curlew and the rather more prosaic sound of my breathing, since I was still re-discovering my hill fitness.

After a couple of hours we were at the summit of the Schil, the hilltop which straddles the border. Before us was England. Behind us, Scotland. And beneath us, a natural blanket of heather and sheep-cropped grass, the perfect place to lie down, side by side, hands loosely touching but no more. We lay like that for maybe half an hour, letting the sun chase away the last remnants of winter chill from our bones. I concentrated on the scratchiness of the heather stalks beneath my shirt, the feeling of the short grass beneath my bare toes, the warm, familiar tickle of Jackson's hand perfectly still beside mine.

Distant voices interrupted our reverie. We sat up like a pair of synchronised swimmers, pulled our boots back on, and began the walk down to the village, wordlessly speeding up as

295

we saw dark shadows rippling in slow waves across the hills away to the West.

Already the column clouds were massing, with the threat of a springtime storm…...

ACKNOWLEDGEMENTS

A huge thank you to all of my friends, especially those who read the early drafts of "Out of Shot," suggested improvements and offered encouragement. And especially to KW, who read the original rough version, one chapter at a time. Without you demanding to know more about Jackson and Claire, and nagging me (in a good way) to keep on writing, their story would have remained in my head, probably forever.

And without Andy...there would be no book. The novel you have in your hands now, whether in printed or digital format, is the result of many hours of hard work and dedication, sitting at the computer, in order to turn my manuscript into a finished product. For that, and for everything else - thank you.

BIOGRAPHY.

Since graduating from Newcastle University with a degree in English Literature, DS Joyce has worked in the television industry as a journalist, director, producer, camera operator and editor.

Working in the dramatic landscapes of the Scottish Highlands provided the inspiration for debut novel "Out of Shot."

When not filming or writing, DS likes nothing better than to get together with friends and go hill-walking or holidaying on the Greek Islands and further afield. Home life is currently split between Scotland and Northumberland. The latter may well be the backdrop for a second Claire Armstrong mystery.....watch this space!

Printed in Great Britain
by Amazon